He must have been crazy.

Six weeks in the cramped quarters of a camper with the woman he had hoped never to set eyes on again? A constant reminder of all that he'd lost, the bitterness of regret, the pain of loneliness and self-recrimination?

He'd spent the best part of fifteen years resenting Jill Preston, and now he'd agreed to spend the next few weeks in constant contact with her, protecting someone he didn't know and couldn't care less about.

And he couldn't back out. He'd given his word.

Hank groaned. He *had* to be crazy.

Dear Reader,

It's another great month for Silhouette Intimate Moments! If you don't believe me, just take a look at our American Hero title, *Dragonslayer,* by Emilie Richards. This compelling and emotionally riveting tale could have been torn from today's headlines, with a minister hero whose church is in one of the inner city's worst neighborhoods and whose chosen flock includes the down and out of the world. In this place, where gang violence touches everyone's lives—and will continue to touch them throughout the book in ways you won't be able to predict—our hero meets a woman whose paradoxical innocence will force him to confront his own demons, his own inner emptiness, and once more embrace life—and love. *Dragonslayer* is a *tour de force,* not to be missed by any reader.

The rest of the month is terrific, too. Marilyn Pappano, Doreen Roberts, Marion Smith Collins, Beverly Barton and new author Leann Harris offer stories that range from ''down-home'' emotional to suspenseful and dramatic. You'll want to read them all.

And in months to come look for more irresistible reading from such favorite authors as Justine Davis, Linda Turner, Paula Detmer Riggs, *New York Times* bestsellers Heather Graham Pozzessere and Nora Roberts, and more—all coming your way from Silhouette Intimate Moments, where romantic excitement is always the rule.

Yours,

Leslie J. Wainger
Senior Editor and Editorial Coordinator

ONLY A DREAM AWAY

Doreen Roberts

Silhouette® INTIMATE MOMENTS®

Published by Silhouette Books New York

America's Publisher of Contemporary Romance

SILHOUETTE BOOKS
300 East 42nd St., New York, N.Y. 10017

ONLY A DREAM AWAY

Copyright © 1993 by Doreen Roberts

All rights reserved. Except for use in any review, the reproduction or utilization of this work in whole or in part in any form by any electronic, mechanical or other means, now known or hereafter invented, including xerography, photocopying and recording, or in any information storage or retrieval system, is forbidden without the permission of the publisher, Silhouette Books, 300 E. 42nd St., New York, N.Y. 10017

ISBN: 0-373-07513-8

First Silhouette Books printing August 1993

All the characters in this book have no existence outside the imagination of the author and have no relation whatsoever to anyone bearing the same name or names. They are not even distantly inspired by any individual known or unknown to the author, and all incidents are pure invention.

®: Trademark used under license and registered in the United States Patent and Trademark Office and in other countries.

Printed in the U.S.A.

Books by Doreen Roberts

Silhouette Intimate Moments

Gambler's Gold #215
Willing Accomplice #239
Forbidden Jade #266
Threat of Exposure #295
Desert Heat #319
In the Line of Duty #379
Broken Wings #422
Road to Freedom #442
In a Stranger's Eyes #475
Only a Dream Away #513

Silhouette Romance

Home for the Holidays #765

DOREEN ROBERTS

was hooked from the moment she opened the first page of a Mary Stewart novel. It took her twenty years to write her own romantic suspense novel, which was subsequently published, much to her surprise. She and her husband left their native England more than twenty years ago and have since lived in Oregon, where their son was born. Doreen hopes to go on mixing romance and danger in her novels for at least another two decades.

To my son, Regan,
for his help in the stage techniques,
and in the hopes that
he'll make his dreams come true

Prologue

The hand that held the pen moved slowly across the paper, printing out the letters one by one, as if it were picking its way through a mine field. The tip of a pink tongue protruded from the writer's mouth, working back and forth across a full bottom lip.

At last it was done. And this one was good. Real good. If this didn't put the fear of the devil in them, then nothing would.

The lips smiled, enjoying the anticipation of the terror the words would cause. The danger would be real, but where would it come from? That's what fear was all about. The unknown. The unseen enemy. The wait for the hand of evil to descend.

The writer's fingers curled into the palm. The hand of evil. That was good. It would make a good song title. Maybe Danny Webster would sing it.

A high-pitched giggle, devoid of humor, disturbed the silence of the room. Yeah, Danny Webster could sing it.

"The Hand of Evil." That would make 'em sit up and take notice.

The weird laughter faded. The letters seemed to stand out on the white paper. Danny Webster was going to die. Maybe not today, or tomorrow, but soon. Unexpectedly. Horribly. And *soon*.

With infinite care, the slender fingers folded up the letter and slid it inside the envelope.

Chapter 1

The tavern smelled just like any other bar in town—sweaty bodies, spilled beer and smoldering tobacco. Sitting alone at a corner table, Hank stared at his empty glass. Above his head an ancient speaker competed with the raucous laughter that greeted off-color jokes and the loud boasting of men too young to hold their booze.

Hank wondered if he could manage another beer and still be able to drive. He wasn't used to the squat little compact he'd rented. The telephone call had left him no time to drive to Cedarvale, Colorado, and he'd had to leave his camper behind in Wyoming. He'd made it in time for the funeral. That was the most important thing.

Thinking about the funeral aggravated his thirst, and he shoved his chair back from the table. It hit something solid and an explosive curse from behind him swung his head around.

Through a haze of smoke he saw angry eyes glaring down at him, almost hidden beneath thick, bushy brows. The guy's belly hung over the large buckle of his belt, which struggled to hold up a pair of washed-out jeans. A plaid shirt gaped open at his throat, exposing a thatch of reddish hair, the same color as the unruly mustache sprouting beneath a purple-veined nose.

Hank opened his mouth to mutter an apology, but the brute gave him no chance. A hand the size of a football reached out and grabbed the collar of his shirt. A blast of warm, beery breath hit him in the face as Purple Nose leaned over him.

"That was my shin, fella. I reckon you need glasses. Or maybe a bruised nose will learn you to watch what you're doing."

Okay. So he should've looked behind him. But it had been just a little bump. And this big oaf had enough fat on him to cushion the blow. Obviously the bastard was looking for trouble.

Hank lowered his chin and stared at the chunky knuckles just an inch or two beneath his nose. "If you let go of me now," Hank said pleasantly, "I'll forget what you just said."

The thick, hairy wrist twisted, tightening the collar of his shirt painfully against his Adam's apple. "Oh, you will, will you? Well, fella, I ain't about to forget what you did to my shin. Reckon you need to be learned a lesson."

He tried to swallow but couldn't. If it hadn't been for that he might have controlled himself. He was getting better at it all the time. He'd tried hard to keep his hands clean since the suspension. He knew what would happen if he got into any more trouble. It could mean the end of his career on the rodeo circuit.

Much as he enjoyed a good fight, part of him hoped the big guy would get the message. "Look," he said, barely making himself heard with his strangled voice, "I don't think either of us is in any shape to scrap. One of us could get hurt. So let's just forget it, okay?''

The fist twisted, cutting off his air. He couldn't just sit there with this fat punk slowly choking him. After all, he had a reputation to protect. Hank Tyler had never backed away from a fight yet.

He knew what the odds were. Hell, he'd faced down enough bruisers to figure it out. The guy outweighed him, and judging by the tree-trunk neck and massive shoulders, looked as if he could throw a formidable weight behind a punch. However, he also swayed on his feet, and his slurred speech indicated a belly full of booze.

Deciding that he had the advantage in speed and accuracy, Hank made up his mind. Very deliberately, he lifted his boot and slammed the heel into the guy's shin.

Purple Nose let out an outraged howl and relaxed his grip. Hank cleared his throat. "You got one more chance to walk away," he said without too much hope as he rose to his feet.

The big guy answered by grabbing a chair with one hand and flinging it to one side. It crashed against a table, sending glasses rattling and slopping their contents over the laps of the men sitting there.

Someone jumped up, swearing. Without turning his head, Purple Nose jabbed out a hand and sent the guy sprawling.

Hank swallowed. He had a pretty good buzz on himself. Something told him he could lose this one.

Grunting, the big guy lumbered forward, murder gleaming in his small black eyes.

In desperation, Hank drew back his fist and drove it into the swaying jaw. His knuckles connected right on target. The guy's head snapped back, and by all the rules of logic, the drunk should've collapsed like a punctured tire. Instead he swayed violently back and forth, then his eyes cleared and the rest of his face turned purple.

By now the tables close to them had cleared, and a circle of noisy onlookers formed around them. Hank sent up a silent prayer and prepared to defend himself.

Across the room, Jill Preston paused in the doorway, her gaze drawn immediately to the men facing off in the corner. Her mouth tightened when she recognized the taller one. He hadn't changed much in fifteen years.

As soon as she'd heard he was back in town she knew where she'd find him. Hank Tyler was predictable in only two respects. His fondness for certain taverns, and his inability to resist a fight.

She saw the huge bear of a man wave his fists in Hank's face and sighed. She had to be crazy. Didn't she have enough problems without taking on a troublemaker like Hank Tyler? If it wasn't for the fact that she was desperate, and he was exactly what she needed, she'd turn around and run as fast as she could in the opposite direction.

The big man took a quick jab and met nothing but air. A chorus of jeers rippled through the crowd watching the scene. Apparently incited by their reaction, the massive shoulders flexed.

Knowing what was coming, Jill pursed her lips and began to work her way toward the bar.

Hank saw nothing but the bully. He kept his eyes glued on the bunched fists circling in front of him. A massive paw shot straight at him, whistling past his ear as he ducked to the right. The quick move put him off balance and he stumbled, helped by a hefty shove from Purple Nose.

For a moment he thought he'd lost it. Then, with a twist of his body, he miraculously regained his feet. His years of sliding off the back of a rampaging bull had paid off. All that twisting to keep his balance had now become instinct.

Purple Nose seemed a little taken aback. Hank took advantage of that, and went for the wide expanse of paunch. Knock the wind out of him first, then drop him with an uppercut. His fist sank into soft flesh.

The guy had to be superhuman. Either that, or the bum had drunk too much to feel. He did little more than grunt.

Hank eyed the bunched fist coming at him and twisted down and away. Not quite fast enough though. A rabbit punch exploded on the back of his neck and sparkling dots danced in front of his eyes.

He swayed, his spirits dropping like a penny down a well. Okay. So he'd picked a damn boxer to argue with. Didn't mean he had to go down without a fight. He shook his head, and the room swam, sending the onlookers circling around him in a haze of shapeless faces and bodies.

Voices hummed in his ears—muffled shouts of encouragement. He didn't know if they were for or against him. At this point he didn't care. He saw Purple Nose looming up in front of him. A blur of movement, then sharp pain crashed through his head.

His nose felt numb. He touched it and his fingers came away wet with bright red blood. The fog cleared.

He was mad now. Mad as a hornet. He heard the warning in his head, but he no longer heeded it. He wanted to punch that purple nose so bad he could taste it.

He could feel the roar building inside him, smoldering, steaming, swelling with the pressure. His muscles bunched, and he concentrated all his thoughts on his shoulder, arm and fist. Only one shot. If he had to get that close, that's all he had.

He swayed his body to the right as Purple Nose came at him again. At the last minute he changed direction, jabbing hard and fast, his entire weight thrown behind the punch.

With a grim sense of satisfaction, he felt his fist connect. Surprise washed across the face in front of him, the bloodshot eyes rolled up to the ceiling, and Purple Nose went down like a sack of oranges dropped from a truck.

Hank didn't have time to gloat. Already two more thugs were on him, anxious to test the victor. With his back to the bar, Hank unleashed the full extent of his fury.

He was no longer in control. His fists flew in all directions, reaching where they could. Glasses and bottles crashed around him, but he barely noticed. He put three more down before four of them jumped him all at the same time, taking him down to the floor.

Just before he passed out, he could have sworn he saw a pair of silver sandals with three-inch heels, and the prettiest pair of ankles he'd seen in a decade.

"Jeez!" muttered one of the men, his knee firmly pressed into Hank's back. "This one's a fighter."

"He must be," Jill said wryly, looking down at the still form. "It took four of you to control him."

The rest of the men climbed to their feet. "That's what we're here for," one of them said, slapping the dust from his jeans. "If we'd waited much longer he'd have wrecked the bar."

"I think he was getting some help." Jill glared pointedly at one of the young men who had jumped Hank and was now nursing a bruised jaw.

"Aw, come on, Jill. He should know better than to pick a fight in a local bar, being a stranger an' all."

Jill shook her head at the man who had spoken. "Hank Tyler's no stranger to this bar. He just hasn't been around in a while."

One of the other men looked at her in surprise. "Hank Tyler? The rodeo champ?"

"Ex-rodeo champ," someone else said. "He got suspended some time back. Thought I recognized him."

On the other side of the bar the barman grunted. "Are you gonna stand there B.S.-ing all night or is someone gonna help me clean up this mess?"

"What we gonna do with him?" one of the cowboys asked, prodding Hank's unconscious body with his foot. "After the amount of beer he's guzzled tonight he's gonna be out for a while. Anyone know where he lives?"

"Probably at his mother's house," Jill said, feeling a twinge of sympathy in spite of herself. "He came into town for her funeral."

Several murmurs of condolence greeted her words, but she barely heard them. She was too busy trying to make up her mind. The opportunity was too good to pass up. If she wanted to take advantage of the situation she had to do it now.

"How about a couple of you helping me get him home?" she asked, smiling at the nearest guy.

The cowboy nodded. "Sure. Where's his mother live?"

"Not his mother's house." She turned and started for the door. "My apartment. It's only a few blocks from here. Just follow me home."

She glanced back to see them pick Hank up from the floor, then walked out the door, wondering if she was possibly making the biggest mistake of her life.

Looking down at him later, lying peacefully on her couch, she was even more apprehensive about her impulsive decision. The Hank she'd known had been twenty-five years old, brash, confident and painfully outspoken.

She'd had more than one fight with him, and the last time she'd seen him, they had been ready to kill each other. He was not going to be at all happy when he realized where he was.

He looked a mess. Blood splattered his denim jacket and his jeans wore beer stains darkened by dust from the floor. She might as well try to clean him up some before he woke up, she decided.

Leaving him alone for a few minutes, she ran warm water into a bowl and found the antiseptic. He hadn't moved when she got back and she set about repairing some of the damage to his face. She had to admit there were some changes, after all. Long hours in the sun had weathered his skin and deepened the lines in his forehead and around his eyes. A day's worth of dark stubble covered his firm jaw, it felt scratchy against her hand as she carefully dabbed at his split lip.

One eye looked puffy, and would be sporting a spectacular bruise in a day or two. She remembered the stony glint in his gray eyes the last time he'd spoken to her, and again felt a pang of apprehension. She had the distinct feeling she would live to regret her rashness in bringing him home.

Gently she smoothed his dark hair from his brow where a reddish lump had formed. He wore his hair longer now, and it still grew thick and wavy on his forehead, though strands of silver gleamed in the light from the lamp behind him.

Heartbreaker, the girls had called him. They had flocked around him, fascinated by his good looks and devil-may-care attitude. Jill's mouth twitched. Even with the bruises, he was more of a heartbreaker to look at now than he'd been fifteen years ago.

His shoulders jerked, and she snatched her hand away, her heart skipping wildly. He was coming around. Quickly she gathered up the first-aid items and took them back to the kitchen. She didn't want to be the first thing he saw when he opened his eyes.

* * *

He woke up slowly, moving in and out of the black fog, feeling more and more pain each time he surfaced. He was almost afraid to open his eyes, in case those men were standing over him, waiting to pound into him again.

God, he hurt everywhere. It hurt to breathe, it hurt to move—damn, it hurt to think. He wondered if anything had been broken. It wouldn't be the first time. But as he got older, bones took longer to mend, bruises took longer to fade. He probably looked a mess.

Which raised another question. Where the hell was he? Not on the floor of the bar, judging by the soft surface pressing into his back. Only one way to find out. He opened his eyes.

Actually, only one of them opened. The other had swollen shut. Light blazed into his head, intensifying the pain for several agonizing seconds before fading to a dull throb. Then, to his amazement, something cool and damp settled on his brow.

Hank rolled his good eye sideways. He seemed to be lying on a couch in someone's living room. A slender hand wearing an opal ring hovered just above his nose.

"I'm glad to see you're awake. I was beginning to get worried."

The voice sounded pleasantly low and unmistakably female. The faint hint of perfume that drifted across his bruised nose intrigued him. Spicy and interesting.

Anxious to see the source of all this femininity, Hank shifted his head. Bad mistake. Even the sound of his groan hurt.

"I'd keep still if I were you," the voice advised. "You took quite a beating."

"Who are you?" Spoken through a split lip, the words sounded caustic. He tried to soften them. "Where am I?"

"You're in my apartment. I had you brought here after you did your best to destroy the Black Steer."

He opened his mouth to speak and tasted blood. He closed his eyelid. The damp cloth shifted, covering his eyes. Another dabbed at his lip. "You'd better lie still for a while. And don't try to talk. It could hurt."

He agreed wholeheartedly with that. Besides, the soothing touch of her fingers felt real nice. And her perfume definitely did things to his blood. Even in his sorry state. He wondered if she looked as good as she smelled. He wished he'd had time to look at her face before she'd covered up his eyes.

"You put up quite a fight before they took you down," the voice said.

He felt his strength returning. It must have had something to do with the grudging note of admiration he'd heard. He felt better by the minute.

"In case you're wondering why I brought you here," the voice continued, "I have a job for you, if you're interested. I want to hire you as a bodyguard."

He digested that for a moment. Bodyguard? For who? The owner of that intriguing voice? He made an attempt to form the question but a velvet finger touched his lips.

"Not yet. Give it a chance to heal."

Dammit, he couldn't stand it a minute longer. Braced against the pain, he lifted his hand and dragged the cloth from his eyes.

Shock coursed through him, clearing the rest of the fog from his mind. He couldn't believe he hadn't recognized her voice. He sure as hell recognized her face.

"You've got damn nerve," he mumbled, trying to make it sound as harsh as he felt. "What makes you think I'd have anything to do with you, of all people?"

She gazed back at him, looking the way she smelled. Sultry. Dark brown velvet eyes, pouty lips, and shiny dark hair that danced around her head in an unruly froth of curls.

Older perhaps, fuller in the face—and figure, he couldn't help noticing. The years had been good to her. His mind managed a quick calculation. She'd be thirty-four now. She looked damn good for thirty-four. A woman in her prime.

He had to struggle to remind himself of all the reasons he resented her. Bitterly resented her. He'd thought about bumping into her again, now that he was back in town. He'd rehearsed all the things he wanted to say to her. Right now he couldn't remember a word.

"I had hoped the years had matured you, Hank Tyler, and that you would be more tolerant and less condemning."

"Yeah? Well, sorry to crush your hopes, sweetheart, but I've got a long memory."

He struggled to sit up, trying to ignore the blinding pain that crashed through his head.

"You're going to hurt yourself if you don't lie still," Jill said calmly.

He sent her a lethal look from his one good eye. All he wanted was to get out of there, hopefully with his dignity intact. He couldn't imagine why she had thought for a single moment that he'd be interested in anything remotely connected to her. Let alone work for her. The idea was ludicrous.

Even so, he had to acknowledge something. She'd been right about the pain. What with that and the effects of the booze, he doubted he'd make it to the door. Maybe if he gave it another minute or two. Rigid with frustration, he lowered his head back to the cushion.

"As long as you're lying there with nothing better to do," Jill added, "I might as well give you the story. Then you can make up your mind if you want the job or not."

He wanted to tell her that nothing she said would come close to changing his mind, but he wasn't going to waste the pain of talking on her, so he said nothing, just stared up at the ceiling and tried to pretend he wasn't lying there listening to the honeyed voice of Jill Preston.

"I need to hire a bodyguard," she began, "for Danny Webster. He's a country singer and I'm his manager. He's been getting threatening letters. They've been coming for some time, but lately they seem to be more menacing, and it's making him very nervous. To the point of affecting his singing."

She'd piqued his curiosity, though he barely moved his head. It wouldn't do to let her think he was interested in anything she said. Apparently she didn't have a husband. The opal ring was on the right hand and her left hand was bare. Angry at himself for noticing, he shut off the speculation.

"We are leaving on a road tour in three days," Jill continued, "traveling through three states. Danny is young and highly temperamental. Something like this could seriously damage his performance. This tour is vital to his career, and I don't want anything to ruin it. I've played down the importance of the letters as much as possible, but I'm concerned enough to consider a bodyguard."

She stood. He turned his head slightly to accommodate his limited vision. She looked even better standing up. She had obviously taken care of her figure. Real good care.

"I can't tell Danny that, of course," she said, moving across the room and out of his sight. "If he thought the letters could be for real, he would simply refuse to go on the tour. He could lose the one big chance of a lifetime. Tours like this are not usually offered to lesser known singers like Danny."

In spite of himself, his lips moved. "Why me?"

"I heard about your suspension. I knew you would miss the summer season. I figured you could use the money."

So she knew about that. That made it all the more crazy why she would want to hire him. She had to know why he'd been suspended. Hank eased his shoulder down so he could look at her.

She stood at a window, looking out at the night. She wore a bright yellow shirt tucked into tight jeans. Skin-tight jeans. Dragging his gaze away, he lifted his wrist. Two in the morning. He must have been out the best part of an hour.

"You're a rebel, Hank Tyler. You talk with your fists, you act first and think later. And unless you've changed over the years, no one can tell you what to do."

He cautiously worked his mouth. It felt a tad better. He looked back at her. She'd dropped the curtain back in place and was heading toward him. She walked with a slight swing to her hips that could grab a man's attention and hold it.

"I need a man like you, Hank." She stopped in front of him, looking down at him with those soft, dark eyes. "Not only are you physically capable of the job, you've had the experience of working with a band. I would simply tell Danny that I hired you as road manager for the band. He would never have to know the real reason you're traveling with us."

Maybe if she hadn't mentioned the band right then, he might have held it all in. But that particular memory opened up the wounds again. His anger gave him the strength to swing his legs to the floor and sit up.

"Lady, I got to admire your nerve. You don't care whose toes you tread on, do you? You always were too damn ambitious to see straight. Not to mention selfish as hell."

Her cheeks flamed, but she held her temper, as she sat in a chair opposite him. "And you always were too stubborn and unreasonable to understand."

His mouth stung when he swore, but he ignored it. He'd waited a long time to say it all, and nothing was going to stop him now. "Understand? I understand one thing. Because of you my only brother hasn't spoken to me in fifteen years. I saw him for the first time at our mother's funeral, two days ago. We stood on opposite sides of her grave and never spoke to each other. He left right after the service, flew back to Tennessee that night."

For the first time he saw genuine sorrow in the brown eyes. "I'm sorry," she said softly. "But if you hadn't fought with him over his marrying me, none of that would have happened. He couldn't forgive you for interfering in his life, or for the terrible things you said about me."

"He was too young to get married. You filled his head with all those fancy ideas and talked him into marrying you. Then you turned him against me. Wouldn't let him have anything to do with me. God knows what lies you told him—"

"I had nothing to do with it, Hank Tyler. You did that all by yourself. I admit the marriage was a mistake—"

"You bet it was a mistake. Two years it lasted, wasn't it? If that. Two years, and you walked out on him. That's how much you wanted him. You destroyed the relationship between two brothers and it was all for *nothing.*"

Her eyes grew stormy, setting off sparks that seemed to bounce right into his face. "I destroyed nothing, and you know it. That was between you and Perry. He might have been young, Hank, but he was still an adult. He made his own decisions. I didn't turn him against you. He was sick of you running his life and resenting anything he tried to do that wasn't your idea."

Hank tried to shove himself forward, off the couch, and grunted when pain shot up his back. "I had to run his life. I'd been responsible for him since he was two years old. He always listened to me, until *you* came on the scene."

"And showed him that he was capable of making his own decisions."

He made a sound of disgust. "Which turned out just dandy for him, didn't it?" He felt the blood trickle warmly down his chin and swiped at it with the back of his hand.

Jill reached for the cloth to dab at his chin, but he pushed her hand away, cursing.

"Look," he muttered, "get someone else to baby-sit your paranoid protégé. We'd be at each other's throats the whole time, and that wouldn't be good for artistic temperament. Besides, people in the public eye get this stuff all the time. It's just some jealous screwball out for kicks. You and your country crooner are overreacting to the whole thing."

She got up and crossed the room, pausing in front of a small desk. Opening it, Jill reached inside and withdrew a pile of envelopes. "I'd like you to read a couple of these and then tell me if I'm overreacting," she said, coming back to hand them to him.

He didn't want to read them. He wanted to get out of there, right then, before she could say anything to change his mind. Not that he had the slightest intention of changing it, of course. He stared down at the white envelopes in his hand.

"Go on," she demanded, "read them. Since you're so knowledgeable on the subject, I'd appreciate your opinion."

He heard the challenge in her voice and, as usual, rose to meet it. He noticed his hand tremble slightly as he withdrew the single sheet of paper, torn crudely from a notebook. He had to stay off the booze, he told himself. He was getting too old to handle it anymore.

The scribble was hard to read, but as he made it out his stomach crawled with disgust and disbelief. This wasn't the work of a harmless screwball. The vehemence behind the crude words appeared horrifyingly clear. Whoever wrote this note meant business.

He tried to keep his expression blank as he slipped the paper back into the envelope. As if needing to convince himself, he read a couple more. They were all the same. Frightening and deadly.

He handed her back the sheaf of envelopes. "I take it you've contacted the police?"

She nodded briefly. "Of course. Like you, they assured me it happens all the time, and for the most part, nothing ever comes of it. In any case, they can't do anything unless someone actually carries out the threat."

She laughed, a little dry sound in the back of her throat. He realized, then, just how scared she felt behind all that calm talk.

"I guess it would be a little late by then," she said, and twisted the cloth she held into a tight ball. "They did suggest I hire a private detective, but that would let Danny know I was taking this whole thing seriously. So far I've managed to persuade him it's nothing to worry about."

She must have done a good job on him, Hank thought. Apparently she had a lot of influence over her client. He found it hard to equate this cool professional with the hot-headed star-struck teenager he'd known back then. "You're probably right, at that," he said without much conviction.

She shrugged. "I hope the police are right, and that it is just some crank getting his kicks. But Danny's performance is suffering because of this, and at this stage in his career I can't let anything disrupt what we've worked so hard to achieve. Besides, I'd feel better if I knew there was someone around to protect him. Just in case."

Just in case was right, he thought. He didn't like the look of those letters one bit. But he wasn't about to tell her that. No point in frightening her any more than she already was. On the other hand, if the letters were for real, this Danny Webster could be in serious trouble. And that meant that his manager was also in the line of fire.

Hank didn't like that. He didn't like that at all. But what the hell could he do about it? Carefully he ran his finger across his swollen eye and down his bruised nose. He could, of course, sign on for the ride, and keep an eye on things for her. She was right. He had nothing better to do and he could use the money.

Damn. What the hell was the matter with him? Hadn't she caused him enough pain and grief? How could he forget that she'd created a permanent rift between him and his brother? How could he forget the reason for it wasn't so much Perry getting married that had upset him, but the woman he was marrying?

He could never forgive her for coming between him and Perry. But worse, he couldn't seem to forget the way he'd once felt about her.

"It's all right," Jill said, breaking into his churning thoughts. "I can see how much you hate the idea. And you're right. It wouldn't have worked out. We have too much resentment between us to survive six weeks cooped up in a small space together. I shouldn't have asked."

He should have felt relieved, but he didn't. "So what will you do?"

Again she gave him that tight little shrug. "It's too late to do much about anything now. I guess we'll just go ahead with the tour and keep our fingers crossed."

He frowned at her, feeling his skin tighten across the bump on his forehead. He didn't feel right about this, and he resented the spot she'd put him in.

"It's okay," Jill said again, checking her watch. "I understand. Just forget it. I'll drive you home."

He didn't want to go back to the dismal motel room. He hadn't been able to bring himself to stay at his mother's house. Too many memories. Sighing, he pushed himself to his feet. His head swam and he swayed, grabbing on to the nearest thing to keep his balance. It happened to be Jill's shoulder.

She grabbed his arm, steadying him. "Look, you're in no shape to make it back tonight. It's late. You're welcome to stay on my couch for the night. You'll feel better after a good sleep, and I'll take you back in the morning."

It was the last thing he wanted to do. But he was exhausted, hurting, and couldn't see worth a damn out of his one good eye. It would be nice just to lie down right here and go to sleep. Before he realized what he was doing, he'd sat himself back on the couch.

"I'll make some coffee," Jill said, and hurried from the room.

He took a look around as best he could. Simply furnished, the room bore the stamp of a country girl with the blue gingham cushions and deep, comfortable armchairs. A small stereo sat in one corner with magazines piled on top of it, and the television set next to it shared its stand with an assortment of stuffed bears.

On the wall hung landscapes of the desert and dry, craggy mountains—hot, sultry images that warmed the room. His vision blurred and he shook his head.

"Here," Jill said, handing him a steaming mug. "Drink this, it will help clear your head."

He hadn't heard her come back. For a moment he felt disoriented, as if this were a dream he'd had before. He took the mug from her and sipped the sweet, black coffee. She'd remembered. No cream. A spoonful of sugar.

His head throbbed painfully, and he wanted very badly to go to sleep. But he couldn't get rid of that voice of conscience screaming in his ear.

Dammit, why him? Why couldn't she have picked some other sucker to bat those big brown eyes at and ask for help? If he walked away from her now and something happened, he'd never forgive himself. He had the time, he had the experience, and worse, he was the only one who could help her now. The only one she could trust.

And judging by those letters, she could really use someone she could trust.

"I'll leave you alone, to get some sleep," Jill said, heading across the room.

Sleep. Just the thought of it made his eyes close. But there was something he had to say first. Something important. And he'd better get it out before he could change his mind again. He finished the coffee and put it down carefully on the table in front of him.

Jill came back carrying a pillow and blankets. "The couch is comfortable," she said, leaning over him to slip the pillow behind his head. "Danny has slept on it a few times."

He tried not to notice the subtle, yet exotic perfume. He tried to ignore the glimpse of smooth skin at the open neck of her shirt. For a moment panic swept over him. He couldn't do it. He'd be crazy to do it.

"I'll do it," he said, loudly and clearly, hoping the words would chase away his misgivings.

She straightened at once, and even with his hazy vision he could see the startled surprise on her face.

"Pardon?"

"I've never guarded anyone else's body before, but I reckon I've done a pretty good job of protecting mine at times, so I'll give it a shot. I'll be your bodyguard." And may heaven help us all, he added silently.

Chapter 2

Jill stood looking at him with that dumbfounded expression on her face.

He tried to sound casual. "Six weeks, you said?"

She nodded slowly, almost as if she'd changed her mind and regretted asking him.

"So what's the deal?" He wanted to get it all settled before he lost his nerve.

She stared at him for a long moment, then said quietly, "You get a percentage of the take, just like I do. In return, I would expect you to keep an eye on Danny without letting him know why you're there. I need him relaxed and confident."

"I reckon I can do that."

"The three of us would stay in the motor home, it's more convenient than motel rooms and will give Danny more security."

"And the band?"

"The Wildwoods. Danny's backup. Slim, Gary and Gary's wife, Tiffany. They'll be traveling behind us in their own rig with the equipment. I'll tell them I hired you as a bodyguard, since I don't think they'll go for the road manager, but I don't want to tell them about the letters. The least people who know about that the better."

He nodded, then a thought struck him. "How come you don't use one of them for a bodyguard?"

"They'll be a little busy taking care of the hundred and one details of a road tour. You must remember how much time and concentration that takes. Besides, neither Slim nor Gary are the type to put up a fight."

"Not even with a gun?"

Her expression hardened. "No guns. I won't allow a gun on the premises. I've heard too many horror stories, and you know how temperamental people can be in this business."

He needed to think about that. "That widens the odds a little," he said after a pause.

"That can't be helped." She turned, shrugging her shoulders, as if trying to shake off some sense of foreboding. "Maybe the letters are nothing more than a sick joke. Maybe whoever wrote them has no intention of following us on the road. But if this person is serious, and is some kind of groupie, he or she will know the schedule. They always do. Unfortunately, we can't manage without advance publicity."

"How does Danny feel about hiring a manager for the band?"

"I haven't told him yet. I wanted to talk to you first. He'll accept it. He trusts me."

Hank felt a sudden burning curiosity about the young man he was supposed to protect. But that could wait. His burst of energy had been temporary. He could feel exhaustion creeping over him again, making his limbs heavy and his head ache. As well as the rest of his body. He closed his good eye.

"I'll let you sleep," Jill said softly. "We can talk in the morning."

He barely had the strength to mumble an answer. He knew no more until he opened his eyes, both eyes this time, and found daylight warming the room.

It took him a moment or two to remember where he was. And when he did, the jolt to his stomach brought him fully awake.

He must have been crazy. Six weeks in the cramped quarters of a camper with the woman he had hoped never to set eyes on again? A constant reminder of all that he'd lost, the bitterness of regret, the pain of loneliness and self-recriminations? He'd spent the best part of fifteen years resenting Jill, and now he'd agreed to spend the next few weeks in constant contact with her, protecting someone he didn't know and couldn't care less about.

He pulled himself upright and groaned as the stiffness of his sore muscles reminded him of his fight the night before. He had to be crazy. But he couldn't back out now. He'd given his word. Besides, much as it galled him to admit it, he wouldn't have a minute's peace wondering how she was doing, riding through all those strange towns with the possibility of some kind of maniac on her trail.

Face it. He hadn't signed on to protect Danny Webster. He'd agreed to go to protect Jill Preston. And he had a very uncomfortable feeling that if he didn't watch out, he was the one who was going to need the protection—against his feelings for a woman that, try as he might, he had never quite been able to forget. For all the wrong reasons.

Standing in the bathroom, Jill faced her own misgivings. She'd once heard Hank Tyler described as a hell-raising, hard-hitting, outspoken rabble-rouser with a reputation for causing trouble. That had been a long time ago, but so far nothing she had seen had given her cause to think anything had changed.

He'd brought back a lot of bad memories, talking about Perry last night. She wondered if he knew about the baby she'd lost, and her heart filled with pain, as it always did when she thought about the little boy who'd never had the chance to draw breath.

If Perry had been more understanding about that, they might have made it together. But Perry was relieved when the baby was born dead. He hadn't wanted it in the first place. It would have interfered with his plans.

It was the reason she'd left him. His callous disregard for the dreadful sorrow she was trying to deal with had been the last straw. But she couldn't explain that to Hank. He had never understood her side of things, and it was too late to expect him to do so now.

She had all the trouble she needed dealing with Danny. It was a toss-up as to whether she'd hired the perfect man for the job of protecting the singer, or added to her problems by aggravating the tension that she fully expected on the tour.

Leaning closer to the mirror, she applied a light coating of copper lipstick. She would have to explain to Hank about Danny. It was hard to predict how the singer would react to her hiring a new "manager." She just hoped Danny would be on his best behavior. The last thing she needed was for him to throw a tantrum. She could lose her bodyguard before they'd even started.

Bracing herself, she left the bathroom and walked down the hallway to the living room. With luck, Hank would be feeling better after his night's rest.

Pushing open the door, her gaze went straight to the couch. Her heart gave a little jerk when she saw it was empty. For a moment she thought he might have changed his mind and left without telling her.

Then she saw him standing by the window, and her rush of relief unsettled her. She didn't want to depend on him just yet. They still had a ways to go before it was time to leave for the tour. And he had yet to meet Danny. She couldn't tell how he'd react when he first saw the singer. She had no way of knowing if he'd see a resemblance between Danny Webster and the brother he'd alienated so many years ago.

She'd forgotten how tall he was. He turned around to look at her, his unbuttoned shirt swinging open to reveal his bare chest. She realized he was broader in the shoulders than she remembered. She hadn't had much time to think about it last night. She couldn't imagine why she should notice it now.

"Good morning," Hank said, sounding wary.

She braced herself, wondering if he'd changed his mind. "Hi. I hope you slept well."

"Well enough."

She walked into the room, close enough to get a good look at his face. "You look a little better this morning, though I think you'll have a black eye for a while."

"At least I can see out of it." His fingers strayed to his jaw as he worked it from side to side.

His beard was even more pronounced, she noticed. "If you want to shave, there's a razor and blades in the bathroom cabinet. Feel free to help yourself."

He nodded, his gaze sliding away from her to focus across the room. "Thanks. Any chance of some coffee?"

"I'll make some." She padded across the room on bare feet, uneasily conscious of the awkwardness between them. At least they were being polite to each other. If they could manage that for the duration of the tour it would help. She filled the coffeepot with water. It would also be a miracle. She jumped when his voice sounded close behind her.

"Aspirin would help, if you have some."

Concerned, she spun around, looking up at him with a worried frown. "You have a headache?"

"A mild description of the hammering going on in my head, but yes, I have a headache. My back doesn't feel all that great, either."

She pursed her lips. "Well, if you insist on brawling in a bar like some itinerant bum you really can't expect too much sympathy."

"Lady, sympathy is the last thing I expect from you."

The glint in his eye was unmistakable. She turned her back on him. "You'll find aspirin in the bathroom cabinet as well. Help yourself."

She expected him to leave and was surprised when he said quietly, "I didn't start the fight, you know."

"Maybe not. But you sure did your best to finish it."

This time he did leave, and she relaxed her shoulders. It would be worth it, she promised herself, to know that Danny had some measure of protection. Even if she was worrying about nothing. She just didn't need the extra worry on top of everything else she had to hassle with.

She could handle Hank Tyler. He couldn't intimidate her fifteen years ago when she was still a kid. He sure as hell wasn't going to intimidate her now that she was a mature woman with all those years of experience behind her.

She kept repeating that to herself as she drove to Danny's apartment later that morning in the clear, late June sunshine. Hank sat next to her, silent and withdrawn, after insisting that she take him to meet the guy he was hired to protect.

There was no point in putting it off, Jill told herself as she pulled into the apartment building parking lot. The sooner they got acquainted, the easier it would be to get the tour off to a good start.

Hank climbed stiffly out of the car, a sure indication that he was still feeling the effects of his battle the night before.

His face was an interesting patchwork of pink and purple, but his lip had gone back to its normal size and his eye, though bloodshot, appeared to be healing nicely.

Freshly shaved, he looked almost presentable, she thought as she rang Danny's doorbell in the foyer. True, his dark gray shirt was torn and splattered with blood. She'd offered to wash it for him, but he'd declined. He wore his denim jacket over it instead, and with his jeans and Western boots, looked every inch the rodeo cowboy. All he needed was a Stetson.

She wondered if he'd been wearing a hat last night in the bar, then forgot about it as the sleepy voice sounded over the speaker.

"Yeah?"

"Danny, it's me. Let me in. I've brought someone to meet you."

"Okay, c'mon up."

The security door buzzed and Jill slipped through, followed closely by Hank. Now that the moment was at hand, she was anxious to get it over with. "Don't forget," she warned Hank as they stepped into the elevator, "not a word about the letters. As far as Danny is concerned, you don't even know they exist. You are here strictly as a road manager, nothing more."

He nodded, his mouth tight.

For the second time Jill wondered if he had second thoughts about hiring on with her. He hadn't said as much, but she was still surprised by his change of mind last night, and still half expected him to change it back again.

She didn't get a chance to say any more as the elevator jerked to a halt and the door slid open. Stepping out into the carpeted hallway, she waited for Hank to join her, then pointed to the door at the end of the passageway. "That's Danny's apartment."

"Are you going to tell him we knew each other before?" Hank asked sharply.

Surprised by the question, Jill frowned. "I hadn't thought about it, but I suppose it would be a good idea. It would explain why I felt secure in hiring you at the last minute."

"I just wanted to get the story straight, that's all."

She could hear a definite edge to his voice now. Please, she prayed silently, don't let Danny mess this up.

Reaching the door, she pressed the bell and waited, her heart beginning to thump. The door opened, and Danny's face smiled at her. He was wearing a pair of faded jeans and nothing else.

He looked as if he'd just climbed out of bed, she thought, noting his long, blond hair straggling over his bare shoulders and his pale blue eyes half closed against the light.

At that moment he looked years younger than his age of twenty-four, and she sensed Hank's tension as she said with a smile, "Good morning, Danny."

"Hi," he drawled, in the low, husky voice that sent the groupies wild. "You're early."

"No, you're late." She looked at her watch. "It's almost eleven."

He was about to answer her when his gaze slid past her. With a sinking feeling, she watched the shutters snap down over his face. Before she could speak, he demanded harshly, "Who's he?"

"Let us in, Danny," she said quietly, "and I'll explain."

"I'm not letting anyone I don't know into my apartment." He folded his arms across his thin chest and glared at the man standing silently behind her.

She started to speak, but Hank forestalled her. Moving forward, he held out his hand. "Hi, there, Danny. Jill has told me a lot about you. It's a pleasure to meet a talented singer, and I'm sure looking forward to hearing you perform."

She had to hand it to him, Jill thought. It was exactly the right thing to say. Although he ignored the outstretched hand, Danny's expression gave just a little.

"Danny," she said quickly, "this is Hank Tyler. I knew him many years ago, when he was managing the band I was singing with. I ran into him last night and he's looking for work. I told him the Wildwoods were looking for a road manager and he's offered to go with us on the tour. Isn't that great?"

Danny's heavy-lidded eyes slid over Hank from head to foot. "What do we need a road manager for?" he muttered. "Seems to me we were doing okay all by ourselves."

"Now you know we need a manager." Jill reached out and patted his arm. "We need someone to help organize the setup, make sure the bookings have been taken care of, check out the advance publicity, take care of the dozens of small problems that crop up on a tour like this. I explained all this to you yesterday."

"Yeah, but—"

"Can we please talk about this inside?" To her relief, Danny shuffled backward, and she stepped past him into the living room. As usual, articles of clothing lay everywhere. It looked as if someone had tossed a laundry basket full of wash in the air and left everything where it landed.

Wincing at the sight, Jill gestured at Hank to follow her, then started around the room, picking up shirts and socks from the carpet. A pair of jeans had been draped across the back of the couch and she snatched them up, too. "Sit down, Hank. You too, Danny."

Hank chose a leather armchair, but Danny remained where he was, leaning against the wall, arms folded, his face tight with suspicion. "What's wrong with your face, man?" he demanded, staring rudely at Hank.

Hank's eyebrows arched, but his expression remained pleasant. "I fell off a horse."

"Hank rides in the rodeo," Jill explained quickly. "He's taking a year off, that's why he's looking for work."

"Yeah? The rodeo?" Danny unfolded his arms and pushed himself away from the wall. "If a horse did that to me, I'd sure get the hell out of that business and fast."

"Well, some of us wear better'n others." Hank stretched out his long legs in front of him.

Danny flung himself down onto the couch next to Jill. "So what'd you say your name was?"

"Hank. Hank Tyler."

"What kind of bands have you worked with?"

"The Back Trackers Country Band for one," Hank said, beginning to sound irritated.

"I told you, Danny," Jill interrupted. "Hank managed the band I sang with. A country and blues band, like yours. He's—"

"I don't see we need a road manager." He gave Jill a reproachful look. "I got you for my manager. Why do I need another one?"

"You don't," Jill said evenly. "But as I've already told you, the band could use some help. You know how disorganized Slim and Gary are, and I don't have time to keep an eye on them and give you my full attention, too."

That seemed to appease him. "Yeah, that makes sense. Let's not forget who's the star, right?"

"Right. After all, this tour is very important to your career. I want to make sure that everything is done right, so that you have nothing to worry about except getting up there in front of that mike and giving them your very best performance."

His face broke into a grin. "Don't you worry none about that. I'll give 'em what they want and then some. I'm the best damn country singer to hit the boards and they're gonna know it. I get this gig over and done with and I'm on my way to the top."

He jiggled his knee rapidly up and down, bouncing Jill on the springs. She smiled at him, and laid a hand on his shoulder. "You'll make it, Danny. If this goes right, it could mean a recording contract and stardom. That's why it's so important that we have enough staff along with us."

His smile vanished, and he slumped back on the couch. Once more, he lowered his lids and stared broodingly at Hank. "I don't care for strangers," he muttered.

"Hank's not a stranger, not to me. And once you get to know him, you'll like him." Jill glanced across at Hank and caught his expression as he rolled his eyes up to the ceiling in mock despair.

"Anyway," she added quickly, hoping Danny hadn't noticed, "we have to settle this right away. You have a luncheon engagement in less than an hour, and you have to get showered and dressed."

To her relief, Danny nodded his grudging approval. "Okay, if you say we need him then I guess it's okay." He jerked to his feet, as if propelled on a spring. "As long as he doesn't get in my way, we should get along fine." Without looking at Hank again, he left the room.

"Nice guy," Hank murmured, with more than a touch of sarcasm. "That's insecurity?"

Jill touched a finger to her lips. "I'm going to run Hank home, Danny," she called out. "I'll be back for you in half an hour. Make sure you're ready."

From just a few feet away, Danny sang out, "Don't panic, I'll be ready."

Nodding at Hank, Jill made for the door. Outside in the hallway she breathed a sigh of relief. "Well, that's one hurdle over with."

"Do you always do that?" Hank asked as they waited for the elevator.

She glanced up at him, noting with apprehension his formidable frown. "Do what?"

"Baby him like that."

She stifled her resentment. After all, she'd expected his reaction. "You have to know Danny to understand him. He is extremely talented, but he's had a lot of grief in his life. He never knew his parents, they died when he was very young. He won't talk about his childhood, it's too painful for him. He's still a little boy inside, afraid to trust, afraid to believe in his own talent. He expects it all to be snatched away from him any moment. He buries that fear beneath a show of arrogance, which is nothing more than bravado. Underneath all that, he's terrified."

"And you're trying to be all things to him, including his mother."

The door swung open and swallowing her quick retort, she stepped into the elevator. "All I'm trying to do is give him the confidence to be all that he can be. It isn't easy to step up to that mike in front of a crowd of roughnecks who expect too much for their money and are not shy about letting you know if they don't like your performance. That can be devastating to someone far more stable than Danny is."

"So why does he do it?"

She stabbed at the button with her finger. "Why do writers write? Why do climbers climb mountains?" She looked up at him, annoyed by his disapproving expression. "Why do you ride the rodeo?"

His shoulders lifted in a dismissive shrug. "It's all I know."

''That's not true and you know it. There are a hundred things you could do instead of punishing your body day in and day out.''

''The money's good.''

''It's only good if you are. What about the years you don't do well? What about all those new guys coming up behind you, younger, stronger, more agile, better able to take the grinding rides and the pounding your body takes every time you hit the dirt?''

His gray eyes glinted as he looked down at her. ''Lady, you're beginning to depress me.''

She felt a quiver of some long-forgotten emotion. There had been a time, before she'd married Perry, when she'd gone weak-kneed every time Hank Tyler had looked at her that way.

He had a way of shifting his gaze to her mouth, just briefly enough to make her wonder what it would be like to be kissed by him. She'd spent many a night imagining him taking her into his arms and smothering her mouth with a deep, passionate kiss.

Much later, when she'd thought about it, she'd put it down to simple, adolescent reactions to a man older and much more experienced than her age group.

Now, however, when his brief glance touched her mouth, the swift stirring of excitement was far more primitive than anything she'd felt then.

Disturbed by the notion, she was glad when the elevator jerked to a halt. ''Face it,'' she said, as she waited for the door to open. ''You're in rodeo because it's what you do. It's who you are. Just like Danny. He has to sing.'' The door opened and she stepped outside.

They left the building in silence and she waited until they were back in the car before saying, ''I guess if you want to change your mind, this is a good time to do it. We leave the day after tomorrow, and I have too much to do to talk about this again.''

He didn't look at her, and she studied his profile. He had a strong nose and a chin that reflected his stubborn nature. She wondered if the years had softened his hard, relentless attitude about things he didn't understand. Somehow she doubted it.

Remembering that moment in the elevator, she wasn't sure if she really wanted him to accept the job. He disturbed her too much, and brought back too many memories she'd sooner forget. She felt a moment's apprehension when he finally answered her.

"I said I'd do it and I will. But I might as well tell you up front, I'm not crazy about the idea."

"Then why are you doing it?"

He glanced sideways at her. "Like you said, there are some things you gotta do."

And that, she decided, would have to be enough for now.

It had begun to rain by the time they were ready to roll, heading for Westoaks, their first stop in Colorado. Jill had been rushing about for two days, and was looking forward to the long drive that would take them into their first stop late that night. She enjoyed driving, and Hank had offered to split the time at the wheel, giving her the rare opportunity to relax for a while.

Danny seemed excited and on edge at first, but soon settled down, lulled by the steady hum of the engine and the gentle sway of the roomy vehicle.

The camper had two tiny bedrooms partitioned off from the rest of the interior. The third partition housed a miniature shower stall and toilet.

The living quarters consisted of a narrow table, with benches around three sides of it, the kitchen counter with sink, fridge, small oven and burners, and two long couches that converted into a double bed.

Hank had been assigned the couches, while Danny and Jill took the bedrooms. It seemed like a workable arrangement, Hank thought, as they sped along the wet road to the accompaniment of swishing windshield wipers and the soft strumming of Danny's guitar.

It was his turn to drive, and Jill was somewhere in the back, relaxing with a book. The freeway miles were monotonous, the steady rain making it difficult to see. He needed his concentration to keep the unwieldy vehicle inside the lane, yet his mind kept wandering back to the woman behind him.

She had changed, in more ways than one. She still had the spirit and the fire that had made her such a hothead years ago, but it had been channeled into something much more controlled, a quiet determination and a sense of purpose that he was forced to admire, in spite of his personal feelings about her.

Oh, he still resented her, he reminded himself. He couldn't wipe out what she'd done, nor the years of misery she'd caused him. But he had to admit, she'd matured into quite a woman, both in looks and temperament. It was too bad he couldn't forgive her for what she'd done. It might have been a very interesting trip.

A waft of perfume warned him she was close behind him, and his hands tightened on the wheel.

"We should be coming into town soon," she said, moving into the passenger seat next to him. "I have the maps here, so I'll act as navigator."

He nodded briefly. He didn't want to look at her. He knew what she looked like. Those tight jeans she wore accented her curvy hips, and her pale green sweater clung snugly to her full breasts.

She wore little makeup, just a touch of color on her mouth and above her dark eyes. Her clear skin was the color of sun-warmed sand, and her nut-brown hair gleamed as it curled about her face. Oh, yeah. He knew what she looked like.

"The next exit," Jill said, pointing at the sign ahead.

He narrowed his eyes. "Okay."

He saw the ramp up ahead and flicked on the indicator, pulling the camper over gradually as they drew closer to the exit. The next few minutes were taken up with maneuvering the traffic lights and stop signs, while Jill quietly and efficiently gave directions.

They had to pass through town to reach the theater, and already dusk had darkened the streets. Brightly colored lights from a movie theater splashed across the road, reflected in the puddles left by the rain, then vanished as he plowed on, almost blinded by the beams from the headlights of oncoming cars.

Jill pointed out the theater finally, and he saw the entrance to the parking lot, hemmed in by oak trees on either side, their soaked branches swaying in the wind.

He slowed, peering through the wet splatters on the windshield, and caught a glimpse of a trailer hitched to a pickup parked at the edge of the lot. His shoulders ached, still not quite recovered from the bar fight. He longed for a soak in a hot tub, preferably with a foaming beer in his hand.

"The Wildwoods made it," Jill said as he pulled up alongside the darkened trailer. "They must be celebrating already."

He'd been wondering what had happened to the backup group. They must have left earlier that morning. He stepped on the brake, shifted out of gear and cut the engine.

"What would you have done for a relief driver if I hadn't come along?" he asked Jill as she leaned forward to switch on the interior lights.

"I would've managed without one. I don't mind driving. I'm used to it."

She moved out of her seat, and he rubbed the back of his neck. He had to be getting old. The thought depressed him.

"Don't you ever get tired?" he said as he stepped down into the bed of the vehicle and stretched his cramped muscles.

"Sure I do. Exhausted. But it's part of the job." She looked up at him. "You okay?"

"Yeah, I'm fine." He couldn't see Danny, he had to be in his bedroom. "Just hungry."

She reached up to a cupboard and opened it. "There's a tavern across the street. I saw it as we pulled in. You can probably get something to eat there if you want."

For a moment he let his gaze wander over her body as she stretched up her arms. Firm-looking breasts outlined the sweater. Just made to fit into a man's palms, he thought. A spasm of need shook him, and he clamped down on the treacherous thought.

Hank felt relieved when Jill added, "I'll fix something for Danny and myself here."

She took out a couple of cans and shut the door. "He's been sleeping for a few hours, he'll be hungry when he wakes up. You go ahead. You'll probably find the gang in there. Just introduce yourself. I told them about you so they'll know who you are."

"How will I know who they are?"

She put the cans down on the counter. "You'll know. Just head for the sexiest-looking blonde in the place. That'll be Tiffany."

Considering how badly he wanted a beer, he was having a tough time getting out of there. "I guess it's okay to leave Danny? I'm supposed to be guarding him, remember?"

"Oh, I think he'll be okay this one time." She glanced up at his hair. "It's still raining. You'll need your hat and a jacket."

He almost smiled. Seems her mothering didn't stop with Danny. He turned away before he could give in to the impulse. "I'll get them."

"Oh, and I have a key for you. I'm going to have a hot shower later, so I might not hear if you come back."

He felt a twinge along his spine and shut off the image before it could form. "Well, just make sure you lock everything up real good behind me."

"I will. Here."

He looked back at her, then took the key she offered him and slipped it into the back pocket of his jeans. "Don't wait up."

"I don't intend to. Enjoy your supper."

He didn't feel right about leaving her and Danny alone, considering the reason he'd been hired. But right then he needed to get out of that enclosed space and give himself some room. His mind was playing tricks, and he didn't like it. Some good, hot food, a couple of beers and any company other than this warm-eyed woman would chase away the erotic thoughts that plagued his mind.

It had been a long time since he'd been bothered by those kinds of thoughts. Too long. He needed to put some distance between himself and the source of his problem. Without looking at her again, he grabbed his hat and jacket and let himself out of the camper.

Striding across the deserted parking lot, hat in hand, he let the cool, wet wind play with his hair. It felt good, like washing the cobwebs from his mind. Now that he was out of the camper, he could think straight again.

It was the combination of hunger and fatigue, he told himself as he headed for the lights gleaming through the trees ahead of him. And it was the first day, after all. It was natural that he'd feel uptight and edgy around her.

After everything she'd done, he'd better get his mind off that track and fast. She was the last person on this earth he wanted to waste those thoughts on.

Of course, being in such close quarters with a woman, any woman, was bound to have a physical effect on him. He was only human, and it had been longer than he realized, he thought ruefully as he paused at the edge of the curb to wait for a gap in the traffic.

Across the street, the door to the tavern opened, letting out a babble of chatter and the strident sounds of a rock band. He didn't care much for that kind of music, but right then any noise was welcome, if it drowned out the turbulent thoughts chasing through his head.

He dashed across the street, then paused to jam his hat down over his wet hair before pushing open the door of the tavern.

The music clashed in his ears when he stepped inside. The smoke-filled humidity threatened to cut off his breath as he edged his way through a crowd of chattering women to the bar.

Reaching the counter, he caught the eye of the bartender and ordered a beer. "You serve food?" he asked as the bearded, black-eyed guy lifted a burly tattooed arm and slapped a foaming mug down in front of him.

"Upstairs," the barman grunted, snatching the bill from Hank's hand.

Pocketing his change, Hank picked up the mug and drained half of it before fighting his way to the narrow staircase. At the top of the steps a young waitress greeted him with a grimace. Her black-smudged eyes looked through him as she mumbled, "Dinner?"

He felt older than ever. "Yeah." He looked around. A dozen or so tables were squeezed into the rectangular room, with three of them lined along the windows that looked out onto the street.

At the middle table by the window sat three people. One of the men wore a cowboy hat and a checked shirt. He sat back in his chair, with a cigarette hanging from his thin lips. His face looked drawn, as if he'd gone without sleep for several nights, and he had a look in his dark brown eyes that suggested he could be mean if crossed.

The other man was older, and had more flesh on his bones. His light brown hair was thinning on top, and hung limply below his earlobes. He had a beer clutched in his hand, and he talked rapidly, his attention on the woman seated opposite him at the table.

Looking at her, Hank could see why. She sat with one arm draped over the back of her chair, the golden bangles around her wrist gleaming in the lamplight. The scooped neck of the black T-shirt she wore flirted with decency, leaving little to the imagination as it strained low across her prominent breasts. Something told him this had to be Tiffany.

Her smooth, wrinkle-free face had been skillfully made-up to accentuate her sea-green eyes, and her baby-doll mouth puckered in a permanent plea to be kissed. Shimmering hair floated about her shoulders in a fluffy cloud of gold, and she wore the bored expression of someone who'd seen it all and was waiting for someone to give her some excitement.

Maybe five years ago, Hank would have been happy to oblige. Now he just felt tired looking at her.

As if sensing the scrutiny, the green eyes glanced in his direction, then widened with interest.

Realizing he'd been caught staring, Hank looked over at the waitress. She'd slapped a greasy menu on an empty table and stood waiting with ill-concealed impatience.

He made his way over to the table, conscious of calculating green eyes following his every movement. Judging by the sudden silence at her table, the blonde wasn't the only one who was interested.

He sat down, placing his beer in front of him. "Steak sandwich," he said without looking at the menu. "Medium rare."

"You want salad with that?"

"Bowl of soup, as long as it's not clam chowder."

"Minestrone."

"That'll do."

The waitress shuffled off, and he picked up his beer. Over the rim of the glass, his gaze clashed with the blonde's. Very slowly, she looked him over. He didn't have to look at the mean-faced cowboy to feel the bite of his hostile glare.

Hank pushed back his chair and stood. With his beer in his hand, and watched by three pairs of eyes, he sauntered over to their table.

Chapter 3

"**Y**ou wouldn't be the Wildwoods, by any chance?" Hank directed his question at the older man, who seem startled.

"Er...y-yes," he stammered, but Mean Face jabbed him into silence with his elbow.

"Who wants to know?" he muttered, the cigarette flipping up and down in his mouth as he spoke.

Hank smiled without humor. "My name is Hank Tyler. I'm your new manager."

"Well," the blonde said, drawing out the word as if she were licking her lips. "Nice to meet you, Hank. I'm Tiffany. Jill has told us all about you."

She made it sound as if he were an X-rated movie. He nodded in her direction, but didn't take his eyes off Mean Face.

"Gary," the thin lips said. "Tiffany's *husband.*"

The emphasis on the last word made the message loud

and clear. Hank switched his gaze to the other man, who looked decidedly uncomfortable. "I take it you're Slim?"

"Yeah," Gary said, answering for him. "And we know why you've been hired, big boy, so don't go throwing your weight around, okay? We run things our way, and we don't need no one telling us different. Got it?"

Oh, he got it all right. Not for the first time, Hank wondered what the hell he'd been thinking of when he accepted this job.

"Oh, cool it, Gary," Tiffany said, reaching for a lipstick-smeared glass of wine. "We all got to work together for Danny's sake, right? As long as we keep him happy, we're happy."

"Yeah," Slim muttered, scowling at Gary, "we don't need any more trouble than we already got."

"Who asked you?" Gary snarled the words out of the corner of his mouth, but his gaze remained steadily on Hank's face.

Hank raised his hands. "Look, guys, I don't want to cause trouble. I've been hired to do a job and I'll do it the best way I can. I'll try not to tread on anyone's toes, but I have to tell you, Danny's well-being comes first. I'll do whatever I have to do to maintain that, and if it means acting like a road manager once in a while, then I'll do it. You don't have to listen, okay?"

Gary answered with a shrug, but he dropped his gaze. Slim looked relieved, while Tiffany batted her long eyelashes at Hank. "Should be an interesting ride," she said softly.

He flicked his gaze over her, then abruptly turned and went back to his table. The waitress brought the steak and he tried to ignore the three muttering together across the room. He'd almost finished his meal when the muttering suddenly got louder.

Without lifting his chin, Hank glanced up from under the brim of his hat.

Gary had hold of Slim's arm, his face red with temper. The older man dragged his arm free and muttered something Hank couldn't hear.

Gary's fists clenched, but Tiffany's hand on his arm apparently made him think twice about using them. He nodded at his wife, and all three of the Wildwoods got up from the table. In silence they filed out of the door, but not before Tiffany had sent one last glance in Hank's direction.

Hank was left hoping the argument wasn't about him. Whatever it had been about, there seemed no doubt that the members of Danny's backup group were on very shaky ground. He could feel the hostility hovering in the room long after they'd left.

He had a couple more beers in the bar before he felt able to face his own predicament. He was not looking forward to going back to the camper. He could only hope that both Danny and Jill were sound asleep in their respective bedrooms and that he wouldn't have to face either of them until morning. He'd had enough tension for one night.

Finally, he paid his bill and left, welcoming the rain that still sprinkled down from a black sky. The traffic had dwindled to nothing now, and he crossed the empty street, his footsteps echoing in the damp night.

Both the trailer and the camper were in darkness, and he began to breathe easier. At least he'd get a good night's sleep, he hoped, before facing whatever tomorrow would bring.

He sauntered across the parking lot, taking his time, breathing cool, clean air into his lungs to clear out the smoke from the tavern. With his hat tipped low over his brow, and his hands shoved deep into the pockets of his jacket, he didn't see the shadow move until it was almost in front of him.

He stopped abruptly, trying to adjust his eyes to the gloom. He didn't have to see her face clearly to know who she was. The wave of perfume reached him first, then she laughed, a soft, low sound that prickled his spine with warning.

"Hi, handsome. I wondered how much longer you were going to be."

"What do you want, Tiffany?" Stupid question. He knew what she wanted. He wondered where her husband was. Asleep, he hoped.

"Just wanted to say good-night, that's all. And to tell you not to worry about Gary. He talks that way to everyone." She stepped closer, and he hunched his shoulders.

"Go home, Tiffany. I don't need that kind of trouble."

"Trouble?" Her soft laugh floated in the darkness. "What he doesn't know won't hurt him. Besides, don't tell me a big, strong guy like you is afraid of someone like Gary? From the look of your scars, big guy, it wouldn't be the first time you've tangled with a fist."

She leaned forward, bumping against his arm. She had to be freezing. She wore no jacket, and the major portion of her breasts gleamed white and smooth in the darkness. "Come on, sugar," she whispered, snuggling up against him, "just one, tiny little kiss can't hurt, can it? You know you want to."

It was time to duck out, Hank decided. He stepped away from her, fishing for the key Jill had given him. "Sorry to disappoint you, kiddo, but all I want right now is to get my head down for some shut-eye. Go back to your husband if you're looking for action. That's where you belong."

He had to admit, she was persistent. "He can't give me what I want," she said softly. "But I just know that you can. You know it, too."

He opened the door, then looked down at her. "All I know," he said, keeping his voice low, "is that I'm not interested in anything you can offer. You're a little too wet behind the ears for my taste. Is that plain enough?''

Her teeth gleamed white in the darkness. "You got it wrong, sugar," she whispered, "I'm more experienced than you think. Just wait until you've been on the road awhile. I'm going to look very good to you, and I'll be ready and waiting. All you have to do is say the word."

Before he could answer, she had slipped away in the darkness. Cursing under his breath, he stepped inside the camper and closed the door, then felt his way down toward the couches. His shin bumped into something, and he realized that Jill had unfolded the bed and made it up for him.

Silently thanking her, he pulled off his clothes and slipped between the sheets. But tired as he was, he couldn't sleep. Somehow he had trouble shutting off the thought of Jill lying on the other side of the thin partition. He'd spent the last fifteen years wishing he and Perry had never set eyes on her. Now here he was, cooped up in this damn camper with her.

All his life he'd been inclined to bite off more than he could chew. Somehow he'd always managed to land on his feet. But right now, he could see all kinds of wrong paths opening up in front of him, each of them loaded with booby traps.

He'd been on this job one day and already he was getting bad vibes. He couldn't help wondering what kind of disaster waited for him on the road ahead, and how in the hell he was going to avoid it.

Jill woke up the next morning listening to the birds welcoming the sun and the faint hum of early morning traffic. Even on weekends, it seemed that some people found a reason to be on the road at the crack of dawn.

She smiled to herself, thinking of all the dawns she'd seen on the road. At least on this trip they could sleep in a little.

Hearing a sound from the bathroom, she reached for her watch. A little before seven. Danny always slept late, in preparation for the grueling evening ahead of him. It had to be Hank.

Her heart skipped at the thought, and she frowned. She'd been awake when he'd come back last night. The idea of him sleeping on the other side of the wall caused all kinds of unwelcome sensations. Not for the first time, she questioned the wisdom of suggesting he share the camper with them.

Yet what else could she have done? She'd hired him to take care of Danny, and he wouldn't be much help to them if he was down the street in a motel. And there was no way Gary would have let him sleep in the trailer, even if they'd had room.

In fact, Jill was constantly amazed that Gary allowed Slim to stay with them. She had never seen anyone quite so possessive about his wife as Gary was. Not that he didn't have cause to be. Tiffany flirted with anything in pants.

Still, the fact remained that things could turn out to be very awkward having Hank living in—though it was a little late to worry about such things now. She'd known when she'd suggested it that the intimacy of their shared quarters could prove to be extremely awkward.

But for Danny's sake, she would have to make the best of it. She just hoped that Hank would do so, too.

She slid her feet out of the bed and reached for her robe. With Danny there she had no reason to feel uncomfortable, she told herself. After all, Hank had spent the night in her apartment earlier that week, and she had survived that.

Even so, she felt her heart thumping as she edged the door open and looked around it. He was still in the bathroom, she could hear the shower running.

The smell of coffee was too inviting to resist, and she edged her way down the bed toward the kitchen area. She had to step over bedclothes and his brown Western boots. His hat lay on the table, and he'd draped his jeans over a chair.

The water shut off in the bathroom, and she stared at the jeans. He could, of course, have taken a clean pair of jeans in with him. Losing her nerve, she decided not to hang around to find out. It would be incredibly embarrassing if he walked out of there in his underwear.

She started back to her room, but almost immediately the bathroom door opened. Whipping around to face the other way, she felt heat surge to her face. She stooped to pick up the bedclothes, trying desperately not to envision a half-naked man standing a few feet away. Hands shaking, she went to the bed and folded it back into a couch.

There was silence for a moment behind her, then she heard the soft sound of the door being gently closed. Her breath came out in a rush, and she hurriedly folded the sheets and tucked them into the drawer. Then, with a great deal of noise, she returned to her cubicle and loudly closed the door.

Breathing hard, she sank onto the bed. That was too close for comfort. Obviously Hank had not been fully clothed, or he would have come out. She couldn't blame him for not wanting to get dressed in the closet they called a bathroom. It was barely big enough for her to turn around in. A man of Hank's size would have real problems.

She closed her eyes, willing her mind not to envision how he must have looked standing in the doorway. She didn't want that picture on her mind when she faced him.

The bathroom door opened and closed, and she sat for a few minutes longer, trying to find the composure to go back into the kitchen. Then she heard another door open and slam shut. Crushed, she realized Hank had left the camper.

She tried to tell herself it was just as well, but her disappointment stayed with her as she took her turn in the bathroom.

Danny had joined her for a late breakfast. When Hank returned, he avoided her gaze as he stepped inside, directing his greeting at Danny, who mumbled an unintelligible answer, his mouth full of toast.

Feeling ridiculously flustered, Jill asked brightly, "Have you eaten?"

His gray eyes flicked over her and away. "Yeah, down the road a ways. I didn't want to disturb anyone that early."

"Oh, you needn't have worried. I'm always up early, and Danny can sleep through a tornado." She got up and reached for the coffeepot. "Want some?"

"No, thanks. I've had too much already." He glanced at his watch. "What time is the band setting up?"

"They usually start around four. Danny and I get there about five for a sound check and rehearsal, then we get something to eat before we go back at seven.

"So what do you do for excitement in the meantime?"

"We sit around and look cool," Danny muttered.

Jill sent him a reproachful look, which he ignored. "Sometimes we go sight-seeing, depending where we are. Sometimes I go shopping, or else I stay here with Danny while he rehearses, or works on a new song."

She looked back at Hank. "Did I tell you Danny writes some of his own songs?"

"Yeah? I'd like to hear them."

He seemed genuinely interested and, encouraged, Jill said, "How about it, Danny? When you're finished with your breakfast?"

Danny lifted a disdainful shoulder and went on reading the music magazine spread out in front of him.

"They are really very good," Jill said firmly, "and I'd like to get an outside opinion from someone who knows what he's talking about. You might not know this, Danny, but before Hank got into rodeo, he was managing some very popular groups. He told you about the Back Trackers Country Band, remember?"

Danny lifted his head and, looking up at Hank, said grudgingly, "Yeah, I heard of them. They were doing pretty good back in the seventies."

"For a while, yeah," Hank said, taking off his hat and laying it on the couch. "I got them their first recording contract."

Danny frowned. "Why'd you give it up, man? That must have been good money."

Hank's gaze slid over to Jill. "I lost interest in the music business," he said, his voice suddenly curt.

Anxious to break the small, awkward silence that followed, Jill said quickly, "Danny, why don't you play Hank a couple of your songs while I clean up these dishes?"

To her relief, Danny shrugged, then slid along the table to where he could stand up. "I'll get my guitar," he said. "It's in my room."

Left alone for the moment with Hank, Jill busied herself collecting the dishes.

"I'll be honest about his talent," Hank said quietly behind her.

His voice did odd things to her stomach. He had the kind of lazy drawl that dropped now and then to a sleepy growl. Incredibly sexy. Startled by the thought, she said quickly, "I expect you to be. I wouldn't have asked otherwise."

She dumped the plates in the sink and turned on the faucet. Concentrating on the subject with an effort, she added, "But I have complete faith in him, Hank. He is good, and he's going to the top. I don't care what we have to do to get there, but that boy is going to have his chance. He deserves it."

"You sound like you're real fond of him."

She glanced warily at him over her shoulder, but he was looking down at the open magazine on the table.

"I'm very proud of him," she said. "I'd be proud of anyone who has fought against the kind of odds Danny has and hung on to his dream. It's that kind of discipline and dedication that will get him where he wants to be. And I'm going to see that nothing stands in his way again. Nothing."

"He reminds me of Perry."

The abrupt words, spoken in a cool, clipped tone, hung between them like an accusation.

She turned to face him, knowing that she'd been waiting for this moment. "Danny might resemble him in appearance, but his personality is nothing like Perry's. He doesn't have Perry's confidence or his independence. Danny is sensitive, and needs careful handling. I hope you remember that and won't treat him the way you treated your brother."

He lifted his face, his eyes silver slits of anger. "Well said, considering how well you treated Perry."

"What happened between Perry and me is our own business. I am not going to defend myself to you, because you would simply accuse me of lying. As you always did."

He looked at her for a long moment, and she saw a flicker of uncertainty in his eyes. "So try me."

She was tempted. But she knew him too well. He would never hear a word against Perry, and no matter what she told him, he wouldn't believe her. He never had. And it was just too painful to talk about that time just to have it all thrown back in her face.

Yet, how she wished they could both forget about the past and be friends. She would really have liked to have him for a friend. Basically, in spite of his somewhat disreputable reputation, he was a nice guy. He'd always been dependable, honest and straightforward.

In spite of his disapproval of her, he'd always treated her with respect, and she knew that his loyalty to his brother, if somewhat misplaced, was born out of love and a very real sense of responsibility.

She couldn't deny the fact that she was attracted to him. She only had to look at him, and see his gaze so intent on her face, as it was then, and her stomach did wild things. That was something else she couldn't let him know about.

Danny chose that moment to reappear, guitar in hand, and she was saved from answering him. She hoped that Danny's singing would calm her crazy reactions to the one man she should be avoiding like the plague.

Danny was on his third song when a rap on the door interrupted him. Breaking off mid-phrase, the singer scowled as the door opened and Tiffany danced in, wearing a bright smile and a white T-shirt that advertised the fact she wasn't wearing a bra.

Jill glanced instinctively at Hank, wondering if he'd met the exuberant singer the night before. Judging by the wary look on his face, she thought wryly, apparently he had.

"Morning," Tiffany sang out, giving Hank a look loaded with promise. He merely nodded, and she turned her attention to Danny.

"I was over at the theater early," she said, handing him a sheaf of letters. "Got your fan mail. Looks like we should have a good house tonight."

"Thanks." Danny picked up the letters and without so much as a glance at Tiffany, disappeared into his tiny bedroom with them.

Tiffany's smile vanished as she gazed at the closed door. "I don't know why he can't stay and chat for a while. I went over there especially to get his mail."

"You know he likes to be by himself when he reads it," Jill said, stacking plates back in the cupboard.

"Yeah, well, it could've waited for a few minutes." Tiffany flung herself down on the couch and spread jeans-clad legs out in front of her. "Don't know what he sees in a bunch of screaming kids who should be doing their homework instead of scribbling weirdo letters to performers."

Jill paused with her hand in the air as Hank said quietly, "Weirdo letters?"

"Yeah, you know." Tiffany slapped a hand to one of her generous breasts and adopted an expression of exaggerated adoration. "Oh, Danny, I would just *die* for a kiss from those sweet lips." She gave a trembling sigh. "I'll be in the front row tonight, wearing a red sweater, so please, Danny, please blow me a kiss!"

Her face screwed up in a look of disgust. "Yech! How could he fall for that stuff? Most of them have never seen him before in their life. Half of 'em don't even know what he looks like until they get into the theater. All they know is what they read in the local newspaper."

"So, you read Danny's mail?"

Jill shot Hank a look of warning, but his attention was concentrated on Tiffany.

"I don't have to. I can guess what's in them." Tiffany pushed herself up from the couch. "I'd better go before Gary comes looking for me. He's in a lousy mood this morning and you know how irritated he gets when I hang around with Danny."

She paused in front of Danny's door and grinned up at Hank. "Not that I can't handle him, of course. So, if you've got nothing better to do later, sugar, how about you and me taking in the local sights? I'm sure I can find something to interest you."

Jill hid a smile as Hank's eyebrows twitched. "Thanks, but I'll pass," he said, reaching for his hat. "I've got some business to take care of."

"Too bad," Tiffany said loudly. "I could've used the company."

"How about using your husband's company?" Hank muttered, jamming his hat onto his head.

"Gary bores me." Tiffany moved to the camper door and opened it. "If you change you mind, sugar, I'll be across the street in the tavern."

"I won't change my mind."

Seemingly unperturbed, she lifted a provocative shoulder and smiled at him. "In that case, darlin', I'll see you at the theater. 'Bye."

"Not if I see you first," Hank muttered as the door closed behind her.

Jill was about to speak when Danny's door flew open. His eyes looked huge in his white face, and his hair flew in all directions, as if he'd been running his hands through it. He held a sheet of paper in his hand, and Jill didn't need to read it to know what it was.

"Danny—" She started forward, but Hank was closer.

"What is it?" he asked sharply. "What's wrong, Danny?"

Danny looked at him as if he'd forgotten Hank was there.

"It's okay, Danny," Jill said quickly. "You can trust him."

Still looking at Hank, Danny crumpled the letter in his fingers. "It's nothing," he muttered. "Forget it." He disappeared behind the door and closed it with a bang.

"I'm sorry," Jill said, looking at Hank's frustrated expression. "It must be another of those letters. Give him time, he'll come around."

Hank nodded. "I sure hope so. I'm not going to be much help to him if he doesn't trust me."

As if in answer, the harsh strum of a guitar vibrated from Danny's room. Taking advantage of the noise to cover her voice, Jill murmured, "I was hoping he wouldn't need your help."

"Yeah, I know what you mean." He took off his hat again and laid it on the couch. "It looks as if our letter writer knows the schedule."

Jill brushed a shaky hand across her brow. "I really didn't expect the letters to follow us on the road. This could mean big trouble with Danny."

"As long as it's only letters, we might not have that much to worry about."

She sent him a fearful look. "You think the person who's writing them could be here in town?"

"I don't know what to think at the moment. But I'd like to get a look at the envelope."

"If he hasn't torn it up." She picked up a dishcloth and began aimlessly wiping down the counter. "He usually gives the letters to me. He doesn't know you know about them. I guess he doesn't want you to know."

"Maybe you can talk him into changing his mind about that?"

She wished she didn't feel so confused. Confused and frightened. "I . . . don't know. I don't want him upset and worried by them, yet on the other hand, if he doesn't take them seriously, he could get hurt."

She shook out the cloth and draped it over the sink. "You have to understand Danny. He's excitable, highly strung. It doesn't take much to tip him off balance and the result can be...unpredictable."

"You could always cancel the tour."

"No," she said sharply. "You know as well as I do that that would be disastrous for his career. Apart from the financial aspects of it, his reputation would be damaged. He'd be labeled unreliable, and you of all people should know that in this business that could mean the end of his career before he's had a chance to get started."

"But the kid is talented. He has a good voice, he's got the looks and the presence, and he writes a pretty good song. He'd pick up again where he left off. Under the circumstances—"

"No!" Unwittingly, in her need to convince him, she raised her voice. "Not under any circumstances. This is Danny's big chance and I'm not going to let it slip through our fingers."

She hadn't realized the strumming had stopped until Danny's door flew open. One look at his face told her the worst. His eyes glittered with fury as he glared at Hank.

"What the hell business is it of yours what we do?" he demanded, his shrill voice rising almost to a shriek. "You're only the damn manager, you got no right to butt in. Get the hell out of here and go do what you're paid to do, instead of sitting around bullsh—"

"Danny!" Jill stepped forward, hand raised in protest, but Hank forestalled her.

"It's okay. I'm leaving. I want to take a look at the theater, anyway, and check out a few things." Without looking at Danny again, he picked up his hat and let himself out the door.

"And good riddance!" Danny shouted, aiming a furious kick at the door.

Jill dug her fists into her hips, more angry than she ever remembered being with him. "Sit *down*," she ordered at the top of her voice, "and you listen to me."

He jammed his thumbs into the pockets of his jeans and shoved his chin down on his chest.

"I said, sit down, Danny," Jill repeated more quietly.

She waited while he shuffled over to the couch and dropped onto it.

"Now," she said, folding her arms and standing over him. "I want you to promise me you will never, and I mean *never*, talk to Hank that way again."

"I don't like him," Danny mumbled. "I don't like him staying in here with us."

"Now I told you he would be staying with us in the motor home. There isn't room in Gary's trailer, with all the equipment. It's a lot more convenient than a motel room, besides saving us money."

Danny changed his tactics. "I didn't like the way he was talking to you."

"He was only trying to help. I'd asked his opinion and he was giving it to me." She hesitated, then took a chance. "That letter you got this morning. It was another one of those bad ones, right?"

Danny nodded, but refused to look at her.

"I'd like to have it, Danny."

"I tore it up."

"I don't think you did." She sat down next to him without touching him. "Danny, I told Hank about the letters. I'd like him to see it."

He looked at her then, with fear in his eyes. "Why? What'd you tell him for?"

"I wasn't going to. But I know how worried you've been, and you won't believe me when I say it's nothing to worry about, I thought it might make you feel better if someone like Hank saw it. He can tell you what he thinks."

"I don't care what he thinks," Danny muttered, staring down at his bare feet.

"He thinks you've got what it takes to get to the top. And he's in a position to know. Do you care about that?"

She held her breath while he thought about it. Then his shoulders lifted in a shrug. "Yeah, I guess so."

"Then you'll show him the letter?"

His foot tapped ceaselessly on the floor. "If you say so. But I still don't care what he says."

Wisely, Jill left it at that.

Hank could see no movement from the Wildwoods's trailer as he set off across the parking lot. It would be some time before they were due to set up. He planned on staying out of their way as much as possible. In fact, he thought, remembering Tiffany's sly look as she left the camper that morning, the less he saw of the group members the better.

Establishing his presence there was purely for Danny's benefit, since everyone else knew the real reason he was going along. Though they didn't know about the letters, which, judging by the performance he'd seen from Danny this morning, was a good move.

The theater manager, a pale-faced young man with glasses and a permanent frown, greeted him distractedly when Hank found him in his office. His lighting man had wrecked his car the night before, he explained to Hank, and he didn't know if he was going to show up.

"Don't worry," Hank told him, "I know enough about it to take care of it." He went on to ask a few technical questions about the setup, then added casually, "By the way, who collects the fan mail for the performers here?"

"It comes to me, with the rest of the mail." The manager rubbed his forehead with nicotine-stained fingers. "Usually junk mail, of course, and bills."

"So you gave Danny Webster's mail to a member of the group this morning?"

"Yeah, the blonde. Tiffany." For a moment, the bespectacled eyes glazed over. "Some looker, huh?"

Hank smiled. "If you like the type. Did you notice if there were any letters from out of town?"

The manager's gaze sharpened behind his glasses. "No, I didn't. Is there a problem?"

Hank shook his head. "It's just that Danny was expecting a letter from his hometown and it hasn't turned up yet. I just wondered if maybe Tiffany dropped it on the way back to the trailer. You know how these women have their minds on everything except what they're supposed to be doing."

"Yeah." He said it as if he would like to be the one on her mind. "Well, it could come in today's mail. It hasn't arrived yet."

Hank got up from the chair. "Well, I'll go and take a look around, if it's okay with you?"

"Sure." An impatient hand waved a dismissal. "Let me know if there's a problem."

"You'll be the first to know," Hank said dryly.

He spent an hour checking out the stage area and auditorium. The time when Danny would be most vulnerable would be on stage, in full view of several hundred people. Hank needed to know all the angles and areas where possible danger could be lurking.

He was still inclined to believe that the letters were more of a psychological threat than a physical one, but he was there to do a job, and it didn't hurt to be cautious.

By the time he was through, he was hungry again. He was reluctant to go back to the camper, but his conscience told him he should check back there to see how things were going.

On his way out, he stopped by the manager's office. The mail had arrived, and there were several letters for Danny. Hank took them, promising to deliver them, and left.

Outside the building he sifted through the mail. There was one from Cedarvale. He stared at it for a long moment, then shoved it in his back pocket.

The sun had dried all the puddles from the night before, and he enjoyed the clean air as he walked back to the camper. Now that the clouds had virtually disappeared, he could see the white-tipped peaks on the blue smudge of the Rockies in the distance.

The buildings on the other side of the street had been there for a hundred years by the look of them, and the old-fashioned shop fronts intrigued him. He could imagine the gun fights that must have taken place along these streets in the days before progress and industrialization had buried the old world, leaving only lingering memories.

He would have enjoyed living then, Hank thought as he crossed the parking lot. Things might have been just as violent, if not more so in the old days, but it was a lot less complicated.

He thought of the letter stuffed in his pocket, still unsure what to do about it. It had been mailed the day before from Danny's hometown. Whoever had mailed it knew exactly where he was, and could even be right here, waiting for an opportunity to carry out the threats.

To reassure himself, he patted the inside pocket where he'd stashed his revolver. Somehow, it made him feel better just knowing it was there.

He tapped on the door of the camper first, wary of using his key. He'd had a narrow shave that morning. He couldn't help wondering what Jill would have done if she'd turned around and seen him standing there, stark naked.

More to the point, he wondered what he would have done. Preoccupied, it had never occurred to him she could be in the room. That was one mistake he wouldn't make again. He had enough problems keeping his mind off his wayward libido, without tantalizing himself that way.

The door opened and Jill looked down at him. "Forget your key?"

He shook his head. "Didn't want to barge in on anything."

A pink flush stole across her cheeks. "Oh, that's okay. Danny's asleep, and I was catching up on my reading."

She turned away and disappeared, leaving him staring after her thoughtfully.

Standing at the kitchen counter, Jill tried to recover her composure. If he didn't stop giving her those devastating looks she would have to quit looking at him. The last thing she needed was for him to know how he affected her.

"Have you had lunch?" she asked, opening the door of the tiny fridge. "I can offer a ham sandwich, or spaghetti and meatballs?"

"I'll take the sandwich."

His deep voice, coming from so close behind her, seemed to vibrate up her spine. She grabbed the sliced ham and a jar of mayonnaise and slammed the door shut. "Coming right up. Coffee?"

"Got any beer?"

"No, you'll have to make do with cola."

"That's fine."

She opened the fridge again and took out two cans.

He sat down at the table, and she avoided looking at him as she made the sandwiches.

"I've got something to show you," he said, and threw a pile of letters on the table.

She caught her breath. "For Danny?"

"Yes. There's one more." He reached into his back pocket and pulled out a crumbled envelope. "I thought you might like to take a look at that before giving it to him.

Postmarked Cedarvale, no return address. Recognize the writing?''

She stared down at the crudely printed words and nodded. Her hand shook as she picked up the letter. ''You think I should open it?''

He shrugged. ''It's your decision.''

She stared at it for a moment longer, then quickly slit it open with her nail. The folded piece of paper was the same as all the others, torn from a notebook. Ice ran along her veins as she scanned the scrawled words.

Shuddering, she threw the page down on the table. ''I can't believe that anyone could be this vindictive. Whatever has Danny done to deserve this?''

''Nothing, probably.'' Hank reached for the letter and read it. ''This is a sick mind we're dealing with. And they're the most dangerous.'' He read out the last part of the letter again to her. '' 'You can't run from me, Danny. I'm right behind you. I'm watching your every move.' ''

Shaking his head, he folded the letter and put it back in the envelope. ''That's the part that worries me, more than the rest. If whoever wrote this is on our trail, it's only going to be a matter of time before Danny knows it.''

She stared at him. ''What do you mean?''

Hank looked grave as he looked up at her. ''All they have to do is mention one tiny incident that happened on this tour, and Danny will know for sure that someone is following him all the way.''

Jill sat down and curled her fingers around a can of cola. ''He'll go to pieces.'' She sent a desperate look at Hank. ''Do you think we should talk to the police?''

''What can they do? They told you they can't do anything unless someone makes a move. It's still possible it's just a crank out for kicks. And if we get the police involved, Danny will know there's something to worry about.''

"God, what are we going to do?" How she hated this helpless feeling. She'd always been so in control of everything, always sure of the answers. Now she was treading on shifting sands, not knowing where to take the next step, and she didn't like it.

"We're going to try not to worry," Hank said firmly. "Though from now on, I'm not leaving you and Danny alone. We stick together as much as possible, it will make it that much harder for anyone to get to him."

She nodded, too miserable to speak. It seemed as if her worst fears were being realized. Danny's life could well be in danger, and there didn't seem to be too much she could do about it.

Chapter 4

"If it's any consolation," Hank said gruffly, "I still don't think it's likely anything will happen. From what I've heard, people who do things like this rarely carry out their threats. If this person was serious about hurting Danny, he certainly wouldn't want to advertise the fact and warn him. How would he know we wouldn't call in the police?"

She raised her eyes to look at him. "I guess."

Once more his gaze seemed to stab right into her soul. "I'll try to monitor Danny's mail and grab any more of these before he sees them."

"Okay." She hesitated. "Thanks."

For a moment something flickered in his eyes, then with a curt nod, he reached for a sandwich. "All right, now let's eat. I'm hungry."

The lighting man turned up that afternoon at the theater, his left arm in a sling and a large bump on his head, but anxious to do his job. It was one less thing for Hank to worry about, he thought with relief. Danny seemed moody and preoccupied, barely listening as the monitors were set up and tested.

Tiffany played guitar and Gary the keyboard, both of them providing the vocal backing, while Slim was on drums. Danny's arrangements called for him to accompany himself on guitar for four of the numbers.

"Hit the snare again," the sound man ordered as Slim performed a light drumroll.

Slim did so, and a moment of silence followed before the sound man spoke again into the speaker.

"More snare, and give me the high hat."

Slim's sticks vibrated on the small drum, then flicked the cymbals.

"Check. Let's do a run-through."

Standing in the wings, Hank looked down at Jill standing beside him. "We never used a sound board in the old days."

Jill smiled. "Modern technology. It's surprising the difference it can make to a small group like this."

"Yeah, but I can't help thinking of it as cheating. Makes me wonder if anyone worries about technique anymore. The electronics do it all for them."

"Not really. All the sound board does is balance the sound to blend the instruments. The musicians still have to play them."

Hank watched as Tiffany raised a hand, asking for a boost on her monitor. Her voice was fading, she complained, when the keyboard took over the melody. After a moment or two of adjusting, she was satisfied, and the song began again.

"That's one of Danny's songs, isn't it?" Hank asked, recognizing the melody he'd heard that morning.

Jill nodded, her face lighting up with pride.

Hank listened intently, his head to one side. He waited until the song had come to an end, then said, "He's good. Did he do his own arranging?"

"Yes, he always does for the numbers he writes." She glanced up at him. "I told you he was going to the top."

If she had anything to do with it, Hank thought grudgingly, the boy would have a damn good shot. The problem was, it took more than talent to make it. He wasn't at all sure that Danny had the temperament to withstand the rigors of a singing career.

Although he had to admit that Jill had matured into a dedicated, ambitious and determined woman, she was going to need more than drive to reach her goal. She was going to need patience and a firm hand, not to mention a great deal of luck. And Danny was her biggest obstacle.

That much was evident later in the rehearsal when Danny suddenly stopped singing and turned to glare at Gary. "You're off-key, man," he complained. "Probably that skinful of beer you had last night."

Gary's scowl was lethal. "I ain't sung off-key in my life, and what I do in my spare time ain't none of your damn business."

"Yeah?" Danny slid the strap of his guitar over his head and laid the instrument down on the chair next to him.

Hank heard Jill draw in her breath. She took a step toward the stage, then halted, her eyes on the singer.

Danny sauntered over to the keyboard and stuck his face close to Gary's. "Who pays your wages, man?"

"The audience pays my wages," Gary said, his face turning mean.

"Come on, guys, lighten up," Tiffany said, looking hopefully over at Slim.

Slim just gave a disdainful shake of his head and tapped lightly with his sticks on the drums.

Jill went to step forward again, but Hank laid a hand on her arm. "Let them handle it," he said quietly.

He could feel her resistance, but she stayed where she was.

"There wouldn't be an audience if it wasn't for me," Danny said, wagging his finger in Gary's face.

Gary snatched the hand in front of him and held it. "Keep doing that, fella, and you won't ever play guitar again."

"Gary!" Tiffany said sharply. "Drop it."

"Grow up, kid," Slim muttered out the corner of his mouth, sending a disgusted look at Danny.

Gary looked across at Tiffany, who glared back. After a moment he shrugged and dropped Danny's hand. "Okay, let's do it again. I'll try to stay in key."

Surprised at Gary's capitulation, Hank looked across at Tiffany. He sure had things pegged wrong, he thought. It looked as though Tiffany was the one in control there, not her husband.

"Just make sure you do," Danny said, earning another vicious scowl from Gary before sauntering back to the mike.

Hank felt Jill's muscles relax and realized he still had hold of her arm. He let go quickly, disturbed by the sudden hot leap of his pulse. He moved away from her, angry with himself for the momentary lapse.

The rehearsal came to an end, and everyone seemed satisfied with the way it had gone. Jill and Hank started across the stage toward Danny, but before they reached him, Tiffany slid up to the singer and wound an arm around his neck.

"Just keep giving it to 'em like that tonight, sugar," she breathed, gazing up into his face, "and you'll have them on their knees."

Hank shot a look at Gary. He'd lifted his head and fixed his gaze on his wife, who seemed not to notice his fierce scowl. For a moment it looked as if Gary were preparing to intervene. He straightened, his fists clenched at his sides, and took a small step forward. Then, just as Hank feared he might have to wade into another fight, Gary halted.

Hank looked back just in time to see Danny shove Tiffany's arm none too gently from his shoulder.

Tiffany shrugged, and walked over to Gary. "How about taking me for a nice juicy steak?" she said, her glance still straying over to Danny.

"Why don't you get Danny boy to buy you one?" Gary muttered.

Tiffany turned her attention back to her husband. "Aw, honey, don't be like that. You know how I love to eat supper with you. We can go to that steak house on the corner and find us a quiet booth to sit in."

Gary looked down at her, his face stiff and unyielding.

Tiffany tried again. Pushing her body against his, she said softly, "You could buy me some wine, sugar. You know how good I can be when I'm drinking wine."

Gary's scowl faded. "Yeah, I know." Putting a possessive arm around his wife's waist, he walked off stage with her.

"Gross," Danny muttered, looking after them.

Hank watched them go, feeling almost sorry for Gary. The guy had his hands full with that woman, that was for sure, and it looked as if the poor sucker was real smitten with his wayward wife. Which made Tiffany's attentions all the more dangerous, no matter who was the target.

Later that evening, Jill sat with Danny in the dressing room, trying to calm the singer's nerves. She refused his demands for a whiskey bottle, as she did before every performance.

"You know you can't sing when you've been drinking," she told him as he paced back and forth across the narrow strip of carpeting. "If you want a drink, you can have one after the show."

He didn't answer her, and she knew he was concentrating on the opening number, going over and over it in his mind. She still felt uneasy about not telling him about the letter, but there didn't seem to be any choice. The least little problem would upset him now, and it was crucial that he stay in control.

She looked up at him, feeling a faint stir of pride. He looked very appealing, with his long blond hair settling on his shoulders, and the silver blue eyes gleaming in a face tanned with makeup.

He wore tight black jeans, and a black fringed jacket over a white shirt. After a couple of songs he would discard the jacket, which usually produced appreciative screams from the younger fans.

Once in a while an unruly fan could cause a problem. The theater had provided security, but Jill was thankful that Hank was out there, keeping a special eye out for trouble.

The tap came on the door, and Danny spun around, his face taut with tension. "I look okay?"

Jill rose, and put an arm around his narrow shoulders. "You look great. Just relax, go out there and do what you do best."

"Is the recording scout in the audience?"

She could feel the tremble go through him and gave him a slight hug. Danny didn't like too much physical contact, and she was careful not to get too close. "I don't know. As I told you, they didn't tell me which concerts they would attend, so try not to worry about it. Just go out there and enjoy yourself."

"Enjoy myself?" Danny stepped away from her, and reached for his guitar. "How can I enjoy myself with all this thumping around going on in my stomach?"

Jill smiled. "You know very well that the minute you step out there and hear those cheers, you're going to feel just fine."

"Yeah, yeah." He slung the wide embroidered strap over his shoulder and grinned at her. "Okay, boss. After you."

She opened the door and he walked through it. She could almost feel the vibrations coming from his body as she followed him. Standing with him in the wings, she listened to the murmur of voices that would soon erupt into a roar.

From across the stage Gary lifted his thumb at her in the recognized signal. She nodded, already feeling the warmth from the stage lights. It would be hot out there, and by the time Danny came off, he would be drenched in sweat.

"Okay, Danny?" she said quietly, and the singer nodded, bouncing on the balls of his feet like a sparring boxer.

The backup group took up their positions and the stage manager looked at her, waiting for her signal to go out and make the announcement. She smiled at him. "All set."

Danny stopped bouncing as the voice spoke clearly over the speakers, welcoming the audience, then introducing the Wildwoods. The voices rose in anticipation, increasing in volume until they drowned out Slim's drumroll.

Jill felt her own body tense as the voice boomed louder. "And now, here he is . . . all yours . . . Danny Webster!"

The Wildwoods exploded with strummed chords as Danny strode onto the stage, and were quickly drowned out by a shattering wave of earsplitting screams. Danny paused in front of the mike, and launched into his first song, apparently unconcerned that no one could possibly hear him.

Jill waited until the screaming had subsided and Danny had settled in to his first set. Satisfied that everything was going well, she left the stage and made her way down to the front aisle, where she knew Hank had stationed himself. Reaching him, she tapped him on the arm.

He seemed startled, and glanced down at her. "Everything okay?"

"Seems to be. How about out here?"

"Looks good at the moment." He turned his head to scan the excited crowd. "Good opening."

"Thanks. I'll tell Danny that."

He didn't answer and she was about to move away when another onslaught of screams threatened to deafen her. Glancing at the stage, she saw that Danny had taken off his jacket and tossed it aside.

At the same moment, she heard Hank mutter something under his breath. A flurry of movement caught her eye, and she followed his gaze, her nerves jumping. Heading straight for the stage, mouths wide open, hands waving in the air, a large group of young girls raced one behind the other.

A security guard stepped forward, and Hank moved closer to the stage. Jill watched, aware of tiny chills chasing down her back. If anything was going to happen, now would be a perfect time.

She watched in dismay as the human wall of frenzied excitement rushed toward the stage. She saw a second security guard join the first, then another stepped out from the opposite side of the theater. Hank had positioned himself center stage, arms folded across his chest, looking relaxed in spite of the small screaming army bearing down on him.

Danny seemed confused, as if he wasn't sure what to do next. He half turned toward the group behind him, who were playing the intro for the next song.

Gary looked up in surprise when Danny missed the cue. Slim broke the drum phrase and deliberately began again. Tiffany managed to pick up the melody and after a second or two, Gary joined her.

The fans surged forward, surrounding Hank. His expression changed to controlled alarm. The guards rushed to help and together they held off the girls who were trying to climb onto the stage.

Jill left them to it, and tore through the side door that led to the wings. Danny's gaze met hers as she reached the edge of the stage and her pulse jumped. He looked scared to death.

"Sing," she mouthed at him, and made movements with her hand as if she were singing into a mike.

The Wildwoods started the intro for the third time, but Danny still had that frozen look on his face. Jill held out her hands to him in silent appeal. "Please?" she mouthed.

Tiffany's voice came in strongly as she sang the final phrase of the intro, as if willing Danny to join her.

Weak with relief, Jill saw him turn and take the mike from its stand. He began to sing, quietly at first, but then, as the fans began to quiet down, he regained his confidence, and once more his voice soared throughout the auditorium.

The fans were quiet now, standing with enraptured expressions on their upturned faces as they swayed to the slow, sultry tempo of the music.

Jill's rapid heartbeat began to subside, and she took several deep breaths. Hearing a movement in the shadows of the partitions behind her, she turned and met Hank's worried gaze.

"It looks okay for now, but I think I'll stay here for a while, just in case we have to get him off stage."

She nodded, turning back to look at Danny, who now seemed relaxed and in control. "I don't understand it," she murmured, "this has never happened before."

"What do you mean?" Hank said sharply.

She glanced back at him over her shoulder. "Well, he's not all that well-known. Certainly in these small towns. He hasn't played anywhere except close to home. I'm surprised he's generated this much excitement at first sight. You know how long it usually takes to build this kind of attention.''

"Yeah," Hank muttered. "I was wondering about that."

"It's very gratifying, of course," Jill continued, "and it's something Danny will have to get used to. I just didn't expect it so soon. Neither of us were prepared for this."

Hearing no response, she glanced back again. To her surprise, Hank had disappeared. Shrugging, she turned back to watch Danny. Obviously Hank must have decided the danger was over. At least for now.

She didn't see him again until the concert was almost over. They had prearranged for Danny to leave the theater while the fans were still waiting for a second encore, encouraged by the continued presence of the Wildwoods.

Just as Danny reached the end of his last number, Hank arrived in the wings. He looked grim, but then, Jill thought as she waited for Danny to finish taking his bow, she had rarely seen Hank looking anything else but grim.

Danny gave his final wave and strode toward her, flushed from the heat and excitement. She could tell he was strung out, and hoped she wouldn't have a problem calming him down again.

"I need to give them one more song," Danny said, already turning back toward the stage.

"No," Hank said, with an abrupt movement of his hand. "You get out now, before they start crowding the back door."

Danny's look of elation vanished under a scowl. "Who the hell do you think you're ordering around?"

Sending Hank a frown of disapproval, Jill said quickly, "I really think it might be best, Danny. Those fans are very excitable and could get out of control. They could end up scratching your face or something and that wouldn't look too good at your next stop."

To her relief, that seemed to make sense to Danny, and after another scowl at Hank, he muttered, "Okay. Let's go. I need a drink, anyway."

Hank led the way, followed by Danny, with Jill behind him. The Wildwoods would follow, after they'd packed up the gear, which would take about an hour.

Outside, the cool night air felt wonderful against Jill's flushed face. Drawing level with Danny, she touched his arm. "You did a great job tonight, Danny. I'm proud of you."

He seemed preoccupied and didn't answer. Hank, who was a step or two ahead, suddenly halted. Right in front of them, five young girls stood in a line, holding up small books in their hands.

"No autographs," Hank said, his voice cutting through the chorus of pleas.

"Hey, man," Danny said, stepping forward, "I decide if I want to give autographs."

"You hang around one minute longer and you're going to have the entire audience screaming down your neck. You want that?"

Hank grabbed hold of Danny's arm and the singer shook him off, his face tight with fury.

"Don't you touch me, man, you hear? You don't ever touch me."

"Danny," Jill urged, "he's right. You have to get back to the camper."

"Oh, come on, Danny, you can sign my book, can't you?" one of the girls called out.

A chorus of "Oh, please, Danny" followed, and Hank took a step toward them. At that moment, a loud scream erupted across the darkened parking lot.

Hank swore as more shapes darted toward them. "Get him back in the theater," he ordered, and turned to face the mob.

Frantically, Jill tugged at Danny's arm. "Come *on.*"

Danny went, and the two of them tumbled through the door and ran for the dressing room. Once inside, Danny threw himself down on a chair and ignored all her attempts at conversation.

It seemed an eternity until Hank finally opened the door and stuck his head in. "Okay," he said, flicking a glance at Danny, who sat slumped in a chair, "it's all clear now. They're gone."

"Thank heavens for that." Jill got up, stretching her weary limbs. "How is the group doing?"

"Nearly finished." He opened the door wider. "You can go home now," he said, looking at Danny.

The singer got slowly to his feet and, without a word, walked through the door.

"He's tired," Jill said as she followed him.

"Yeah, so am I." Hank closed the door behind them and caught up with her.

"How did you get rid of them?" Jill asked as once more they stepped outside.

"I took their autograph books and promised to deliver them, signed by Danny, to the manager's office in the morning."

Jill frowned. "How many?"

"Just the five. They promised not to tell the others."

Danny, who was ahead of them, reached the camper first and leaned up against the wall. As he did so, a shape detached itself from the rear and moved toward him.

Hank started forward, then pulled up as Tiffany's lilting voice said, "Hi, Danny. I couldn't go to bed without telling you what a great job you did tonight."

"Thanks," Danny muttered, and turned his back on her.

"I was really proud of the way you handled that mess of fans." Tiffany placed a hand on Danny's arm. "You did real good, sugar."

With an abrupt movement of his arm, Danny shook off Tiffany's hand.

"Good night, Tiffany," Jill said firmly. "We're all very tired. We'll see you in the morning."

Tiffany turned to look at Hank, her face pale in the light from the street lamps. "You did good, too, sugar." She wrapped her arms across her breasts. "So masterful. You can handle me like that any time."

Danny made a sound of disgust, and Hank stepped up to the door to unlock it. "Good night, Tiffany," he said evenly.

To Jill's relief, the woman shrugged and walked slowly back to her trailer.

Once inside, Danny seemed anxious to get to bed. He downed his shot of bourbon much too quickly, though Jill chose not to comment. She felt drained of all her energy by the time Danny had showered and finally shut himself in his cubicle.

"Coffee?" Hank asked as she sank down on the couch with a tired groan.

"Are you going to make it?"

"Sure. There are some things I'm good at."

He sounded defensive. She opened one eye and looked at him. "Thank you."

"You're welcome."

She watched him measure coffee into the filter cup. "That was quite an experience tonight," she said, trying to find something to say.

"Yeah."

His tone of voice caused her to sit up. "Is something wrong?"

He flipped the switch on the coffeepot, then sat down on the couch opposite her. "That little demonstration tonight was paid for."

She stared at him, trying to make sense of the words. "I beg your pardon?"

"The fans, all that screaming and jumping around. Someone gave away free tickets for the concert, on condition that the takers act like a bunch of hysterical freak-outs. All except for the little group that met us at the back door. They're genuine. They come from Cedarvale and are following the tour."

Stunned, she continued to gape at him. "But who . . . ?"

Hank shrugged. "I don't know. I talked to the manager, he didn't know anything about it. He thought it was a publicity stunt." He narrowed his eyes. "It wasn't, was it?"

"Of course not." Jill caught her breath. "Unless . . ."

"Unless what?"

"Unless Tiffany had a hand in it. It's no secret she's crazy about Danny, she could have done this to surprise him."

"If she knows anything at all about the kid, she'd know he isn't ready to handle that. It could have sabotaged his entire performance."

Jill sighed. "I just wish she'd leave him alone. It's obvious Danny wants nothing to do with her, yet she will insist on hanging around him. Apart from the fact that Gary could get nasty about it, it's upsetting Danny. He doesn't like too much physical contact, it bothers him."

"So I've noticed," Hank said dryly.

Instinctively she jumped to the singer's defense. "You upset him, jumping down his throat like that. You know how sensitive he is—"

"Yeah, yeah. I know how sensitive he is. You never let me forget it."

Sensing a confrontation, Jill leaned back and closed her eyes. "I'm just doing my best to take care of him."

Hank got to his feet and opened a cupboard to reach for the mugs. "Well, hang on tight, lady. Sometimes no matter how hard you try, they slip out from under your fingers when you're not looking."

Knowing he was talking about Perry, Jill said quietly, "I don't think we need to go into that again."

"Look, I'm only trying to save you a lot of grief. You're putting all your life into that kid. And the minute he's got a foot in the door he'll dump you so fast you won't see it coming. I've seen it happen a hundred times."

She could feel resentment stirring. He was doing it again. Interfering in something that was none of his business. They were both tired, and this wasn't a good time to have an argument. "I told you before," she said, choosing her words carefully. "Danny isn't like Perry. He appreciates what I'm doing for him. And he needs me."

"And Perry needed me until you came along and filled his head with lies."

Suddenly she'd had enough. She was too weary to argue with him, and too sure of his reaction to bother trying to defend herself. "I'm going to bed," she said, standing up.

He looked at her, the coffeepot in his hand. "What about your coffee?"

"I've changed my mind. I don't like the company."

"That's nothing new. You always did resent me."

She paused, and looked back at him. "Haven't you got that the wrong way around?"

"I don't think so."

He put the coffeepot down, and something about the way he did it sent shivers down her back. "You resented the authority I had over Perry. I wouldn't let him do what you wanted to do, and you didn't like that, did you? You were always used to getting your way and it bugged you like hell to know I wasn't going to give in to you.''

She took a step closer to him. Raising a finger, she shook it at him. "You were the one who was unreasonable. You didn't want Perry to have anything to do with me, because you were too damn afraid it would wreck your plans for him. Your plans, not his.''

"Well, you did a damn good job of that, without any help from me.''

"Did it never occur to you that Perry was as much to blame for what happened as I was? Or are you still too bullheaded to admit that?''

"Bullheaded? Whose idea was it to go off and get married when neither of you had a dime to buy a cup of coffee? Are you gonna stand there and tell me that was Perry's idea? He never wanted to get tied down to a woman. All he thought about was making music.''

"No, that's all you thought about.'' Recklessly, she lashed the air with her hand. "And for your information, it was Perry's idea to go to Las Vegas. He knew you wouldn't stand for him being married to me. I wasn't good enough for your precious brother.''

"It wasn't that.'' His voice was hard now, and cold with anger. "I knew Perry wasn't ready for marriage. He wasn't responsible enough.''

Too tired to control her temper any longer, Jill walked up to him. "That was your opinion. And that's all you cared about. What you thought, what you decided, what you knew was best for him. Well, let me tell you something, mister, your brother turned out to be just like you. Stubborn as all get out and mean as hell.''

His eyes glinted at her, like moonlight on cold steel. "Lady, you haven't seen me when I'm really roused.''

"You have a short memory, Hank Tyler. I can remember a night when you practically threw me out of the house.

Everyone within five miles of us must have heard you bellowing like a wounded elephant.''

Her heart skipped as he grabbed her upper arms. He brought his face close to hers, so close she could feel his breath on her cheek. A faint aroma of earthy cologne seized her senses, and her breath seemed to freeze in her throat.

His skin was leathery, burned by hours in the sun, and his clear gray gaze seemed to fasten on her mind, erasing everything from it but the sensation of being close to him, his fingers searing her flesh.

Her awareness of his masculinity seemed to leap higher and higher as she stared into his eyes. She saw an answering response flicker in his gray gaze, then vanish.

"You got a lot to answer for, lady," he said softly. "Don't ever forget that. Don't push me too far, or you might be sorry you ever came looking for me."

He let her go, and straightened. "I'm going to step outside for a breath of fresh air. I'll have my back against the door if you need me."

Before she could answer, he strode to the door, flung it open, then slammed it shut behind him.

Shaken, she poured herself a cup of coffee, and sat down with it grasped in both her hands. She shouldn't have said all those things to him. For one thing, they weren't true. He and Perry were not at all alike. Not in looks and not in personality.

She glanced at Danny's door, half expecting him to fly out of there demanding to know what all the noise was about. He had to be sound asleep to ignore all that.

She sipped at the coffee, her mind slipping back to the past. She could see herself as she was then—young, frightened and confused. She'd married Perry on a crazy impulse and was already half regretting it when they'd faced Hank with the news.

Perry had warned her that his older brother would not be too happy about the marriage. Neither of them had expected the rage with which Hank had greeted the announcement.

He'd demanded that they get an annulment, and when Perry had adamantly refused, he'd thrown them both out, telling them he never wanted to see either of them again. Perry had taken his brother at his word and apparently had not had contact with Hank since.

Jill sighed and rested her mug on the table. Hank Tyler was the one to blame for what had happened, not her. Yet he still carried a grudge, even after all these years. She wondered now why she'd wanted to hire him. Maybe, deep down, she'd wanted to set things right between them.

A rueful smile curved her lips. If so, she was doomed to disappointment. Nothing, it seemed, was likely to break through that stubborn wall of resentment. And she wasn't helping matters with her quick temper.

She wondered how he'd react if he knew the physical effect he had on her. One thing she knew for certain, she never wanted him to find out. Some things were far better left dormant.

Standing, she yawned and stretched her arms above her head. It was going to be a long six weeks.

The next few days passed swiftly as the tour got under way. Much to Jill's relief, the screaming mob did not appear again. She questioned Tiffany about the paid stunt, but the singer flatly denied any knowledge of it. Jill wasn't sure whether or not to believe her, but she decided to drop the issue, since it hadn't been repeated.

Danny didn't comment on the absence of the unruly crowd. The small group of fans who had asked for his autographs appeared at each show and created enough noise among themselves to unsettle him. In spite of them, he managed to give a good performance, and since Hank had decided the groupies were harmless, Jill stopped worrying about them.

In any case, Hank seemed to have them under control, and spent some time chatting with them at the end of each performance. Jill couldn't help admiring the way he handled them.

"You know, Danny should sing more ballads," Hank said one night after the singer had shut himself in his cubicle. "He has the voice for them, and he doesn't use his full range in those fast numbers."

Jill finished wiping up the mugs she'd rinsed out and set them down on the counter. "I agree he has the voice, but he doesn't relax enough to carry off the body language. He's too tense, and it shows in the slow songs."

"Then work with him." Hank stretched his legs out as far as the space between the couches would allow. Jill tried not to notice the hard thigh muscles straining against the denim.

He surprised her when he added, "You know all the moves for the romantic ballads. As I recall you used to be real good at it."

Taken aback by this rare compliment, Jill glanced at him. He held her gaze for a moment, then looked down at his boots.

"Thank you," Jill said lightly. "I didn't know you'd noticed."

"I noticed."

The treacherous quiver of excitement raced through her body. "I don't know if I can remember how," she said, reaching up to put the mugs away in the cupboard.

"It's not a case of remembering. To some people it just comes naturally. You're one of those people. You could always sell a song with the way you moved."

Feeling ridiculously pleased, she turned and smiled at him. "Thanks again. I appreciate the kind words."

She'd tried to sound casual but to her dismay, he muttered, "Yeah, well, don't let it go to your head. I just hate to see good talent not used to its full extent. Especially when you can coach him."

Stung by his tone, she answered without thinking. "Are you suggesting I'm not doing my job?"

He stood, staring down at her, his gaze unfathomable. "All I'm suggesting is that you can do better. But then it's none of my business, is it? I'm just the bodyguard."

She cut off her retort as he turned away and headed for the door.

"I'm going to get a breath of fresh air. Don't worry, I'll be within calling distance." He opened the door and closed it quietly behind him.

She uttered a grunt of exasperation. He could be so damn infuriating. And the worst of it was, he was right. She had been reluctant to consider any changes to Danny's act, knowing how it unsettled him. Hank's suggestions were valid, and constructive. And as usual, she'd reacted badly.

She finished tidying up and went to bed, wishing that she and Hank could be together five minutes without arguing about something.

Thanks to an accident on the road the next day, they arrived at their next stop much later than scheduled. It was a mad scramble to get everything set up and checked out, and tempers were frayed by the time everyone was ready to eat.

With little time to spare, Hank suggested they eat at a fast-food restaurant. Since the weather had turned warm, Tiffany wanted to eat her hamburger at an outside table. In the end, everyone sat outside, enjoying the last of the warmth from the sun.

Danny was wound up, as usual, and talked nonstop, until Jill had to tell him to quit talking and finish his meal or they'd be late for the performance.

Gary and Slim left to go to the men's room. The minute they were out of sight, Tiffany leaned across to Danny and put a hand on his arm.

"How're you doing, sugar?"

Danny shook her off with a scowl. "Quit bugging me."

Jill watched warily as Tiffany laughed. Sliding out of her seat, the singer wound an arm around Danny's neck.

"Now you know you don't mean that, sugar. You know you love it when I get close to you."

Danny shoved his chair back with a loud scraping noise. "I told you to quit bugging me. Lay off me, Tiff, or I'll—" He broke off, leaving the sentence unfinished.

Tiffany, however, seemed determined to be difficult. "Go on, Danny, honey, tell me what you'll do. I might like it."

"Tiffany!" Jill said sharply. "Leave him alone."

"Oh, quit mothering him." Tiffany sidled closer to Danny's chair. "He's a big boy, aren't you, sugar? You know what you want, don't you?"

Swearing, Danny rose to his feet, knocking his chair over. At that moment Jill saw Gary and Slim threading their way through the restaurant to the door. Someone had to do something and quickly. Already people were staring in their direction.

Up until this point, Gary had held his temper, but he would only be pushed so far. And she was very much afraid that moment was fast approaching. She shot a look of appeal at Hank, praying he'd be able to prevent a confrontation before it got out of hand.

Chapter 5

Hank rose, reached for Tiffany's arm and pulled her down onto her chair. "Sit," he growled, "and quit acting like some cheap whore."

Danny picked up his chair and sat down on it, just before Gary emerged from the restaurant. Tiffany shot a speculative look at Hank, and ran the tip of her tongue over her lips.

Gary was deep in conversation with Slim, and appeared not to notice anything amiss, for which Jill was immensely grateful. If Hank hadn't intervened, things could have taken an ugly turn. Gary's jealousy over Tiffany had caused more than one serious confrontation, and he was not in the best of moods that evening.

Jill thought about the situation again that evening as she watched the show from the wings. She had to admit, Hank was proving indispensable on this trip. She would have found it very difficult to handle all the problems without him.

She watched Danny swing into another fast number, and thought about Hank's advice. Maybe she should start working with him more, she thought, then smiled, thinking about Hank's comments on her own performance.

That had been a long time ago. And Hank had always kept his distance from her, almost as if he were afraid of her. She almost laughed out loud at the thought. She couldn't imagine Hank being afraid of anyone, least of all a woman. It was more the other way around.

Taken aback by the thought, she considered it. Was she afraid of Hank? Or just the sensations he aroused in her? Disturbed by the track her thoughts were taking, she closed her mind to them and concentrated once more on Danny's performance.

Leaving the theater with Danny later, Jill found Hank already talking to the groupies, who were all laughing at something he'd said. As soon as Danny appeared, they rushed to his side, all babbling at once.

Jill saw Danny's face tighten up as they approached and she gave his arm a gentle squeeze. "Just relax and be pleasant," she murmured. "Hank will get rid of them if they're a nuisance."

Danny gave a curt nod, but managed a thin smile as the girls reached him. He answered a few of their questions, then Hank stepped in.

"Okay, girls, give him a rest. He's been working hard and needs his sleep."

"Oh, come on," one of the girls complained, "we just got here."

"How about a kiss, Danny?" another one added.

To Jill's dismay, Danny's expression changed to one of disgust.

Hurriedly, Hank pushed between him and the girls. "That's enough for tonight. Remember our deal. You behave like ladies and I let you talk to him for a while after the show. You don't want to spoil a good thing, now do you?"

Reluctantly the girls moved away, calling out "Good night" as they left.

"God, how I hate that," Danny said, pushing a hand into his hair. "They freak me out, those people. What do they want from me?"

"Just a little attention, that's all," Hank said quietly. "It's something you'll have to get used to, Danny, if you want to make it big in this business. Your life's not your own anymore. You'll have to share it with your fans and be pleasant about it. They'll be the ones who can make or break you."

"Yeah, well, I might have to do it, but I don't have to like it."

"Well, don't worry about it now," Jill said, sending Hank a warning look. "Hank's right, you need your sleep. I'm just glad we have him along with us. I told you hiring a road manager would be a good idea."

The look Danny sent Hank suggested he didn't share her opinions, but he said nothing and ambled off toward the camper.

Hank shrugged. "Not winning any popularity contests, am I?"

"Don't take any notice of him," Jill said, watching the singer's slim figure cross the parking lot. "He's just tired."

"Yeah, tired of having me around. I'm surprised he hasn't demanded that you fire me."

Jill looked up at him in surprise. "It isn't that bad, surely? What has Danny been saying to you?"

"It isn't anything he says." Hank kicked a loose stone, sending it skittering across the ground. "It's in his eyes when he looks at me. I get the impression he'd be a lot happier if I'd get lost."

"I'm sure you're imagining things," Jill said, feeling uncomfortable. "Danny looks at everyone that way."

"Maybe. Everyone but you, that is."

Danny had reached the camper now, and stood with one shoulder supporting his weight against the wall.

"He trusts me," Jill said, feeling a faint stir of maternal affection. "He finds it very difficult to trust people. It took me months to reach him, and there were a lot of times when I almost gave up."

Hank started to answer her, then broke off with a soft curse as a voice floated out of the darkness behind them.

"Hey, sugar, wait for me. I wanna say good-night."

Hank sighed. "Doesn't that woman ever give up?"

Jill uttered a short laugh. "Not as long as there's breath in her voluptuous body."

"So I figured." Hank slowed his pace. "Why don't you go ahead? I'll deal with her."

She didn't bother to look at him. "Good luck." She strode on, miffed by the thought that he hadn't sounded too reluctant, and angry with herself for letting it matter.

Inside the camper, Danny threw himself down on one of the couches. "I'm hungry," he said, one hand rotating over his stomach. "I only had that hamburger for dinner."

"I'll fix you something." Jill opened the tiny fridge door. "I've got some hot dogs. And the buns should still be fresh. Fancy one of those?"

"Yeah. Make it two." He got up and headed for the bathroom.

Jill reached for the pan and dropped two of the wieners into it. Running water into the pan, she decided she could eat one, too, and dropped another one in. Hank could probably eat a couple, too, she thought. She'd better find out before she cooked them.

She put the pan down on the stove and went to the door to open it. Looking out, at first she could see nothing while her eyes adjusted to the light. Then she blinked.

The moon rode high in the sky, bathing the parking lot in a wash of pale light. Two people stood several yards away, locked in a passionate embrace. They broke apart, and Jill heard Tiffany's soft laugh as she looked up into Hank's face. Very quietly, Jill closed the door.

She leaned against it, feeling a wave of revulsion. He was certainly living up to his reputation. She was shaking with anger. How dare he? To take such a risk right under Gary's nose was not only stupid, it was downright dangerous. It could jeopardize the tour. And with someone like Tiffany. Where was his brain? Steaming, Jill stomped back to the stove. In his pants, like most men's. Let him get his own supper, damn him. She took one of the wieners out of the pan and put it back in the fridge. She'd lost her appetite.

Out in the parking lot, Hank grabbed Tiffany's arms, and broke the deadlock around his neck. "What the hell do you think you're playing at?" he demanded, thrusting her away from him.

Her laugh seemed to echo across the dark, deserted street. "Oh, come on, sugar, you know you've been dying for a little kiss ever since you laid eyes on me."

Trying to control his anger, Hank took a deep breath. "Sorry to disappoint you, lady, but the thought never crossed my mind."

She sidled up to him again. "You're just saying that, aren't you, honey? If you're worried about Gary—"

"I tell you what I'm worried about. I'm worried that if you don't stay out of my hair I'm going to do something drastic."

She pouted, looking up at him with soulful eyes. "Like what?"

"Like getting you fired. You and your husband. Danny doesn't need you, anyway. There are plenty of backup groups who would kill to work with him."

He was getting through to her at last, Hank thought, watching her eyes fill with anger.

In a low, fierce voice, Tiffany muttered, "Oh, yeah?" She dug her fists into her hips and thrust out her full breasts. "Well, Danny might not want to work with other groups. He likes the way I sing. He won't want to start again with someone strange. He's very fond of me. You'll see, he'll do anything I say."

Hank laughed. "Boy, have you got that wrong. How dense can you be, Tiffany? You're just part of the group to him, that's all. So you're a good singer. Good singers are a dime a dozen. And Danny will do what Jill tells him, no one else. Face it, Tiffany, you're nothing to Danny but a thorn in his big toe."

Her face contorted, and for a moment she looked real ugly. "Yeah? Well, who needs him, anyway? He's nothing but a spoiled, conceited jackass who's too wrapped up in himself to see what's going around him. He can rot in hell for all I care." She twisted around and started to walk away.

Hank was beginning to feel sorry for her when she turned back and said viciously, "As for that puffed-up hag who won't let him up from under her painted thumbnail, she can rot, too. She's welcome to him. Danny Webster is a kook, and one of these days he'll get exactly what's coming to him. And nobody could deserve it more."

Hank watched her stalk off, wondering uneasily if she was simply suffering from the pangs of rejection, or if there was something more sinister behind her last remarks.

When Danny came out of the bathroom, Jill made an effort to pull herself together. It wouldn't do to let him see how mad she was. He already had it in for Hank, apparently, and she didn't need to add fuel to the fire.

She waited, hovering anxiously, while Danny ate his hot dogs and washed them down with a beer. She dreaded the moment when Hank would come in, and she'd have to act as though nothing had happened.

Nothing had, she reminded herself as she rinsed out the pan. So he'd kissed another man's wife. If he wanted to make a jackass of himself, that was his funeral. As long as Gary didn't find out and cause an uproar, there wasn't a whole lot she could say about it.

Her temper didn't improve when Danny had gone to bed and Hank still hadn't put in an appearance. She should have been relieved that she hadn't had to face him, yet the thought of him out there with Tiffany burned in her stomach like acid.

She went to bed and lay there fuming, knowing that by now Gary and Slim would have finished packing up the gear. Where was he? Where was Tiffany?

Angry with him and furious with herself, she pummeled the pillow. One thought kept staring her in the face, and at last she had to admit it. She was jealous. Somehow he'd become more important to her than she'd realized. Heaven help her, she was actually jealous.

She rolled onto her back and groaned quietly. It was laughable, really. Here she was, getting all fired up about a man who bitterly resented her. She didn't need this. She didn't need the aggravation, she didn't need the complications, and she certainly didn't need the pain.

Wishing she'd never heard of Hank Tyler, Jill closed her eyes and made a determined effort to go to sleep and forget the two people who were laughing together outside.

She heard him come in a little while later, and decided to have a word with him the next day. He'd been hired to keep an eye on Danny, after all, and he could hardly keep his mind on his job if he let someone such as Tiffany distract him so easily.

By the next morning Jill had changed her mind again, promising herself that she would keep quiet for now, unless it happened again. She was reluctant to let him know what she'd seen, in case he thought she'd been spying on him.

Somewhat to her surprise, Tiffany seemed to avoid both Hank and Danny that day. They crossed the state line shortly after noon. The routines went smoothly, and the concert that night was a huge success. Danny had never sung better, and Jill hoped passionately that the scout had been in the audience.

Although forced to spend a good deal of time in Hank's company, she managed to control her turbulent thoughts, hiding them beneath a cool, offhand manner that had Hank glancing at her more than once in puzzlement.

Danny was in a good mood that night and even managed to joke with Hank as they sat enjoying a beer in the camper after the show. It had been several days now without a menacing letter for Danny, and Jill began to hope that the writer had become tired of the game and had decided to give up.

After Danny had gone to bed, she discovered she'd left her jacket in the theater. "I had better go and get it," she told Hank, "I can't trust Tiffany or the guys to pick it up for me."

"I'll go get it," Hank said, getting to his feet. "What's it look like?"

"No," Jill said so sharply it earned a look of surprise from Hank. Reaching for the flashlight on the shelf above her head, she added, "Thanks, but I could use the fresh air and exercise."

He gave her a long look, then shrugged. "Suit yourself. Want me to walk with you? It's pretty dark out there tonight."

She shook her head. "I'd rather you stayed with Danny." She went out the door before he could answer her.

The lights were still on in the theater, and she relaxed her tense shoulders. The group apparently hadn't finished packing up the gear. She'd given up suggesting that Hank help them, Gary was adamant he didn't want "no rodeo cowboy messing with his equipment."

It had done no good to remind Gary that Hank was a band manager before he joined the rodeo. For some reason, Gary had taken an instant dislike to Hank, and there was no point in arguing with him.

Besides, Jill reflected as she let herself into the theater through the back door, as much as it disturbed her to have him here, she felt a lot more secure when he was close to Danny in the camper. Even if her fears for his safety were proving to be overreaction, after all.

She threaded her way through the maze of partitions, ropes and booms that were an intrinsic part of backstage theater, and headed for the dressing room, where she'd left her jacket.

She was almost there when she heard raised voices coming from the far side of the stage. She heard Tiffany's shrill voice, and Gary's deeper one. They were arguing about Danny.

"I warn you, woman, stay away from that puny punk. It riles me something fierce to see you prancing around him like a mare in heat."

"It don't mean nothing, honey, you know that. Just a bit of fun, that's all. You're the one I'm crazy about, you know that."

"Yeah, well it don't look good when you do stuff like that. You're my woman, and I married you for keeps. I don't want no one else touching you, you hear?"

"Aw, Gary, baby, don't be such a wet noodle. You're just trying to spoil my fun."

"I'm just trying to stop you making a damn fool of yourself that's all. The kid don't like you hanging around his neck, and neither do I."

"Well, sugar, if you don't like it, you sure as hell don't have to stick around."

"Dammit, woman!" Gary's roar echoed throughout the auditorium. "I swear you're gonna push me too far one day. I'll end up doing something you'll regret."

Tiffany's voice dropped, but Jill heard her clearly as she crossed the passageway. "Just make sure you're not the one regretting it, honey. I'd hate to see you locked away for the rest of your born days."

Gary muttered something Jill didn't catch.

"Forget Danny," Tiffany said, and her familiar laugh rang out. "He's not worth getting in such a stew about. He's not gonna be around long enough, you'll see."

Something about the laughingly uttered words bothered Jill. She glanced across the stage as she passed through the wings and saw Tiffany go up on her toes to kiss Gary's flushed face. She saw something else that neither Gary nor Tiffany appeared to notice.

Standing in the wings on the other side of the stage, Slim stood motionless, half hidden by the backdrop. He was staring intently at the couple, as if waiting to see what would happen next.

Jill continued on her way, wondering uneasily how long he'd been there, and if he'd deliberately been eavesdropping. There seemed to be a mounting tension between the Wildwoods, and she couldn't ignore the sense of foreboding she felt when she thought about the scene she'd just witnessed.

It was like watching a steaming volcano, wondering when it was going to erupt. And Danny appeared to be sitting right on top of it.

Returning to the camper, jacket in hand, Jill was prepared to go straight to bed. Hank, however, had just made a pot of coffee, and much against her better judgment, she agreed to join him.

She sat on the couch, and tried to ignore his probing gaze when he asked casually, "Everything okay?"

She wasn't sure what that meant. She'd gone to great pains to keep things on a casual level all day, trying to hide the resentment she felt every time she remembered him with Tiffany. She knew he must have noticed but didn't really expect it to bother him too much.

Maybe he could sense her uneasiness now, after witnessing the scene with the group. Deciding to talk it over with him, she took a sip of coffee, then said, "I'm not sure. I happened to overhear Tiffany and Gary arguing tonight. They were fighting about Danny."

Hank leaned back, his fingers wrapped around his mug. "I wouldn't worry too much about that. I don't think Tiffany will be bothering Danny much from now on."

Jill fought to keep her expression neutral. Was he really that confident he could hold Tiffany's exclusive attention? That must have been quite a session last night.

The thought sickened her and she put her mug on the table. "I'm tired. I think I'll go to bed."

Narrowing his eyes, he leaned forward. "Something else bothering you?"

She shrugged. "It's just that I saw Slim in the wings. I think he'd been eavesdropping, though I don't know how long he'd been there."

"Probably just curious, or didn't want to interrupt a fight."

"No," Jill said slowly. "It was more than that. I had the feeling that Slim was deliberately staying out of sight so that he could hear what was going on. I can't explain it, but it gave me the creeps to see him standing there like that."

Hank sat back, an odd look on his face, as if he expected her to say something else. "I wouldn't worry about it. You can't expect that kind of setup without an argument or two. When you travel in a tight group like that, the least little thing can set you off. And no one knows that better than me."

She looked at him, knowing he was referring to the rodeo circuit. "Yes, I imagine tempers get frayed pretty often in that environment." The question popped out before she could stop it. "Just how did you manage to get suspended, anyhow?"

For a moment she thought he wasn't going to answer. She felt embarrassed that she'd asked him, and wondered if she should find another subject.

He sighed, and put his mug down on the table. Leaning his elbows on his knees, he stared down at the floor.

"I was set up," he said quietly. "Oh, I'm not saying I wasn't at fault, but I didn't start it. I had a run-in with two of the riders on the circuit, and they had it in for me. We were all in the bar one night and they must have laced my beer, because it hit me awfully fast. They kept poking at me until I lost my temper, and they were just itching to take me on."

Remembering how she'd found him on the tavern floor, Jill pursed her lips. It didn't appear to take much to provoke him.

"Anyway," Hank went on, "it might have been okay, except they were all a little exuberant that night and every sucker in the place decided to join in the fight. It was a free-for-all, and it got nasty. By the time it was over, there were four riders on their way to hospital.''

''Including you?''

He looked up at her, and the light reflected in his eyes, making them look almost colorless. ''Not that time. Unfortunately, the promoter wasn't too happy that four of his top riders had to miss the event, and because of my reputation, it was real easy for him to pin it all on me. He complained to the association, they suspended me.''

''And you didn't give them an argument?''

Hank's shoulder lifted, then dropped in resignation. ''What was the point? They'd already made a pretty good case against me. Sometimes my reputation outrates my performance.''

''You have only yourself to blame for that.''

The look he gave her was full of irony. ''Yeah, I figured you'd say something like that.''

Sensing another disagreement, Jill rose with a loud yawn. ''Well, if you'll excuse me, I'm really tired. I'll see you in the morning.'' She made her escape, sensing his gaze on her as she headed for her cubicle.

Hank frowned after her. Something was definitely wrong, and it was more than just the quarrels going on between the Wildwoods. Something had upset Jill, and she didn't want to talk about it.

Hank got up to pour himself another cup of coffee. She'd been cool toward him all day, as if she disapproved of something, but he couldn't imagine what it was.

He sat down again and tilted the mug to his mouth. Dammit, she didn't even want to argue with him. He missed that. He didn't exactly enjoy the confrontations, but at least she was communicating with him. Anything was better than the cool detachment between them.

Cursing, he swallowed the coffee and set his mug down on the table. What a fool he was, getting all riled up over a woman who had destroyed the only real relationship he'd ever had. He'd lost a brother because of her, and he had better make damn sure he never forgot that.

He got up to unfold his bed, unhappily aware that there had been many times in the past few days when he'd done just that—forgotten all about the feud between them. Too many times he'd found his thoughts wandering down the wrong path, especially at night, lying just a few feet away from her.

He punched the pillow and threw it on the bed. She was getting under his skin, and if he wasn't careful, he'd make a wrong move. Then there'd be hell to pay. He kept reminding himself of that as he drifted off to sleep.

He didn't have much time the next day to worry about his problems. The trouble started when Tiffany, who had reached the next stop ahead of the camper, picked up the mail at the theater.

She gave the letters to Danny, who took them into his cubicle to read, and Hank tried to reassure a worried Jill.

"He hasn't had a letter in days," he said as Jill unpacked the groceries they'd picked up at the store. "There's no reason to suppose he'll get one now."

"I guess not." Jill opened a cupboard and began stacking packages inside. "I keep hoping that whoever wrote them has given up. I just hope he won't have a bunch of them waiting for him when he gets home."

"If he does, we'll deal with it when we get back."

He saw Jill's quick glance at him, and realized what he'd said. He was insinuating they'd keep in touch after the tour.

Cursing his stupidity, he muttered, "I'd better go over to the theater and check out things there." Without looking at her again, he left.

Jill slapped a packet of sugar down on the shelf. It didn't matter to her what he did. In fact, she was beginning to wish she'd never hired him. Now that the letters had stopped there was really no need for him to guard Danny. She and the Wildwoods could have handled the situation between them.

Now that she thought about it, getting Hank involved had been a mistake. An overreaction to a problem that wasn't as dangerous as she'd imagined. Once more, she'd been overprotecting Danny, and she had to learn to loosen up or she'd make him more paranoid than he was right now.

Shocked at the word that had crept into her thoughts, she closed the cupboard door with a loud snap. As she did so, she saw Danny standing in the middle of the narrow aisle between the couches, his face white and his eyes wide and staring.

She dropped her gaze to the letter he held in his hand and her stomach gave a sickening lurch.

"Here," he said hoarsely. He thrust the letter at her, and it shook violently in his hand. "Read it. It's another one from the loony."

Her own hand felt none too steady as she took the letter from him and unfolded it. It looked the same as the others, a page torn from a notebook, the untidy letters scrawled in a childish hand.

The vicious words jumped out at her, their menacing message chilling her blood.

You can't escape me, moron, I am watching you all the time. I am just waiting for the right moment to destroy you. You won't even see me coming. Prepare to die, punk. Slowly. Horribly. Soon.

Wondering where Hank was, Jill folded up the letter and slipped it into the pocket of her jeans. "Where's the envelope?" she asked as Danny continued to stare at her with his eyes frozen in fear.

He just shook his head.

She stepped forward, her hand outstretched to touch him, but he backed off with an abrupt, jerky movement.

"Is it in your room?"

Again he shook his head.

Deciding that this wasn't the time to press the issue, Jill said gently, "Sit down, Danny. I'll fix you a shot of whiskey. Just a drop to steady your nerves, okay?"

He sank slowly onto the couch, as if obeying a command without comprehending it.

Again Jill wondered where Hank was. Then she remembered he'd said something about checking out the theater. Why was he never there when she needed him? she thought irritably.

She poured a generous shot of bourbon into a glass and handed it to Danny. He gulped it down in one quick movement and gave back the glass.

After a moment she was relieved to see color creep back into his face. He looked up at her, and his expression tore at her heart.

"What am I going to do?" he whispered.

Jill took a deep breath, and wished she'd had a shot of the bourbon, as well. Sitting down opposite him, she resisted the urge to touch him. "You're going to ignore this one like you've ignored all the rest. You've been getting these letters for some time now, and nothing has ever happened, has it?"

"But it says he's just waiting for the right moment." Danny looked from side to side as if he expected a killer to come out of the shadows any minute and lunge at him.

Jill remembered something Hank had said. "Danny, if this person were serious about his threats, do you really think he'd go to all that trouble to warn you? Not to mention, running the risk of getting caught. I think he's just some poor soul who's jealous of your success and wants to spoil it for you, that's all. Now you're not going to let him do that, are you?''

"I don't know," Danny whispered, his lips hardly moving.

"No one is going to hurt you while all of us are around you. You are never alone, Danny. We make sure of that. So try not to worry about it, okay?''

Danny nodded slowly. "I think I'll go and lie down," he mumbled.

Jill let out her breath. "I think that's a good idea. I'll wake you when it's time to go for the sound check. But I would like to see that envelope. Will you get it for me?''

"There wasn't one.''

She tried not to show her alarm. "Okay, just don't worry about it. See if you can get some sleep.''

She watched him stumble down the aisle to his room, and her heart ached for him. It wasn't fair. He had so much talent, so much to look forward to, and some creep out there was doing his best to destroy his chances.

She unfolded the note and read it again. Whoever it was, he didn't intend to give up, that much was obvious. She could feel her scalp prickling as she stared at the scrawled words. The absence of an envelope could mean only one thing: whoever was doing this was following them on the road.

She thought of the young groupies waiting outside the stage door every night, and another chill chased down her spine. Sure, they were all young girls, but that didn't mean a thing in today's violent world. Any one of them could be hiding a knife or a gun in her purse or concealed in her clothes.

Thoroughly unnerved now, Jill decided she would have to ask Hank to put a stop to the fans getting too close to Danny. In fact, he would have to get rid of them altogether. It wasn't worth the risk.

Absorbed in her thoughts, she jumped violently when the door suddenly swung open, letting rays of warm sunshine slice through the cool darkness of the camper. For a moment her heart hammered uncomfortably, then she saw Hank framed in the doorway.

Reaction made her voice caustic as she said, "Where have you been?"

He started to answer her, then as he stepped inside, he saw her face. His affronted expression changed to one of concern. "What's happened?" he said, coming toward her.

Jill held out the letter. Her hand still shook, and she was taken aback when he closed his fingers around hers. Warmth from the contact coursed up her arm and spread rapidly over her body.

"Hang in there, tiger. Whatever it is, we'll take care of it."

She felt a crazy urge to cry. Not easily given to tears, she chewed her lip, forcing herself under control. He let go of her hand, and she watched him scan the words, his face darkening as he read them.

"Damn," he muttered. "Of all days, it had to be the one I didn't check the mail."

"Isn't that the way things usually happen?" Jill swallowed, annoyed at the tremble in her voice.

His gray eyes studied her face. "You okay?"

She nodded, and pulled in a couple of deep breaths.

"Danny?"

"He's okay. Pretty shaken up at first, but I gave him a shot of whiskey and I think I managed to convince him it's nothing to worry about."

"Didn't convince yourself, though, huh?"

She glanced down at the letter in his hand. "There was no envelope, Hank."

His hardened expression did nothing to comfort her.

"So what do you think?" she asked, knowing he'd reached the same conclusions that she'd formed.

Hank rubbed the back of his ear with his finger. "I think we should be on our guard, but I don't think we have to be paranoid about it."

Her breath caught as she let it out. "I'm worried about the groupies. If someone is following us, it could be one of them. I don't want them near Danny again."

"I can't imagine one of them writing stuff like this, but I'll see what I can do tonight."

She felt a little better. Managing a smile, she said quietly, "Thanks. I'd appreciate that."

He looked down at her, his expression unreadable. "It's my job, remember?"

"Yes," Jill said evenly. "I remember." She turned away, before he could see the disappointment in her eyes. It was ridiculous to feel so let down. After all, he was stating a fact.

Right then, though, she couldn't help wishing that just once, he could have said something more personal.

Danny seemed to be on edge as they walked over to the theater that evening. Jill watched him anxiously, praying that he wouldn't freak out during his performance. This was one show she hoped the scout hadn't planned on attending. When Danny got this uptight, anything could happen.

As they reached the stage door, Hank said lightly, "Maybe I'll come and wait with you in the dressing room until the start of the show. I get bored standing out front by myself."

Jill shot him a startled glance, realizing how seriously he had taken the latest letter. He wasn't taken any chances leaving Danny alone. The thought drew her muscles tight across her back.

"Forget it, man, no way," Danny said over his shoulder as he marched down the narrow passageway to the dressing room. "I don't let no one in the room except for Jill."

"I won't disturb you," Hank began, but Danny cut him off.

He spun around and faced Hank, his eyes glittering, his hand raised as if to ward off the other man. "I told you, no way. You don't listen too good, do you?"

"Danny—" Jill began, but Hank gave her a warning shake of his head.

"It's okay," he said quietly. "I'll just wait out front, as usual." He left, walking off quickly into the maze of partitions.

"That wasn't very polite," Jill said, following the singer along the passageway. "I wish you'd be a little more friendly. You won't have any friends at all if you go around talking to everyone the way you do."

He paused at the door, looking back at her with a scowl. "You turning against me, now? I knew hiring that guy would be a mistake. He's gonna cause a lot of trouble around here."

Jill thought about the kiss Hank and Tiffany had exchanged and felt a pang of depression. "He's a very good manager, and he's been a big help around here. I don't know why you don't like him, he's a nice man."

"I don't like him 'cause he's always hanging around us, that's why." He peered at her, looking almost accusing. "You're not hung up on him, are you?"

Jill covered her sudden confusion with a light laugh. "Don't worry, Hank Tyler is the last man I'd choose to be interested in. I hired him for road manager, that's all. After the tour, we'll probably never see him again. Unless you develop a sudden interest in the rodeo."

Danny looked relieved. "Not likely. I don't like to get too close to horses. You never know when they're gonna lash out at you." He pushed open the door and went in.

Jill followed, determined to avoid any more conversation about Hank at all costs.

Danny waited for his cue, pacing up and down as he usually did. Only this time he seemed more fidgety than she'd ever seen him—pushing his hair around with his fingers, humming snatches of songs to himself—and twice she had to repeat something she'd said to him, since he didn't seem to hear her the first time.

Certain that it was the letter that was upsetting him, she didn't want to comment on his distraction. Instead she kept up a steady chatter about the tour and the different towns they'd be going through, until he turned on her and almost snarled, "Would you keep quiet? I'm trying to concentrate here."

Surprised, she stared at him. He'd never spoken to her in that tone of voice before. "Danny, what's wrong? Something is worrying you, is it the letter? If so—"

"It's not the damn letter, okay? Get off my back and quit bugging me, all right?"

Alarmed now, she sat back, almost afraid to look at him for fear of setting him off. Something was really bothering him. And if it wasn't the letter, what was it that had got him so jumpy he couldn't sit still? And what worried her the most, why couldn't he tell her what it was?

Chapter 6

Really worried now, Jill sat in silence, watching Danny mumble to himself as he crossed and recrossed the strip of carpet in ceaseless motion.

When the tap came on the door, they both jumped visibly. "Five," someone called out, and Jill answered.

"Thank you."

Danny picked up his guitar and slung the strap over his head. He strummed quietly for a moment or two, then said, "Okay, let's get out there."

Knowing how he hated waiting in the wings, Jill glanced up at him, but he was already heading for the door. She jumped up to follow him, once more praying that the scout had chosen some other date to check out the potential recording star.

In the wings, Danny went into his boxer dance, bouncing up and down with a rapid staccato beat that fairly hummed with energy. Jill's heart seemed to be beating in tune with that feverish rhythm. It seemed an eternity until she heard the Wildwoods strike up the opening chords of the introduction.

She gave the stage manager the signal and he strode out into the lights. The murmurs from the audience increased as the excitement caught fire, and as Danny's name was announced, Jill heard the shrill screams of the groupies from the back of the auditorium.

She thought about them waiting outside later and smoothed her damp palms down her jeans. She wore her favorite cream-colored Western shirt. It had long sleeves, with black silk embroidery on the sleeve bands to match the yoke. She wished now she'd worn something lighter. All of a sudden she felt much too warm.

Danny strode on stage and the curtains parted. Jill caught a reassuring glimpse of Hank out front. In black jeans and black shirt, he was easy to spot. Then she forgot about Hank as Danny began his opening number.

All things considered, the performance went better than Jill had expected. Although she could tell Danny was on edge, he sounded as clear and strong as ever, and the Wildwoods were in top form. Even Slim seemed to have been fired by some source of energy. He beat the drums as if he were trying to put a hole in the skins.

The audience cheered and stamped for more at the end of every number, egged on by the enthusiastic yelling and screaming from the groupies.

Jill's shoulders ached with tension as she waited for a rush of fans toward the stage, but although the volume of noise seemed louder than usual, the fans kept their seats.

At long last, Danny launched into his final number. His voice soared, then held the final note, and the music and voices swelled to blend with his. Before the medley had faded, the fans roared their approval.

The curtains closed as Danny walked off, and screams for an encore followed him.

"Just one," Jill warned, and he nodded.

As she watched him stride back on stage, Hank said behind her, "Keep him here for a while if you can. I'm going outside to talk to our faithful fans."

Jill murmured an "Okay," her gaze still on Danny. The singer took a deep bow, and walked toward her again, his hand raised in farewell to the audience.

He reached her, and she smiled warmly at him. "Well done, Danny, you were great."

"Yeah? Thanks. It's too bad the backing wasn't with me, though. They were all over the place tonight."

Jill raised her eyebrows in surprise. "Really? I thought they sounded pretty good. Better than usual, I thought."

He looked down at her. "You didn't hear it? Gary sounded as if he had a cold or something, and Slim was off the beat half the time."

She met his stormy gaze warily. "Well, I'm quite sure the audience wasn't aware of it. They loved it. Listen to them. The curtains are closed and they're still yelling for more."

"What do they know?" Danny said, swinging the guitar strap over his head. He handed Jill the instrument. "Here, hold this. I'm going to have a word with Gary."

Her pulse jumped. "No wait, Danny—" She looked helplessly after the singer as he strode back on stage.

Gary and Slim were busy packing up the speakers, while Tiffany packed away the instruments in their cases. The cheers in the auditorium had quietened to a dull mumbling as the fans filed out of their seats.

Sending a glance at the curtains that hid them from the audience, Jill followed Danny onto the stage. She saw him tap Gary on the shoulder.

"I want a word with you," he said.

"Not now, man," Gary said, without looking up, "I'm busy."

Danny grabbed the shoulder and swung Gary around. "I said now."

"Let go of me, punk," Gary growled, "or I'll flatten you."

Jill hurried forward, still holding the guitar. "Danny, this can wait until later, can't it?" she pleaded, reaching the two men.

"No, it can't wait." Danny crossed his arms in a belligerent stance and faced Gary. "Your backup was lousy tonight. Bad enough to put me off-key."

Slowly, Gary straightened.

Jill sent a desperate look at Slim, who seemed determined to ignore the confrontation. Tiffany stood biting her lip, her eyes gleaming with excitement as she watched the two men facing each other.

Sensing she would get no help from either of them, Jill glanced back at the wings behind her. Hank was apparently still involved with the groupies. She put down the guitar and reached out to lay a hand on Danny's arm.

He shook her off, his gaze intent on Gary.

"Listen, punk, if you were off-key that was your problem, not mine. Maybe if you rehearsed some more you'd have a better ear."

"There's nothing wrong with my ear. It's the two-bit amateur musicians behind me, who don't know what the hell they're doing. That's the problem."

Gary's face burned with anger. "You'd better shut up that fool mouth before I shut it for you."

"Danny!" Jill's voice snapped out the warning, but it was too late.

Danny swore crudely, and Tiffany giggled. Gary sent an enraged glare at his wife, then drew back his fist and drove it into Danny's face.

Danny dropped to the floor and lay still.

Tiffany's gasp was echoed by Jill as she went down on her knees beside the motionless figure. She heard footsteps behind her, and Hank's voice saying harshly, "What the hell's going on here?"

"Damn, I only gave him a light tap," Gary said, sounding subdued now that the fight was over. "He's been asking for it for days, anyway."

"You didn't have to hit him," Jill said, glaring up at Gary. "I could have handled it if you'd given me half a chance."

Hank bent over Danny and turned his chin with his fingers. As he did so, Danny's eyes flickered open, stared vacantly for a moment, then focused.

"What the hell's everyone staring at?" Danny mumbled. He climbed to his feet, shaking off Hank's attempt to help him. Without looking at anyone, he strode off the stage, grabbing up his guitar as he went.

"I'll talk to you in the morning," Jill said to Gary, who shrugged sheepishly. She hurried after Danny, without waiting to see if Hank followed her.

She couldn't see him in the wings, and concerned now, she quickened her pace as she headed for the stage door. Outside in the parking lot, shadows swept across the ground as the clouds sailed over the moon. A fresh wind stirred the dust and, feeling chilled after the warmth of the theater, Jill rubbed her arms.

She looked across at the camper, expecting to see Danny. But the singer seemed to have disappeared. And no lights shone in the camper's windows.

Her heart gave a sickening jolt, and she scanned the entire area. Railings along one side of the parking lot separated them from a restaurant. The other side opened onto the street, where cars swept by, their headlights blazing a path in front of them.

The camper was parked alongside the trailer in the far corner. Wondering if Danny had walked around to the back side of it, Jill started forward.

The door opened behind her, spilling light across the ground. And then she saw it. Propped up against the side of the camper. It was Danny's guitar.

Not bothering to turn around, she kept running. Hank's voice called her name but she was caught up in a rising panic, her heart pounding wildly as she ran.

What if someone had been lurking behind the camper, waiting for a chance to catch Danny on his own? What would she do if she found him lying on the ground, perhaps dying from a knife wound hacked into his defenseless body?

She couldn't bear the thought and raced on, heedless of Hank's repeated calling of her name. If something terrible happened to Danny, it would be her fault. She'd pushed him into this, insisted on him going on the tour, in spite of the letters.

She could never forgive herself if something happened to him. She'd never be able to live with herself again. It would be the end of everything for both of them.

She reached the camper, her breath ragged and uneven. He couldn't be hurt. She was responsible for him. Hank was right, she was like a mother to him. It would be like losing a child. Almost beside herself now, she flung herself around the end of the camper, her eyes searching the ground.

Weak with relief, she saw nothing but the empty space behind the camper and the trailer. Reaction set in and, trembling, she leaned against the camper wall, fighting tears.

Footsteps pounded around the camper and Hank's body hurtled toward her. Pulling up, he said a little breathlessly, "What the hell is the matter with you?"

She looked up at him, realizing her fears were still valid. "I thought . . . I wondered if someone had been waiting for Danny and . . ." She shuddered. "He's not here, Hank. He left his guitar. He'd never go anywhere without that. Where could he be?"

"He's not in the camper?"

"He wouldn't have left his guitar outside."

"Who knows what he might have done. Have you looked?"

"No, there's no light." Feeling foolish, she looked up at Hank's worried face. "Of course, he could be in there in the dark. He has a key."

"Let's take a look."

With a slim ray of hope she followed him around to the door. Her heart sank again when he found it still locked. Picking up the guitar, she prayed they'd find him inside. She didn't quite give up hope until she'd looked into Danny's cubicle and discovered it empty.

Whirling around to face Hank, she stammered, "W-what are we going to do? We'll have to call the police."

"Maybe not." He looked down at his watch. "It's early yet to get that drastic."

For a crazy moment she wished he'd put an arm around her. Disturbed by the thought, she plopped down on the couch. "What else can we do?"

"Look. Danny was upset. He's most likely taken off to be by himself somewhere and is hitting the bars right now. That's what I'd do. That could be why he didn't take the guitar."

He wasn't Danny, Jill thought, but kept the observation to herself. "I just can't sit here and wait for him to turn up," she said, jumping to her feet again. "Even if he did take off, it isn't safe for him to be out there alone. What if the writer of those letters is out there looking for him?

What if he's already got him and taken him somewhere? We have to call the police.''

"And what if he's simply tying one on to soothe his bruised ego? Do you really want that kind of publicity when the cops pick him up?''

Torn by indecision, Jill rubbed her arms. "No...I don't know. What am I going to do?''

"We can go look for him. Get jackets while I go back to the theater and call a cab. I'll meet you back here.''

She waited impatiently for him outside the camper, trying not to entertain the fears that tumbled through her mind. She felt a measure of comfort when she finally saw his tall figure striding toward her.

He was right. Now was not the time to panic. If they hadn't found Danny by morning, God forbid, then she would have to call the police. Right now, the important thing was to stay calm, so that if they did find him, she would be able to handle whatever mood he was in and bring him back to the camper.

Hank reached her and laid a hand on her shoulder. She felt the warmth of it seep into her body and gave him a shaky smile.

"You gonna be all right?" he asked, and she nodded.

"You got a cab?" She handed him his jacket and he slipped it on.

"Should be here in five minutes.''

She drew her own jacket closer around her. Although the night was warm, the wind gave her the shivers. Or maybe it was the sick worry that wouldn't let go of her mind. Please, she prayed silently, please let Danny be okay.

The cab arrived, and Hank ushered her into it. "We're looking for a friend," he told the cabdriver. "We want to hit every bar in town until we find him, starting with the closest one.''

The driver nodded, as if he were used to the odd request, and pulled away from the curb.

Light from the street lamp filtered through the windows, playing on Hank's strong hands resting on his knees. Never in her life had Jill so badly wanted to hold someone's hand. She dragged her gaze away and stared miserably out of the window.

"I'll take a look," Hank said as the cab pulled up outside a well-lit bar. "If he's there I'll give you a shout." He climbed out, and came back a few minutes later. Giving Jill a quick shake of his head, he ordered the driver to carry on to the next one.

That one proved fruitless, as did the next. Jill's feeling of helpless frustration intensified with each stop, until she felt as if her entire body were stretched taut, like elastic strained to the limit.

As the cab screeched to a halt in front of the fourth bar, the driver said, "This is a popular place. Real lively. Always busy, lots of music."

"Sounds like a good place to look." Once more, Hank climbed out of the cab.

Jill watched him disappear through the swinging doors without much hope. It was obvious from the rock music filtering through the windows that this was a crowded bar. If Danny had taken off on his own, she was sure he would pick somewhere quiet where he could be alone to nurse his battered pride.

She was surprised when, a few minutes later, Hank appeared in the doorway, beckoning to her. Hope surged swiftly as she climbed out of the cab, asking the cabdriver to wait, and ran toward him.

"You found him?"

"I found him."

Hank's grim expression tempered her joy but only slightly. At least Danny was safe, that was the most important thing. She followed Hank's tall figure, inching close to him as he pushed his way between the crowded tables to the bar.

Customers stood four or five deep, all trying to get the barmen's attention. A cocktail waitress in a skimpy dress leaned against the counter between two male shoulders, hollering her orders above the deafening music.

Hank glanced back at Jill and indicated with a nudge of his head toward the end of the bar.

Danny sat on a stool, the glass in his hand waving precariously back and forth as he talked earnestly to a middle-aged woman. She appeared to be bored by the conversation.

His eyes were half closed, and his hair fell over his face in straggly strands of blond silk. He looked very drunk, but otherwise he appeared to be unharmed.

Filled with a mixture of relief and anger, Jill fought her way past the crowds at the bar to reach his side.

"You're going to have one hell of a hangover in the morning," she said grimly, her mouth close to his ear.

He swayed backward to look at her, nearly toppling from the stool. Grabbing the edge of the counter, he smiled at her. "Oh, hi! I'm just havin' a little drink and talkin' to thish nice lady."

Jill took the half-full glass of whiskey from his hand and put it down on the counter. Glancing at the interested face of the woman seated next to him, Jill said quietly, "You'll have to excuse us, but we have to leave."

The woman nodded. "S'okay, honey. I was getting tired of listening to his singing anyway. It was almost as bad as his jokes."

Danny's face took on an affronted look. "Now wait a minute—"

"Come on, son, time to go." Hank's firm voice spoke loudly behind her as Jill grabbed Danny's arm.

"I'm not your son," Danny said, pronouncing every word with exaggerated care.

"For which I am truly grateful." Hank grabbed Danny's other arm and nodded at Jill. "Okay, let's go."

Between them, they managed to get a sometimes giggling, sometimes swearing Danny out into the fresh air, where he promptly passed out.

"Just keep your fingers crossed he doesn't throw up in the cab," Hank muttered as they bundled the unconscious figure into the back seat.

"He's not dead, is he?" the cabdriver asked, peering at Danny.

"Not yet," Hank said grimly.

Jill jabbed her elbow into his side. "You can take us back to the theater now," she said quickly.

"You want to go back to the theater?" The driver looked at her in surprise.

"We're being picked up there," Hank said.

The driver shrugged and took off. Within minutes they were standing at the door of the camper, supporting a very miserable Danny between them while Jill unlocked the door.

Glancing at the trailer and the well-lit windows, she said quietly, "Thank heavens the group didn't see this. They'd never let him forget it."

"What makes you think I'm going to?" Hank muttered as he hauled Danny up the steps and inside.

She let him put Danny to bed. The singer was too far gone to protest, and she felt exhausted. It had been one hell of a day, she thought as she made a pot of coffee.

Hank joined her as she filled two mugs with the steaming liquid. "Sleeping like a baby," he told her, accepting the mug she offered him. "I wouldn't want his head in the morning, though."

"I hope it's bad enough to turn him off drinking like that again." She leaned her hips against the counter and took a sip of the coffee. The warmth of it felt good as it crept down to her stomach.

"I just don't understand what set Gary off like that." Hank put his mug down on the counter. Pulling off his jacket, he added, "I know the kid can get a little aggressive at times, but I can't believe he deserved a pop on the jaw. I figured Gary had more control than that."

Deciding she'd had enough of the coffee, Jill put her mug in the sink. "Gary is not as predictable as you think. He might seem to have it all together, but he has a vicious temper. Sometimes even Tiffany can't pacify him."

"Yeah, well, Tiffany doesn't exactly have a calming influence on a man."

Something about the way he said it hit her raw nerves. It had been a long, tiring day, and the fright over Danny had left her jittery. Before she could stop to think, she said harshly, "You had better be careful about your little games with Tiffany. Gary is possessive about his wife, and you could be in more trouble than you can handle if he catches you smooching with her."

Her pulse jumped as his expression hardened. Narrowing his eyes to little more than silver slits, he repeated coldly, "Smooching?"

She lifted her chin. "Don't deny it, I saw you. The other night in Dartville, in the parking lot. She was all over you."

"Is that so? Well, if you'd spied on us a little longer, Mata Hari, you would have seen me firmly removing myself from that little mess. Tiffany came at me like a piranha after food, and it took me a moment or two to peel her off me."

Her face flushed, and wishing she'd never started the discussion, Jill went to brush by him. "Well, don't say I didn't warn you."

He put out an arm to stop her, catching her just above her waist. "You don't believe me?"

It sounded disturbingly like a threat.

"It doesn't really concern me one way-or another." She tried to push his arm away, but the muscle under her fingers flexed.

Lowering his voice, he said softly, "Lady, I can assure you, if I were really kissing someone, you'd damned well know it."

She tilted her head back, intending to demand he let her pass. But something in his eyes froze the words in her throat.

Before she could stop him, he lowered his head and clamped his mouth down hard on hers.

All kinds of thoughts shivered through her mind in those first few seconds. Her initial instinct was to resist, and she raised her hands to shove them against his chest.

But the minute she did so he dragged her closer, slamming his body against her to trap her against the counter.

She pushed against him with her hips, realizing immediately that it was a wrong move. The shock of finding him hard against her belly sent a shudder of excitement winging through her body.

He spread his legs, trapping her even more securely, while his mouth moved relentlessly on hers.

She wanted to resist him, and yet she didn't want to. She had imagined this moment so many times. It shocked her to remember that now. She made an effort to wriggle free, and managed to pull her mouth from his.

He caught the back of her neck and once more his mouth covered hers, warm, seductive, demanding and totally irresistible.

She felt the urge to fight dissolving, melting under the heat that fired her heart and her mind. For a moment she remained passive under the hard pressure of his mouth, then the need rose, swift and undeniable.

She'd wanted this, she silently acknowledged, stunned by the discovery. How long had she felt this way about him?

Eagerly she returned the sensuous pressure of his mouth and body, craving the feel of hard muscle and soft flesh. She couldn't get close enough to him, and she slid her hands around his back in an effort to draw him closer.

She felt a shudder ripple through him and elation made her reckless. His tongue fought with hers, and she felt as if she were riding with him on a fast-moving elevator, higher and higher, fighting the pressure that had her gripped in a mad swirl of desperate need.

She felt a swift stab of disappointment when he lifted his head.

"That, lady," he said quietly, "is what I call a kiss."

She found it difficult to draw breath. Her heart still battered her ribs, and she was quite certain that had the counter not been there to support her she'd sink to the floor.

He let her go and turned away, but she'd seen the fire in his eyes and knew he'd been as deeply affected by the kiss as she had.

Her voice shook when she said, "Thank you for the demonstration. Now, if you've quite finished, I'm going to bed."

She forced herself to move, furious now, to think she'd responded to him in such a blatant display of emotions. Never in her entire life had she felt so...wanton. And she'd take good care she never acted that way again.

From now on, she told herself fiercely as she walked unsteadily toward the bathroom, she'd do her best to stay out of his way.

In the cramped space in front of the bathroom sink, she splashed cold water on her face. It didn't seem to help. She grimaced at herself in the mirror. Her hair tumbled around her face in untidy curls and her cheeks glowed with the remnants of the fires that had ravaged her senses.

This was crazy. Here she was, the wrong side of thirty, and her hormones were on a rampage. She had never wanted a man the way she wanted him. And what was worse, she still wanted him.

She uttered a quiet groan. It was going to be a long night. It was going to be a long tour. She should have listened to her instincts right at the beginning and stayed as far away from Hank Tyler as she could get.

And now she had to get from the bathroom to her cubicle. She just prayed that he was at the other end of the camper with his back to her. She was quite sure that the demands of her body were stamped all over her face. Taking a deep breath, she pushed the bathroom door open.

He'd left. She hadn't heard the door so he had taken care not to let her know he was leaving. Her mouth tightened. What did he think she was going to do? Attack him? Well, he needn't have worried. From now on she'd avoid him as much as possible.

She went to bed and tried not to wonder if he'd gone looking for Tiffany to finish what he'd started. It was a ridiculous, childish thought, and she was much too mature to indulge in such petty jealousy.

She pulled the covers over her head so she wouldn't hear him come in and tried to sleep.

She might have spent more time dwelling on it the next day, if it hadn't been for the disturbing events that morning.

Danny had stumbled out of his room, complaining bitterly of a headache and an upset stomach. Already mad at the world, Jill was in no mood to indulge in misplaced sympathy.

"It's your own fault," she said, slapping a cup of black coffee in front of him as he slumped over the table. "If you're going to behave like a spoiled prima donna, then you have to accept the consequences."

He looked up at her in hurt surprise, but she was past considering his delicate feelings.

"And furthermore," she added, standing over him with a dark scowl, "if I ever see you in that condition again, I'll drop you like moldy cheese and find someone else to spend my time and money on. Someone who'll appreciate me a good deal more than you do."

Danny blinked, obviously stunned by this unprecedented attack. "I appreciate you," he said in his little boy's voice.

Normally, that was enough to arouse her motherly instincts and forget her impatience with him. This wasn't a normal day.

"I'm warning you," she said, fixing him with a stern gaze, "if you screw up one more time, Danny, you and I are finished. I'm getting tired of your tantrums. And so is everyone else."

Danny looked as if he wanted to cry. He got up from the table, his bottom lip in a full pout. "I'm going to my room to practice. Please don't disturb me."

"We're leaving in half an hour," Jill said grimly, "so you'd better get washed up first."

Although Hank sat quietly in the corner, reading a newspaper, she knew he'd followed every word. It annoyed her to think she'd revealed her bad mood, and that he could guess the reason for it.

She almost called after Danny to try to make up for her irritation, but decided it had been well founded. Maybe it was time she came down harder on him, she thought, clearing away the dishes from the hurried breakfast. Maybe then he'd get his act together.

Hank did most of the driving that afternoon, and apart from general conversation about the directions for the next stop, he seemed reluctant to say much to her.

She stayed in the back of the camper, pretending to read, though not one word on the page penetrated her mind. The more she thought about the night before, the angrier she got with herself.

Heartbreaker. What a fool she'd been. She'd heard enough about him over the past years to know all about his bad-boy reputation. How could she have fallen for that masterful routine?

She flipped the page of the mystery novel and stared blankly at the print. She'd been around enough to see that one coming from a mile off. Yet she'd ignored all the warning signs and gone into his arms like a lovesick groupie with an idol fixation.

Another page flipped over. Not only that, she'd taken out her anger on Danny, who really hadn't deserved that harsh a dressing-down. She stared gloomily out the window at the green, low-lying fields that seemed to stretch under an endless sky to the edge of the world.

Somehow, she'd have to find a way to make it up to him. She felt awful now, knowing how sensitive he was. Danny regarded her as the only real friend he had in the world. She'd probably hurt him terribly by being so unreasonable.

It didn't make her feel any better later, when they were settled in their new spot and Danny still hadn't made an appearance. She tapped on his door a couple of times, but received no answer, and decided to let him sleep until it was time for the sound check.

Hank, too, seemed to be avoiding her, taking off the minute they were parked to check out the theater. Jill did some housekeeping chores, trying to ignore the depression creeping over her. This was one tour she would be heartily glad to see end.

Deep in her own thoughts, she was startled when Danny suddenly appeared in front of her. She hadn't heard him open his door.

"Hi," she said, smiling at him, "did you have a good sleep?"

"No." He slumped down on a couch. "I didn't sleep much at all."

"I'm sorry." Jill peered at him in concern. "Still got a headache?"

He shook his head and looked out of the window.

Guessing at the reason for the disagreeable expression on his face, Jill said quietly, "Danny, I'm sorry about this morning. I came down hard on you, I know. Put it down to a bad night, okay? I was worried about you, and when people have been worried about someone they care for, they tend to get angry afterward. I'm sorry."

He flicked a glance at her. "I wish you'd get rid of him," he muttered.

She felt a twinge of apprehension. She didn't need to ask whom he was talking about. "Hank helped me look for you last night," she said gently. "He was worried about you, too. He wouldn't let me call the police because he didn't want you to get bad publicity. He could be your friend, Danny, if you'd let him."

Danny shoved himself to his feet. "Yeah? Well, I don't need friends like him. So keep him off my back, okay?"

Jill looked up at him, startled by his vehemence. "What has Hank done to you that you dislike him so much?"

The blue eyes looked down at her, and she felt chilled by the cold anger she saw there. "Forget it," Danny said harshly. "I just don't like him, that's all. I don't know why you had to hire him. We don't need him."

A minute ago she'd been thinking pretty much the same thoughts. "I hired him for the tour, Danny, and he'll stay until it's over. Once we get back to Cedarvale, neither one of us will ever see him again. But until then, we all have to get along, so I'd appreciate it if you'd at least make an effort to be pleasant."

Danny muttered something crude and thrust himself toward the door.

"Where are you going?" Jill demanded in alarm.

"I'm going to see how the group is doing in the theater."

"Then I'll come, too."

He paused at the door and looked back at her, his face grim with defiance. "No, I want to be on my own for a bit. Is that okay with you?"

She nodded helplessly, knowing she couldn't stop him without raising his fears about his safety. Hopefully Hank would keep an eye on him while he was there. After all, that's what she paid him for.

"Go ahead," she said, pretending indifference. "I'll be along in a little while."

He shut the door on her last words and she flinched. Something had really upset him, and somehow she felt it was more than the lecture she'd given him that morning. It occurred to her that he might have overheard Hank's move on her the night before.

But Danny had been out cold. He always slept like the dead, and he'd been full of whiskey last night. Even so, she felt uneasy as she made her way over to the theater later.

The rehearsal went better than she expected, considering Danny's mood. In fact, he seemed to have snapped out of it and even exchanged a joke or two with Tiffany, watched by a scowling Gary.

Dinner afterward started out on a high note. Hank had arranged for the local reviews to be sent on, and they had finally arrived at the theater that afternoon.

There were glowing reports of Danny's performance, and of the group's backing, putting everyone in a good mood. Until Tiffany, obviously excited about their success, expressed her high spirits by flirting with everyone. Even Slim was a target for her provocative remarks, though he paid no attention to them.

Gary sat watching his wife, his face growing more grim by the minute. Jill knew he would say nothing to Tiffany, he was much too afraid of losing her. But he had to be hurting badly inside. How long would he go on watching her flaunt her body in front of other men, without doing something about it?

She tried desperately to smooth things over, but by the time the meal was over, Gary was taking out his temper on Danny, and they traded vicious insults back and forth. Worried that things would escalate into another full-blown fight, Jill tried to intervene.

"I think it's time we got back to the theater," she said, pushing back her chair. "I'll get the bill."

"I'll get it." Hank signaled to the waitress who came bustling over, notebook in hand.

She laid the bill on the table with a bright smile at Hank. "I'll take it when you're ready."

He nodded and reached for the bill at the same time Jill stretched out her hand for it.

Their hands collided, and Jill snatched hers back as if the contact had burned her.

Hank's clear gray gaze clashed with hers. Without a word, he picked up the bill and handed it to her.

All the bills were paid through the bookkeeping system, which Jill took care of herself. Why he hadn't just let it lie there for her to pick up, she had no idea.

She looked across at Danny, who was watching her, an odd expression on his face. She wondered if he'd seen her violent reaction to Hank's touch and if so, what conclusions he'd drawn.

Tiffany rose from her chair and leaned down to whisper something in Danny's ear. He backed away from her as if she were poison ivy. "Why don't you keep your damn wife under control?" he muttered, scowling at Gary. "Or are you too chicken to tell her to quit pestering me?"

Throwing down his napkin on the table, Gary shoved his chair back. "What's your problem, junior? Can't handle a woman all by yourself?"

Danny's head whipped around. "Listen, man," he said in a low, quiet voice that bristled with menace, "just watch your mouth, okay? I've about had enough of your lip. And your damn woman."

Hank stood. "Okay, guys, let's save it until we get out of here."

Danny shot him a lethal glare. "You stay out of it, loudmouth."

Hank's jaw jutted dangerously, and Jill laid a hand on his arm, her eyes pleading with him.

He shrugged, and picked up his hat. "I'm going back to the theater. I'll see you all back there."

"I'm coming, too," Gary said, "as soon as this wimp gets out of my way."

Danny's chair scraped back loudly, causing people across the room to stare in his direction. "I've had it with you," he muttered, so quietly even Jill had trouble hearing him. "All of you. Once this gig is over I'm going solo. So make the most of this tour, beetle brain, because it's your last with Danny Webster."

He turned and strode out of the restaurant, leaving Gary staring furiously after him.

Chapter 7

Waiting with Danny in the dressing room later, Jill said carefully, "I hope you didn't mean that about going solo without the group."

"I sure as hell did," Danny muttered. "I don't need them, anyway."

"Yes, you do. They're part of your sound. The talent scout will be taking that into consideration when he listens to your performance. Without them, you'd have to work on entirely new arrangements. You could lose the chance of a contract."

Danny stuck his feet out in front of him and stared moodily at his boots. "Yeah, well, maybe I'll think about it."

Jill leaned closer. "Danny, won't you tell me what's really bothering you?"

He looked up, and she felt her heart skip a beat. She could see it now, in his eyes. Stark fear.

Very slowly, he tucked his fingers into his shirt pocket and withdrew a folded note.

She read it quickly, her heart beating faster with each word. It was short and to the point.

It's the next stop, punk. The very next stop. Look forward to your one and only solo performance. I promise you it will be spectacular.

"Where did you get this?" Jill demanded, fear making her voice sharp.

"It was sitting there on the dressing table when I came in. I read it while you were out there talking to the sound man."

"No envelope?"

Danny shook his head.

"Why didn't you tell me about this before?" She stared at him. "You weren't going to show me, were you?"

"I didn't want you worried." He got up and started pacing back and forth. "You said not to worry about them, so I was trying not to worry you."

"God." She passed a hand over her eyes. "Look, Danny, from now on I want you to show me every letter like this that you get, okay?"

He stopped pacing and looked down at her, his face white and strained. "They're for real, aren't they? You just don't want to tell me that."

Jill closed her eyes for a brief moment. It was getting harder to keep up a pretence of unconcern.

Danny stood in front of her, his gaze intent on her face.

"I can't be sure of anything," she said honestly. "But I do believe that someone is doing his best to upset you, and that if you let him get to you, you'll be playing right into his hands."

His hands clenched at his sides, but he said nothing, just went on looking at her with that dreadful fear in his blue eyes. She wanted to take him in her arms and comfort him. She wanted to reassure the little boy who had faced so much unhappiness in the past, but she knew he would never let her reach him.

Instead, she said the only thing she could think of that might make him feel a little more secure. "Hank and I are both watching out for you, Danny. We're here to protect you if anyone should try anything silly. Though I feel sure it won't come to that."

She saw some kind of emotion flicker in his eyes, but it was hard to tell what he was thinking.

"What about the group?" he asked finally. "Do they know about this?"

She felt a shiver of apprehension. The reference to Danny's solo performance really bothered her. Just a short time ago Danny had used those same words, in a voice so low only the group at the table could have heard him.

She didn't want to think that one of the Wildwoods could be responsible for these hateful letters. And anyone could have come into the dressing room and left the note. Yet it seemed too much of a coincidence for the possibility to be ruled out.

Until she'd talked it over with Hank, Jill decided, she was going to hold judgment on that thought. "I think at this point the fewer people who know about it the better, wouldn't you say?"

She felt relieved when Danny emphatically nodded his head. "I don't want you to tell them. You know what Gary's like, he'll use it to dig at me."

"Exactly. This whole thing is upsetting enough without someone making it worse. We'll just keep it between us, and Hank. All right?"

He turned away to pick up his guitar. His "Okay" sounded muffled, but at that moment the summons sounded on the door and a voice called out, "Five."

Jill automatically answered. "Thanks." She was anxious to talk to Hank, to show him the note.

She waited until Danny was well into his second number before going down to the auditorium. Standing at the side door, she caught his eye and beckoned to him.

He came at once, an anxious frown on his face. "What's up?"

She handed him the note and he quickly scanned it. When he looked at her again, she saw her own troubled thoughts mirrored in his eyes. "What do you think?" she asked as he handed the note back to her. "Do you think it could be one of the group?"

He swore quietly, his gaze traveling back to Danny on stage. "I don't know what the hell to think. It sure seems like a coincidence, doesn't it?"

"If it is, it's a lot more likely that it's simply one of them trying to upset Danny," Jill said, hoping he would agree with her. "As you pointed out, it's unlikely anyone would go to all that trouble to warn him, and us, if he meant to harm him. After all, he must know Danny would show us the letters."

"Maybe." Hank shook his head. "But why would someone in the group want to sabotage the tour? They'd be out of work, too, if Danny loses the contract."

"I know. I asked myself that, too. None of this makes sense, does it?"

"Not so far. Maybe we should think about talking to the police again."

"I thought of that, too," Jill said miserably. "But they've already said they can't give us protection without a solid reason. Even if they could, they can't protect us while we're on the road."

"How does Danny feel about this?"

She looked up at the singer, who held center stage, his head thrown back, his fingers strumming furiously on his guitar. "He's upset, of course, but all things considered, he's handling this much better than I expected. It hasn't seemed to affect his performance at all."

Hank followed her gaze, his expression grave. "We have three more stops, right?"

"Yes." Her heart thumped. "But the note said it would be at the next stop."

"That could be just a way of stepping up the pressure, since Danny hasn't reacted the way the writer expected him to."

She looked up at him, feeling a faint stirring of hope. "You think so?"

He nodded. "I'll be extra cautious from now on, but try not to get panicked by this. That's exactly what the writer wants you to do. If Danny realizes how nervous you are, it's bound to affect him."

"I know," Jill said, feeling a little better. "That's one reason I don't want to bring in the police. If he knew we were that worried, he'd go to pieces."

She looked back at Danny, who had reached the end of the number. "I'd better go back, he likes to know I'm out there in the wings."

She turned away, her pulse leaping when Hank spoke her name.

"Jill..."

Looking back at him, she waited, disturbed by the confusion in his eyes. Then he shook his head.

"Nothing. Go back to Danny." He walked back to his position in front of the stage.

Wishing she knew what it was he'd been going to say, Jill made her way back to the wings.

Hank barely heard the next few songs. He didn't know what he'd been about to say to Jill, but he knew whatever it was, it would have been a mistake.

Ever since he'd held her in his arms, warm, passionate and so desirable, he hadn't been able to think about much else. He had been angry when he'd grabbed her, intent on making a point. He'd regretted it the minute his mouth had touched hers, but then something inside him had caught fire, and he was kissing her for real.

Even then, he might have put a stop to it, if she hadn't melted right about then and returned his kiss with such feeling and passion he'd been shaken to the point of almost losing it altogether.

He'd wanted that more than anything. It would have been a big, big mistake. And although he was glad he'd had the sense to recognize that in time, part of him longed to know what he'd missed. And that was the part he had the most trouble dealing with.

Impatiently he dragged his thoughts off the depressing subject. He would have to stay alert now, just in case the writer of those letters meant business. And he didn't need any distractions. Especially the kind that could absorb his entire mind.

Maybe he should start carrying his gun again, he thought as he followed Danny and Jill back to the camper later that night. He'd left it in the camper the past few days, convinced that he wouldn't need it and worried that Jill might discover he had it.

She had been so adamant about him not bringing a gun. If she found out he'd had one all along she'd just about bring the roof down on his head.

Preoccupied with his own thoughts, he barely heard the conversation between Jill and Danny. He drank coffee, muttered a response the few times Jill spoke to him and waited impatiently for them both to go to bed.

He was tired, both emotionally and physically, and he badly needed some time alone to come to terms with everything that churned around in his mind.

At long last Danny muttered a curt "Good night" to him and made his way to his room.

Hank hated the awkward way Jill echoed the words, sending him a brief, cool glance before disappearing behind her door. Yet he had nothing to say to her.

He waited a few minutes until he was sure he would be undisturbed, then dug in his holdall for the revolver. He dug his fingers into each side of the bag but couldn't feel the smooth, hard surface of the gun.

Impatiently, he dragged out the contents of the bag. Underwear, clean shirts, two pairs of jeans, shaving gear, a rodeo magazine he hadn't had time to look at yet, spare towel, sneakers, and an unopened bottle of the best bourbon he could find.

Unwilling to believe his eyes, he sorted through his gear again and again, then hunted the length of the camper. There was no mistake. Someone had apparently searched through his belongings and had stolen his gun.

For most of that night Hank fought with the indecision that plagued his mind. The theft of the gun added a sinister twist to the situation. He should report it to the police. But as Jill said, they could hardly give them protection while on the road.

If he told Jill what had happened, apart from the possibility that she'd tear off his head for bringing a gun with him, the fact that it had probably been stolen would scare her to death. She obviously had a very strong aversion toward firearms.

He didn't want to worry her, or Danny, unnecessarily. Yet he couldn't just sit back and wait for whoever took the gun to use it on one of them.

He flung himself onto his back and stared into the darkness. Somehow he just couldn't believe that one of the group really intended to hurt Danny. Sure, there was a lot of hostility between them all, but surely not enough to want to kill the one person who could bring them all fame and fortune.

Maybe it was all part of a scare campaign. In fact, the more he thought about it, the more he was convinced that the whole business of the letters was simply to upset Danny enough to blow the contract. But who would want to do that?

What he had to do, Hank decided as he wrestled with his pillow, was to find out just who had a real interest in sabotaging the contract. Once he knew that, it should be a simple matter to find out who was writing the letters. And most likely, who had his gun.

In the meantime, just to be on the safe side, he'd suggest that Jill cancel the tour. It might give the letter writer what he wanted, but on the other hand, it would ensure the safety of everyone else. And maybe then he could sleep nights.

Jill was taken aback the next morning when Hank suggested the cancellation. "Has something else happened?" she asked, keeping her voice low in case Danny overheard.

He shook his head, avoiding her gaze. He hadn't shaved yet, Jill noticed, and his hair was mussed where he'd run his fingers through it while talking to her. He looked tired, as if he hadn't slept much, and she felt a stab of tenderness that she immediately suppressed.

It wouldn't do to let herself get carried away again by his rugged appeal. What happened the other night had been a simple matter of too much togetherness and too much tension, she assured herself. She wasn't really that crazy about him. So he'd kissed her and she'd enjoyed it. Apparently he hadn't shared her pleasure in the exchange and had no intention of repeating it. For which she should be incredibly grateful.

Wishing she could be just that, and angry for caring too much, Jill said tightly, "I am not going to cancel the tour. We've come this far and we're going to finish it. We have only three more stops to go. The shows are sold out, the reviews are great and everything looks positive for Danny's contract. I'm not going to risk losing it now. He's lost too much in his life. I'm going to see he has this."

"Suit yourself." Hank got to his feet, and yawned. "I'm going to shave."

She watched him move to the bathroom, wondering why she sensed a new tension in him. More than likely, he was getting tired of being cooped up in such a small space. He was more used to the wide open skies of the rodeo rings and hours spent under a hot sun. All this must seem very confining.

It was even getting to her, Jill thought as she heard Danny moving around in his room. She'd be glad when this tour was over and the verdict on the contract settled.

She and Hank sat sharing a pot of coffee when Danny emerged from his room, his hair tousled and his eyes half-closed. He came and slumped down at the table, uttering a grunt for a greeting.

Jill did her best to bring him out of his black mood, but by the time they left for the next stop, his temper had worsened. Twice he snapped at Hank, and then turned on Jill, displaying a childish temper that irritated her to no end.

Things hadn't improved by the time they'd reached their next stop, and Jill was on edge all through the sound check and rehearsal.

It was apparent by Danny's performance that he was becoming strung out, he fluffed the start of two songs and lost the words to a third halfway through the number.

Even Hank seemed to have absorbed the bad vibes. Jill couldn't help noticing that he paid very close attention to the Wildwoods, and Tiffany in particular, which did nothing to improve her frame of mind.

It was a relief when they broke for dinner and she could relax a little more. Though not for long. All throughout the meal, Gary and Danny exchanged barbs while Tiffany did her best to provoke them.

After one particular heated exchange, Slim suddenly pounded his fist on the table and shoved his chair backward. "I've just about had enough of listening to you all squawk at each other like cock fighters. I just lost my dadburn appetite, and if you can't get along better'n this, from now on I'll find a place to eat by myself."

Abandoning a major portion of his meal on the table, he slammed out of the restaurant, and left the door swinging violently behind him.

Tiffany slumped back in her chair, her mouth drawn down at the corners. "Don't know what's gotten into him," she muttered, pushing her plate away from her. "He don't usually get that fired up over nothing."

"He's just tired," Gary said, looking anxiously at his wife. "He'll be okay by the time we get back."

Tiffany didn't answer, but just sat there playing with her fork.

Gary leaned forward and patted her arm. "Don't pay him no mind, honey. Come on, give me a smile. You can't go on tonight with that pretty mouth all droopy like that."

Tiffany continued to ignore him, and Jill watched Danny out of the corner of her eye, praying he wouldn't take advantage of Gary's obvious distress over his wife's mood.

But Danny seemed preoccupied, and for once ignored the interplay between the Wildwoods.

Looking at her watch, Jill decided she'd had enough, too. "We'd better make a move," she told Danny. "Just about time for you to get dressed for the show."

He got up immediately, and without another glance at the rest of them, headed for the door.

Jill met Hank's gaze, and his raised eyebrows didn't do much for her uneasiness. She took care of the bill and hurried out of the restaurant, with Hank close behind her, catching up with Danny.

As they walked across the parking lot, she made a last attempt to reassure him. "This has been a very successful tour so far," she said, hoping to take his mind off his problems. "What with the good reviews you've had, and some very good publicity, we've had sellouts practically all the way. I imagine the talent scout will be real impressed, no matter which performance he caught."

Danny nodded, though she knew he hadn't absorbed a word she'd said.

She tried again. "Only a couple more performances like this and you should be signing your name to a brand-new contract."

"Then we can all celebrate," Hank said dryly.

Danny stopped dead in his tracks, taking them both by surprise. "I'm not going on tonight," he said, his face white and strained. "He's promised to get me tonight and I'm not going out there."

"Danny," Jill said in a quiet, firm voice, "you have to go out there. For all we know, this could be the one stop the scout will visit. We can't take the chance of losing him now. Not after everything has been going so well."

Shock rippled through her when she looked into his eyes. She saw something desperate in their depths, like that of a cornered wild pony.

"I can't," he repeated, his voice rising shrilly. "What if he's out there? How're you gonna stop him from killing me? He can do it, I tell you. He's here. I can feel it in my bones.''

"You're overreacting—" Jill began, but Hank cut in.

"Maybe the kid's right," he said quietly. "Maybe it's too much of a risk."

"See?" Danny pushed her out of the way in his hurry to get past her. "I told you. You won't listen to me. No one listens to me."

He started sprinting back toward the camper and Jill turned furiously on Hank.

"Now look what you've done. You've freaked him out. It will take hours to calm him down now, and we don't have hours. Thanks to you, he could ruin his entire career tonight."

She rushed off after Danny, before the storm clouds gathering on Hank's face could result in a tirade against her.

Inside the camper Danny threw the worst fit she'd ever seen. Yelling and shouting, he cursed everyone he could think of, including himself for being so stupid as to come on the tour.

Cushions, books, food, cups—anything he could get his hands on—sailed through the air as he screamed his defiance of Jill's urgent commands.

The racket brought Tiffany and Gary to the door. "He's really freaking out this time," Tiffany said, looking as if she was enjoying the spectacle. "You'll be lucky to get him on stage tonight, by the looks of him."

Nerves snapping, Jill whirled around to face her. "I'll have him up there, don't you worry about that. And I can manage it a lot sooner if you'd get out of my hair."

Tiffany looked ready to join in the fray, but Gary tugged at her arm. "Come on, honey, we don't have time to mess with him now. We have to be on stage in twenty minutes."

Tiffany couldn't resist a parting shot. "Well, I just hope we don't have to carry the whole show. Not that we couldn't, if we had to."

Hank shut the door in her face, and Jill turned back to Danny. "You hear that? If you don't make it into the wings on time, they'll just go on without you. Is that what you want? You want to blow your whole career in one night?"

A fleeting thought went through her head that if the letter writer were one of the group, he was certainly getting his money's worth that night.

Danny looked ready to burst into tears. He shook his head, and looked at her so helplessly she felt like crying herself.

"Will you at least take your medication?" she pleaded, holding out the pill she'd shaken from the bottle. "You know it will make you feel better. Please, Danny, you've worked so hard, don't throw it all away now."

She held her breath, until he finally nodded and held out his hand for the pill. She gave him the glass of water and watched him swallow it, then took the empty glass from his trembling hand.

"Now sit down," she said firmly, "and let's talk about this in a calm, sensible manner."

"I can't go on," Danny said brokenly. "I just can't. I don't feel well."

Hank sat down next to him at the end of the couch. He started to speak and Jill shot him a look that warned him to keep quiet.

"You're going to be fine, Danny," she said soothingly. "You know that. The minute you walk on that stage and hear all those cheers and feel the love coming from all those people out there, you're going to feel fine."

"No, I'm not," Danny whined, shaking his head from side to side.

"For god's sake listen to him," Hank said harshly. "How the hell do you expect the kid to sing like that?"

"The way he always sings." Furious at his interference, Jill glared at him. "Stay out of this, Hank, I know what I'm doing."

"I'm beginning to doubt that." His face looked like a thundercloud as he got slowly to his feet. "You know what you're doing, lady? You could be risking his life, that's what. And what for?"

He stepped closer, his jaw jutting dangerously. "For a damn contract you don't even know you're gonna get?"

She tried desperately to hang on to her temper, knowing that it would only upset Danny further. "You don't understand," she said quietly. "And I don't have time to explain it now. So please leave me alone to take care of this my way, okay?"

"Dammit, Jill, think what you're doing." He shoved his hat back on his head with his thumb. "I always knew you were ambitious but I never realized you were blinded by it. Ask yourself who the hell you're doing this for. Is it for Danny, your precious protégé? Or is it for yourself? Could it be you're going after your own success through him?"

Stunned, she felt hot tears of anger sting her eyes. How dare he. Of course she wasn't doing this for herself. So why did she catch a sudden glimpse of herself as he must see her? Could there possibly be a grain of truth in his accusation?

No, she would not allow that. Dammit, she would not allow that. "Get out," she said fiercely. "What the hell does a womanizer like you know about anything, anyway? All you've got on your mind is how to get your next conquest in bed. Men like you make me sick."

She caught her breath as his face turned white, then red. He couldn't have looked more shattered if she'd hit him. Without a word, he ground his heel into the carpet, spun around and flung himself from the camper. She could hear his footsteps striding away like a soldier on a battle march.

She wanted to cry. Damn the man. What was it about him that could reduce her to tears? She never cried. Not since she'd lost the baby. She hadn't shed one tear since then.

Pain, swift and excruciating, sliced through her heart. It was all his fault, stirring up the memories, pain she'd buried so long ago with the tiny white coffin and the small teddy bear.

She felt a knot in her throat and closed her hand over it, as if to smooth it away.

"Are you okay?"

For a moment she stared into Danny's anxious blue eyes, then her mind cleared. "Yes," she whispered. "Of course."

"You don't sound all right."

She managed a smile and cleared her throat. "I'm fine. How about you? Are you feeling better?"

He nodded his head. "Yes, I am. We'd better get to the theater, or I'm going to be late for my call."

Taken aback by this swift turnaround, Jill decided not to question it. Maybe he'd pulled himself together for her sake. She felt a warm glow of pleasure at the thought. She risked a light hug of his shoulders, and he smiled back at her.

"Okay, champ. Let's go." She led the way out the door, pulling a deep breath of the still-warm evening air. She didn't like the sharp pang of dread at the thought that Hank might not be out front when they got there. She could only hope he was.

For Danny's sake, she told herself firmly as they entered the theater. She needed Hank around for one reason only. To guard Danny. After the tour she need never see him again. She refused to give in to the depression she felt at the thought.

Her little rush of elation when she caught sight of Hank in the auditorium stayed with her, comforting, somewhat, the ache that had been left by the confrontation.

Danny's solid performance helped a lot, as well, and by the end of the show, when nothing out of the ordinary happened, Jill was beginning to feel decidedly more at ease.

It was beginning to look very much as if the threats to Danny were nothing more than words on paper, just as the police had predicted. She had even managed to convince herself that the Wildwoods had nothing to do with it.

It was more than likely one of the groupies, mad at Danny because he refused to pay her any attention. Danny never had seemed interested in girls, Jill thought as she watched him take his final bow. But then, the ones he met were the usual star-struck fans who were fascinated by what he did, not who he was.

Only two more stops, Danny. Only two. If he could survive the last two as well as he'd done so far, the contract would be a certainty. It might already have been settled, if the scout had been in the audience. She prayed he had.

Hank was also vastly relieved when the performance was finally over. He'd been on the edge of his toes all night, instincts primed, just waiting for something to happen.

He'd scanned the auditorium back and forth all night, looking for any sign of a gun, even though he knew that it was unlikely anyone would take a potshot from the audience. If they used his gun they'd have to be pretty close to the target to get a sure shot off.

And with the extra security he'd ordered at the theater, that was unlikely. Hank smiled, remembering the manager's surprise at the request. He'd had to come up with a good excuse. The supposed rumor that Garth Brooks was going to make a surprise appearance was a masterpiece of invention. The manager had ordered the guards right away.

Still, he couldn't help letting out a huge sigh when the curtains swung together amid thunderous applause. It was over. Two more to go and they were home free. Once he got through the tricky part of getting the singer back to the camper. And he still had to face Jill.

She refused to look at him when he met her and Danny backstage, and he could hardly blame her. He'd accused her of being self-centered. She had a right to be angry with him.

He had no chance to smooth things over that night. Now that the concert was over, Danny seemed fidgety and on edge again. He kept jumping up and down, saying he was tired of being cooped up in the camper.

"I'm not tired," he said, when Jill suggested he go to bed. "I want to go into town, go to a bar or something. I'm sick of going to bed and working, that's all I seem to do."

"It's only three more days," Jill said, "then you can do what you like. But right now you need your rest. You're getting overtired and that won't help your voice."

"I can't sleep when I do go to bed." Danny flung himself down on the couch again. "I keep hearing the backing for the songs in my mind. Over and over and over again."

Hank got up from the table and reached for his holdall. "Here, pal, I've got something that will help you sleep."

Jill shook her head at him, but he pretended not to notice. He wanted a serious conversation with Jill, and he wanted it in private. He pulled out the bourbon, and Danny's eyes lit up.

"Yeah, man. That's what I call a nightcap."

"Just one," Jill warned. "You had your medication earlier, remember?"

"Ah, that's worn off by now." He grinned as Hank poured a generous shot in the glass. "Make it a double," he urged when Hank capped the bottle.

"I don't think so," Jill said. "Remember what happened the other night."

"One double's not going to hurt him." Hank untwisted the cap and poured another shot.

"Fine. If you know better than I do what's good for him, then you can handle him when he gets belligerent," Jill snapped. "I'm going to bed."

Inwardly cursing, Hank watched her go. He'd done it again. Without meaning to, he'd opened his big mouth and put his boot in it as usual. All he'd meant to do was give Danny enough bourbon to relax him, so that he'd sleep deep enough not to hear what he had to say to Jill.

Instead of that, he'd upset her, and probably widened the gulf between them even more. Mad at himself, he watched Danny gulp down his best bourbon, and wondered if he'd ever get the chance to make things right.

The thought kept him awake again that night, and he knew he would have to do something about it. They couldn't go on sparring with each other this way. They still had two more stops, then another day's trip back home. The tension with Danny was bad enough, without making things worse by fighting with each other.

It was time he cleared the air between them once and for all, he told himself, as the lonely minutes ticked by. And the way to do that was to bring their differences out in the open, where they could discuss them rationally and come to terms with them.

With that thought came a little peace, and he settled down, determined to take advantage of the first opportunity the next day.

It came once they were on the road. Danny, complaining that he hadn't slept well, returned to his room to lie down, and Hank hoped, to sleep.

He took the wheel for the first leg, and after giving Danny time to doze off, he called out quietly to Jill, who sat reading in the back of the camper.

"Any coffee by any chance?"

"I'll make some." She clattered around for several minutes, then brought him a steaming mug.

He took it from her and stood it in the compartment slot. "You going to have some?"

"Yes, I've got it back there."

"Why don't you bring it up here and sit with me for a while. I could use the company."

He could feel the surprise in her stare. "I don't want to distract you."

"You won't distract me," he lied. "I'm sleepy and need someone to talk to, in case I fall asleep. I don't really want to yell back and forth the length of the camper."

After a long moment, she said quietly, "I'll get my coffee."

While he waited for her, he rehearsed the opening lines of his speech. Nothing seemed appropriate. He didn't know where to begin.

She settled down next to him, her coffee in her hand. "Okay," she said after a moment or two of silence, "what do you want to talk about? Got a favorite topic of conversation?"

The words seemed to stick in his throat, and he had to force them out. "I'd like to talk about Perry."

"Oh."

For a moment he thought she was going to get up and leave, and he loosened his grip on the wheel to catch her arm. But then she said quietly, "All right. Where do you want me to begin?"

"Nowhere. I want to do the talking, at least, at first. I want you to understand why I was so mad at Perry for getting hitched like that."

"I know why." Her voice sounded bitter, and he winced.

"No, I don't think you do."

"Sure I do. You thought he was making a big mistake marrying someone like me. I wasn't good enough for your baby brother. You wanted something much better for him than I could give him. Right?"

He swung his gaze from the road for a moment to give her an injured look. "Would you give me a chance?"

She sank back in the seat. "Sorry."

He looked back at the road, which stretched in an endless stream of gray toward the blue gray shadows of distant mountains. Now that he had the opportunity, again the words wouldn't come.

After what seemed like several minutes had passed, he said, "Perry was only two years old when my father walked out on us. Perry never remembered him. I was seven. Old enough to remember and old enough to hurt. I took care of Perry, my mother was too busy working to have time for either of us."

"Yes," Jill said softly. "Perry told me. I'm sorry."

Hank shrugged. He wasn't looking for sympathy. Only understanding. "We both grew up pretty wild. With no father to hold us in check we had too much freedom, and most of the time we were getting into one scrape after another. So my mother sent us to an uncle's ranch for the summers. That's where I learned how to handle horses and cattle. Perry was too young for that stuff, so my uncle taught him how to play guitar."

"He taught him well," Jill said.

Something in her voice caught his attention. He glanced at her, but she sat staring straight ahead, a kind of wistful, sad look on her face. He felt a ripple of shared nostalgia, and something else much more potent and dangerous.

He shifted his gaze back to the road. "Anyway, when I left school, I joined the rodeo circuit and did pretty well. Until my mother contacted me. She was worried about

Perry. He'd formed a rock band, and she was worried about the company he kept. She was terrified he'd get into drugs and end up in trouble. She wanted me to come back and take care of him.''

He paused, and felt Jill look at him, but she said nothing. After a moment's silence, he went on. "I quit the rodeo and took over as manager of the band, kind of learning as I went. Although both of us had our share of rebellion, I knew how to handle it. Perry didn't.''

Out of the corner of his eye he saw her lift the coffee mug to her lips. He couldn't tell what she was thinking, and wondered if all this was as painful for her as it was for him.

''Anyway,'' he said, ''I knew if I wasn't there to keep Perry on the right path, he'd screw up his life. We made a deal. I would help him with the band, on condition he talk things over with me if he had a problem.''

''And then he met me,'' Jill said, her voice oddly flat.

''And then he met you.'' Hank's mouth twisted in a bitter smile. ''I knew he was sweet on you, but I never imagined for one moment he'd be fool enough to marry you.''

''Thank you.''

Hank swore. ''I didn't mean it that way. You were both too young, Perry was unstable at the best of times, I knew he couldn't handle marriage. What really got to me was that he took off and did it without saying anything to me. By the time I knew about it, it was too late to stop it.''

''And you blamed me.''

He started to answer her, but just then a loud bang behind him startled him. His hands jerked on the wheel, swerving the camper and he straightened it, swearing under his breath.

A quick glance over his shoulder reassured him it was only Danny's door banging against the wall that had startled him. But then he caught sight of the singer's face, and tension gripped him in the stomach.

He heard Jill's voice rising on a note of anxiety. "Danny, what is it?"

Hell, Hank thought. *Here we go again.*

Chapter 8

"What's the next stop?"

Hearing Danny's high, thin voice, Hank's nerves jolted. It sounded as if another tantrum was developing. They were on the turnpike and it would be a while before he could get off. He hoped Jill could handle it.

He saw her slide out of the seat and disappear from his view. "You know what the next town is," she said calmly. "Goldwater."

"No, I don't want to go there. I can't sing there. Let's skip it and go straight to Badrock."

Hank heard a scuffle of movement as Danny went to the back of the camper.

"We can't do that." A cupboard door opened and closed. "You know very well we can't let all those people down, they are counting on seeing you tonight. They've paid good money to hear you sing. You're surely not going to disappoint them?"

Hank heard her fill the coffeepot, and thought privately that a strong shot of bourbon would probably do Danny more good.

"I can't help it," Danny answered. "I'm not going into that town and that's final."

"You have signed an agreement, Danny. If you don't turn up, how do you think that's going to look? Do you seriously believe that a recording studio is going to take a chance on someone who doesn't show up for his performances?"

"Tell them I'm sick."

"I won't lie for you, Danny."

Right on, Hank thought in approval. He was dying to say something, but he wasn't going to make that mistake again.

Danny muttered something too low for Hank to hear.

Jill dropped her voice to a persuasive tone. "I don't understand what this is all about. After nothing happened last night, I thought we decided there was no real danger. So why don't you want to go to Goldwater, Danny?"

Silence.

"Danny?"

"I just don't want to, okay?"

Jill sighed audibly. "Did you get another letter? Is that what this is all about?"

Danny must have shaken his head.

"Are you sure you're telling me the truth?"

"Yeah, yeah. I didn't get any more letters."

"Well, we're coming up to our exit very soon. Maybe you should take some of your medication with this coffee."

"I don't need any medication."

"All right, then, drink your coffee. And read the newspaper. Here. And I don't want to hear any more nonsense about not performing tonight, okay?"

Danny mumbled, "Okay."

"Tell you what," Jill said, "when we get back home I'll arrange for a short trip to unwind. Anywhere you want to go."

"Anywhere?"

"Anywhere within reason."

"Hawaii?"

"I'll see what I can do. But you have to promise me no more bouts of stage fright, okay?"

"Okay. I'll try."

"Thanks, honey. Relax. Everything's going to be fine. Just like it always is, right?"

Danny's answering "Right" didn't sound too convincing, but Jill returned to her seat and sat down next to Hank with a sigh. She leaned forward and reached for the map from the dashboard. "Okay, let's take a look where we are."

Frustrated at having his conversation with Jill interrupted, Hank waited for her directions, wondering if they'd really solved anything after all. It surprised him how much he wanted to dissolve the tension between them.

For longer than he wanted to remember, he'd resented her. Now the woman he'd disliked so bitterly no longer existed in his mind. Instead he found himself becoming more and more captivated by the compassionate, caring woman who sat next to him peering at the map.

The brief moments he'd held her in his arms had told him more than he wanted to know. She excited him physically as well as emotionally, to the point where he couldn't seem to think about anything else.

He'd wanted her so badly that night. He couldn't remember when the need had been so potent. He'd tried to tell himself it was the heat of the moment, a combination of tension and the frustration of being cooped up in close quarters with an attractive woman.

But it was more than that, and he knew it. He'd always felt a certain electricity between them, even when he knew Perry was sweet on her. He'd stayed away from her because of Perry. But that spark of interest that he'd felt then hadn't died. Even though he'd convinced himself he despised her.

He couldn't imagine how he'd ever resented her that way. Now the spark had ignited into something far more explosive and dangerous. And he would have to be extremely careful to make sure it didn't burn out of control. Because no matter what had happened since then, she was still as unattainable to him now as she had been then.

The thought depressed him. Watching her work with Danny, so calm and reassuring in the face of his tirades, he had seen a different woman from the one he'd remembered. He could tell how deeply she cared for the young singer. He owed her an apology.

He took the opportunity to tell her so later that afternoon, while Danny was in his room working on a new number. The camper sat in its parking spot behind the theater, and the rest of the group was already there setting up for the concert that night.

Figuring he wouldn't be disturbed for a while, Hank sat down at the table, where Jill pored over the latest reviews. "How's he doing?" he asked as Jill looked up. "Still collecting raves?"

Jill nodded, smiling. "I'm so thrilled for him. These reviews will go a long way toward establishing his name."

"Yeah, well, he deserves it. He might be a pain in the butt, but he works hard. And the kid's got talent."

She lifted an eyebrow. "Wow. Praise indeed, considering the source. I'll pass it on."

"Do that."

She looked at him, her warm brown eyes quizzical. Something stirred in his belly, and he dropped his gaze in case it reflected in his eyes.

"I...reckon I owe you an apology," he said awkwardly.

"For what?"

"For accusing you of pushing Danny for your own ends. I know you wouldn't deliberately risk his life for your own ambitions."

He sensed her withdrawal, as if she didn't want to discuss it. Then she said quietly, "You weren't entirely out of line. I am very fond of Danny, yes. But I'll be the first to admit that my ambition is a factor behind my drive to take him to the top. I think I need it as much for myself as for him."

"You always were ambitious," Hank said, trying to let her off the hook. "There's nothing wrong with that."

She shrugged. "I guess it depends on the motivation behind it, and how you channel it."

He settled back, watching her. "So tell me where all that drive comes from."

She smiled, a wry movement of her lips without any humor in it. "My parents. They wanted me to be like my brother."

She propped her chin on her hands, and he waited, sensing that she wanted to talk.

"I don't know if you remember—Bradley is a lawyer. He's smart, good-looking, successful marriage and children, the whole bit. He did everything right in their eyes, and I did everything wrong."

"Why?"

"Both my parents were very proud of my brother. They wanted me to follow in his footsteps, become a professional. Preferably, a doctor. Or better yet, a surgeon." She uttered a short laugh. "Can you honestly see me as a surgeon?"

"I can see you as a lot of things."

He saw the flush on her cheeks and wondered if he'd said something wrong, but after a minute she said, "All I ever wanted to do was be in the music business. I didn't care if I sang, played guitar or sold concert tickets. My whole world was my music and I couldn't imagine doing anything else with my life.

"My parents argued with me constantly. They kept quoting the odds of making a living in music and pointed out that all kids get those kinds of crazy dreams, but it was rare any of them ever came true. They told me I was wasting my time chasing rainbows and one day I'd wake up and my chances to make something of my life will have passed me by."

"I'm sorry," Hank said softly. "That must have been very discouraging."

She looked at him, as if she wasn't sure if his sympathy was genuine. "It made me all the more determined," she said, lifting her chin in the gesture of defiance he knew so well. "The bad part was, I never did feel that good about my singing. I guess I knew, deep down, that I didn't have the voice to make it, but I wanted so much to prove them wrong.

"I started singing with bands while I was in high school. The minute I was out of there, I joined a full-time band."

Hank's heart twisted at the memories. "Perry's."

"Yes. He was advertising for a singer, I applied, and he hired me. That was just before you came on the scene."

He remembered. He could still see her as he first saw her, hair wild and tumbling to her shoulders, dark eyes flashing with excitement as she belted out a song at the mike.

He had to admit, she was right about the singing. She'd had more heart than voice, but he'd admired her spunk and the emotion she'd put in to every performance. She'd sung from the gut, with an air of experience way beyond her years.

"My parents went out of their way to show me how much they hated what I was doing," Jill said, her finger tracing down the newspaper print. "They never lost an opportunity to put down my singing, my clothes, my hair, my friends, just about everything I did.

"One night, we had a terrible fight. My father told me to get out and never come back. He said I was a disgrace to the family and they were disowning me."

"And that's when you went to Perry?"

"Yes." She sat staring at the newsprint for so long he thought she'd forgotten he was there. Then a shuddering sigh shook her body.

"I had nowhere else to go. Perry and I had been dating awhile then. When he heard what had happened, he asked me to marry him. I was hurt, confused and frightened. His proposal was a shock, and before I really had time to think about it, I'd agreed. I thought I knew him pretty well, and that he'd take care of me. It seemed like the right thing to do at the time."

Hank bit back the comment he was about to make. He'd said enough on the subject all those years ago.

"Anyway, I stayed the night. In the morning I began to have second thoughts, but Perry didn't give me time to back out. We took off for Nevada the next day."

She rubbed her hands together and he saw they were trembling. He wanted to hold them, he ached to hold them and knew he couldn't. He'd made one mistake. He couldn't afford another.

"You were right," Jill said bitterly. "We couldn't make it work. After you'd gone back to the rodeo, Perry was miserable and moody. Every time we had a fight, he blamed me for the rift between you. I begged him to go and see you, but he refused. He had too much pride to make the first move. In the end he would get so angry, I gave up trying. When we lost the baby he—"

"You what?" He was so shocked by the revelation he thought he hadn't heard her right.

She stared back at him, her face registering her surprise. "You didn't know? I thought your mother would have told you."

He shook his head. He hadn't been in contact much with his mother in the last fifteen years. The realization had brought him a lot of pain at the funeral. Almost as much as seeing his brother standing silent and withdrawn on the other side of the grave.

"I'm sorry," he said softly. "What happened?"

She glanced at him, and the pain in her eyes knifed through his heart. "He was stillborn."

"Oh, God, Jill. I'm sorry. I didn't know." He had to force himself not to take her in his arms. How much pain they must have suffered, she and Perry. A sharp longing to have those years back again tore at him, and he turned his head to look out the window. "I wish I'd known."

"Would it have made a difference?"

He faced her again, hating the grief on her face. "As far as Perry and me getting together? I don't know," he said honestly.

She looked down at the clippings in front of her. "Anyway, I guess that was the last straw as far as Perry and I were concerned. He never wanted the baby, I don't think he'd really thought about what it would mean to our lifestyle until it was actually on the way.

"He acted as if it was my fault entirely for getting pregnant, and he even hinted that I'd done it to tie him down so that he couldn't follow his career. He couldn't hide his relief when the baby was born dead."

Hank swore softly under his breath. Perry had always had a selfish streak, but he'd never realized how much until now.

"For weeks after we buried Daniel, I couldn't seem to function properly," Jill went on. "I didn't want to eat, I couldn't sleep, and I couldn't stop crying. I guess it was all too much for Perry. He kept telling me to snap out of it. He didn't seem to understand the grief I was suffering and was callous about the whole thing.

"Then one night he told me that it was just as well the baby died. If he hadn't, Perry said, he would have left me. He just wasn't cut out to be a father. He couldn't stand the thought of being tied down with a bunch of kids."

Her sigh trembled, and anxiously he glanced at her, but her eyes were dry. "I left him the next day," she said, her voice growing hard and bitter again. "I went back to my parents. Even they didn't seem to understand how shattered I was about everything. They told me that if I couldn't live a normal, decent life, then I should expect to get what I deserved."

Hank's vicious curse startled her, and she looked up. Again he had to fight the urge to take her in his arms and kiss away the pain. It seemed as if he'd misjudged her all these years. He'd been blinded by his love and loyalty for his brother.

"I made up my mind right there and then," Jill continued, "that I was going to show them just how wrong they were about me. I knew I wouldn't make it as a singer, but I knew enough about it to recognize talent when I heard it. And I knew enough about the business to know how to market a singer. It took me a while. Those were rough times. I worked in so many greasy spoons I forgot what good food tasted like."

Hank nodded. "I know what you mean. I've had my share of that scene, too."

She smiled. "We must both have strong constitutions. Anyway, eventually I found a singer I liked, and before long I was able to quit working in those places. I had two other clients before I found Danny."

Fascinated by the story, Hank propped his chin on his folded hands. "Where did you meet him?"

"I heard him sing in a tavern one night. He had the entire audience hushed while he sang, and I knew I'd found a winner. Danny's parents are dead, and he was drifting from town to town, earning just enough money to feed him until the next stop. Until I took over. I worked with him, teaching him everything I know."

Her smile broke through the solemn expression. "Almost all I know. You were right about the slow ballads. I intend to work with him on them when this tour is over."

The smile faded as her eyes held his. "Maybe I do want it for myself, Hank. But I want it for Danny, as well. You were right about that, too. He has the talent, and he works damn hard. He deserves to succeed, but he needs me to do it. He needs my drive and encouragement to keep him on that tough road to get there."

He wished he could tell her that Danny would make it. But the truth was, he had serious doubts that kid was stable enough to handle success. He was very much afraid that Jill was building her hopes on a castle of sand, and that sooner or later it would be washed away in the tide of Danny's insecurity.

It was little enough to worry about in view of the problems Danny was facing at the moment. But even if he survived this potential disaster Hank still had grave doubts that Danny would ever be strong enough to cope with the stress of being a star.

He couldn't help wishing he could be there to comfort her if it happened. She would need all the comfort she could get. And it hurt to know that it would have to be someone else who gave it to her.

Jill watched the concert from the wings that night filled with apprehension. Danny had been unusually subdued in the dressing room earlier, with none of the nervous excitement he usually displayed just before a show.

He'd sat in the corner, hugging his guitar as if he were trying to crawl inside it and hide. Although Jill had done her best to find out what was bothering him, he'd just shaken his head and refused to answer.

Thinking about it now, Jill couldn't imagine what had caused his depression. Danny had a lot of moods, but this silent, withdrawn brooding was totally unlike him. Even when she'd first met him, he hadn't been shut off from her the way he was now.

She angled upstage until she could see Hank out front. It reassured her a little to know he was there. She even allowed herself a little smile. He'd actually apologized to her.

Although he had a lot more to apologize for, in her mind at least, it was a small step toward a more amiable relationship. Her smile faded. It would make things easier until they got back to Cedarvale. After that, she wouldn't see him again.

The ache hit her hard, cutting off her breath. She'd tried not to dwell on it. She'd tried to tell herself that it hadn't changed her life, but deep down she knew she would never be able to forget the way he'd made her feel.

Every time she looked at him now, she thought about his mouth on hers, his eyes full of fiery need, his hands on her, promising so much, his body hard for her, wanting her—

"Sounds good, tonight, doesn't he?"

She jumped violently, her cheeks flushing as she met the amused gaze of a middle-aged, chunky man wearing jeans and a white sweatshirt.

He grinned, nodding toward the stage where Danny crooned one of his more romantic numbers into the mike. "Ain't often they get that quiet when a good-looking kid's singing."

Jill smiled back, recognizing the stagehand she'd spoken to earlier. "I know what you mean. I'm sure half the time they can't hear a word of the lyrics above all the foot stomping and hand clapping."

"Ah, yeah, but that's half the fun of country singing." He looked over at Danny. "Sure has improved since I last heard him. 'Course, he was just a real young kid, then."

She looked at him in pleased surprise. "You've heard Danny sing? Where was that?"

"At the Country King Tavern. That was right before he headed out of town. Only his name wasn't Danny Webster then. Reckon he changed it when he left, not so's anyone'd blame him. I reckon I would, too, if I'd been him."

Jill frowned, wondering if the stagehand had made a mistake. "Danny changed his name?"

"Sure. You didn't know?"

"Are you sure you've got the right singer?"

He nodded, looking a little uncomfortable. "Sure as I'm standing here. I'd know him anywhere. He grew up right here in Goldwater, right across the street from my folk's place. His real name is Ricky Mason."

Her heart began beating unevenly. Danny had told her he was born and raised in Tennessee. Why would he do that if he'd grown up in Oklahoma? She remembered something else the stagehand had said. "What did you mean," she asked, feeling as if she were standing on the edge of a very deep pit, "about not blaming him for changing his name?"

The stagehand looked away from her, then back, obviously aware now that he'd said the wrong thing. "Look," he said, "maybe it's none of my business. I'd better get back to the gallery, got some work to do—"

"Tell me," Jill demanded. "I'm his manager. If there's anything I should know about Danny's past I'd like to know what it is."

"Maybe you should ask him to tell you himself—"

"I'm asking you."

He looked unhappily over at Danny, who had begun another fast number. "It all happened a long time ago," he said, his voice so quiet Jill had to strain to hear him. "It was all in the papers so everyone knew about it."

He paused, as though he was trying to justify what he was about to say. "I guess it's okay to tell you," he said finally. "It happened when Ricky was just a little kid. He and his dad, Corey Mason, were the best of pals. Went everywhere together, the two of them.

"I watched Corey teach Ricky to ride a bike, up and down our street. Took him days before he finally would stay on. Corey took that kid with him everywhere, hunting, fishing, bowling, you name it."

Once more, he hesitated. "Ricky was around seven or eight when his dad came home unexpected and found Ricky's mom in bed with another guy."

Jill's mouth felt suddenly dry. "What happened?"

The stagehand looked down at the floor and shook his head. "Tragedy, that's what it was. Should never've happened. Corey took down his hunting rifle off the wall. He told the judge he just meant to frighten his wife, to teach her a lesson. But the gun went off."

Jill clamped a hand over her mouth as the stagehand looked up at her.

"They sent Corey Mason to jail," he said, "for murdering his wife. He hung himself a month later."

Jill didn't remember much of the concert that night. Shaken to the core, all she wanted was time to absorb what she'd heard. Poor Danny. No wonder he'd been so upset about appearing in Goldwater. She could understand why he'd changed his name after he'd left.

According to the stagehand, Danny had lived with a foster family until he was fifteen. Then he'd disappeared one night, and no one had heard of him again until his picture appeared in the local paper, announcing his stop on the tour.

Judging by the ages of most of the audience, they were probably too young to remember what had happened. But how many people were there because they were curious about the kid whose father was a murderer?

And if she wondered about that, Jill thought as she waited for Danny to come offstage, the thought must also be playing on his mind. It explained a lot.

She waited until Danny was in bed that night before telling Hank the story. Speaking in a near-whisper, she repeated everything the stagehand had told her.

Hank seemed as stunned as she was by the news.

"The strange thing is," she told Hank, "Danny helped me draw up the route for the tour. We picked the towns for the size of the population, not too big, not too small, and for the interest in country music, which I had researched beforehand."

"Did Danny pick Goldwater?"

"I can't remember. But it seems odd now that he didn't try to steer me away from this particular route. There were plenty of alternatives."

"There's no chance the guy could have made a mistake in recognizing Danny?"

Jill shook her head, her hands wrapped around her coffee mug. It had been raining that evening, and she felt chilled. "He seemed so certain." She looked up as a thought occurred to her. "He said it was all in the papers at the time. Do you think we could find it in the local library tomorrow? We'd know for sure then."

Hank narrowed his eyes as he stared at her. "It means that much to you?"

She hesitated for several long moments. "Yes," she said finally. "I'd really like to know. If it's true, and it is Danny, I think it's possible there might be a connection with the threats he's been getting."

"Ah, I thought that was on your mind."

"You have to admit it's possible."

"I guess you know that if there is a connection somewhere, we could be stirring up a hornet's nest by poking around into the past."

"I've thought of that." She stared down at her cup, trying to calm the quiver of uneasiness. "But if we don't find out who's behind it, there's no guarantee it's going to stop when we get back home."

"I reckon that's true, but at least the police can take care of it there."

"And what if the threats are real, and someone is waiting for Danny at the last stop? What if that last letter he got arrived early, and the person who wrote it meant for it to arrive today? That would mean he's waiting for Danny in Badrock the day after tomorrow."

Hank shook his head. "We're jumping the gun here. So far nothing's happened to make us think the threats are for real. And what about the chance that it's one of the group? They can't have anything to do with Danny's hometown."

"I don't know." She looked at him, feeling as if she were wandering through a maze of corridors, getting more lost at every turn. "But if we get a look at the papers, maybe we'll find out."

He continued to look at her, his gray eyes pensive as he tapped his fingers on the table. "All right," he said just when she felt she'd have to break the silence. "I'll check out the library before we leave in the morning. Lucky we don't have to hit the road early."

Jill let out her breath. "Thanks," she said, giving him a warm smile. "I couldn't do it myself without Danny knowing what I was up to."

His gaze flicked down to her mouth and hovered there. For a heart-stopping moment she saw a deep, intense longing in his eyes, then abruptly, he shoved himself to his feet.

"I'll get on it as soon as they open. Now, if you don't mind, I'd like to get some sleep."

She nodded, scrambling to her feet. Her heart still thudded at the fleeting expression she'd seen in his gaze. She didn't want to analyze it. She didn't want to hope. There could be no future with him, she knew that. So why did she keep wishing for the moon?

In spite of her good intentions, she found herself thinking about it that night. It wasn't just a physical attraction—she'd had that before. This was something different, something much more profound.

They shared a common interest in music, even though Hank's heart was in rodeo. She was able to talk to him on a professional level. He understood the turmoil, the frustrations, the fears and obstacles that were an integral part of the business. Few people did, unless they were part of the business itself.

But it was still more than that. She liked his quiet strength, his confidence. He was so unlike Perry it was difficult to believe they were brothers. She felt safe with Hank, secure in the knowledge that he'd protect her if the need arose. She had never felt protected before. She wasn't even sure she'd wanted to feel that way. Until now.

He listened when she talked. Really listened, as if he cared and truly wanted to understand. He cared for Danny, too, even though he tried to hide behind a gruff intolerance of Danny's moods.

She remembered what he'd said about Danny reminding him of Perry. That was something else they shared. A common bond with a man who was no longer a part of their lives, but who was just as much a barrier between them as if he had stood there in person.

Perry, who had refused to make amends with his brother. Who had stood silent and unforgiving across the grave of their mother, and had left without a word of condolence between them.

Perry, who had promised her love and protection, and had been unable to give her either. He was the reason there could never be anything between her and Hank. He was the reason she had to bury her feelings and forget the crazy excitement she had felt in his brother's arms.

It wouldn't be easy, Jill thought miserably, but it was something she would have to do. Her only consolation was that it would soon be over, and once Hank was out of her life, she would no longer be tormented by the sight of his dark head bent over a newspaper, his strong hands guiding the wheel of the camper, or the swift, enigmatic expression in his eyes every now and again when he looked at her.

Turning on her side, she tried to ignore the persistent ache under her ribs and willed herself to sleep.

The next morning, Hank took a bus into town to find the library. The shy young girl behind the desk was embarrassingly eager to please, and insisted on hovering over his shoulder while he ran the files through the projector.

He finally had to be firm in his assurances that he could manage on his own. It took him more than an hour to locate the story.

Several issues of the local paper carried the details of the murder, and the ensuing court case. Hank had copies made of them all, deciding that he and Jill could read them later when they had more time.

They had planned to leave around midday, arriving in Badrock late at night. The performance was scheduled for the following night, and the day after that, they would be on their way home.

Jill grew increasingly nervous as the camper drew closer to the town. She couldn't shake the thought that whoever had written the letters planned to attack Danny on the last stop.

She couldn't eat the lunch she'd prepared for Hank and Danny, and after she'd taken a turn at the wheel, her shoulders and neck ached with tension.

She desperately wanted to read the newspaper accounts of the murder, but for once Danny chose not to spend the time in his room. He sat in the back of the camper, strumming the chords of a new song over and over until she felt like screaming at him.

The constant sway of the camper bothered her stomach, something that rarely happened, and she felt as if the walls were shrinking, closing in on her on both sides.

By the looks that Hank sent her now and again, she knew that he sensed her anxiety. She did her best to avoid him. She just hoped that Danny would be too absorbed in his music to notice that she jumped at every little sound.

At one point, Hank had to slam on the brakes and almost jerked her off her feet. Her yelp of fear was way out of proportion, and Danny glanced up at her in concern.

"Did you hurt yourself?"

She smiled at him, angry with herself for her lack of control. "No, just a little anxious. We're so close to the end of the tour, I'd hate to have an accident now."

"I'd hate to have an accident anytime," Danny said, going back to his fingering.

She forced a laugh. "Well, we have a good driver up front, so I don't think we have to worry too much."

He didn't answer, his mind more involved in the tune he was playing on the guitar.

Jill glanced at Hank, who sat hunched at the wheel, his hat pulled over his eyes to shade the sun that poured in through the front windshield.

A deep, intense sense of longing swept over her. For the first time in a good many years, she badly needed someone to lean on. All the confidence, all the independence she had built up since her divorce seemed to have deserted her. She felt frightened, and in that moment, very much alone.

She fought the urge to go up front and sit next to Hank. What was the sense of making things worse for herself? It was time to start forgetting how she felt about him, and prepare herself for the parting, which would come all too soon.

The sun finally disappeared beyond the horizon, leaving streaks of pale gold and purple in the darkening sky. With the night came the cool breezes, which Jill welcomed as she took over the wheel for the last leg into town.

She'd hoped that the concentration needed for driving would keep her mind off her fears, but the thoughts wouldn't lie still. She kept remembering Gary's look of fury the night he'd hit Danny.

Memories of Tiffany hovering over Danny, being rebuffed again and again, returned to haunt her. She saw Slim, skulking behind the backdrop, spying on his two partners. And the groupies, giggling, nudging each other, crowding Danny like normal, excitable teenagers. Could one of them be a potential killer?

She didn't want to think that. She hoped and prayed that she was wrong about that. But one fact kept staring her in the face. If there was a killer out there, this next stop would be the last chance to make a move. If it was going to happen, it would happen right here in Badrock.

Chapter 9

It didn't seem possible to Jill that danger could be ahead. In fact, right then, with the lights of the town twinkling in the distance across the flat landscape, the fragrance of newly cut grass and sun-dried corn drifting through the side window and the warm summer breeze ruffling her hair, the idea of someone lurking in the shadows, waiting to strike a young man down, seemed ludicrous.

So much so, that by the time she finally parked the camper in its allotted slot in the parking lot, she had just about convinced herself that the entire episode of the letters had been nothing more than an elaborate game. A cruel and vindictive game, to be sure, but relatively harmless, nevertheless.

Danny, exhausted by the long trip, went to bed early, leaving Hank and Jill the opportunity at last to pore over the news accounts of the murder.

It was worse than Jill had imagined. "Listen to this," she said, picking up the front page of the paper. She read out the entire story, her voice getting more and more tremulous as she neared the end.

Corey Mason had left his wife and son at home, as usual, while he went on his night shift at a manufacturing plant. Later that night, he'd sliced his hand on a band saw and had been taken by a co-worker to the emergency ward.

Not wanting to disturb his family, Corey had decided not to call from the hospital, but had gone straight home. There he'd found his wife in his bed with another man.

He'd taken his shotgun and shot them both in the head. Both of them had died instantly. Corey had then called the police, and confessed to the crime when they arrived at the scene.

Jill reached the last paragraph, her voice treacherously close to breaking. "They found Ricky Mason in his bedroom. He was cowering behind the bed, speechless, and incoherent from the shock of the terrible scene he'd witnessed."

The paper rattled in her hands as she put it down. She looked up to find Hank watching her, his silver gaze warm with sympathy.

"Oh, Hank," she said, "he was only eight years old. He watched his father kill his mother. It must have been horrifying. Can you imagine . . . ?"

To her utter dismay, a tear escaped. She struggled valiantly, determined not to break down in front of this man who sat watching her in growing concern.

"I think I . . ." She started to get up, and he reached out and caught her arm.

"Jill, it's okay to cry."

She shook her head, her teeth clamped on her lower lip, but it was too late. Maybe it was the weariness of days on the road. Maybe it was the constant fear of danger lurking in every corner.

Whatever it was, it was too potent to fight any longer. Sinking into the chair again, she gave herself over to a flood of helpless tears.

Hank made a soft murmur in his throat. Sliding along the couch, he reached for her and drew her into his arms, muttering words of comfort. She couldn't make them out, but it didn't matter. His voice soothed her as nothing else could. And right then, it was all she needed.

She relaxed against him, comforted beyond belief by the strength of his arms around her, his fingers gently smoothing her hair back from her forehead, and the touch of his lips on her brow.

The tears slowed, and finally stopped, but still he held her, his lips moving softly over her eyelids, her cheeks, her nose, and brushing her mouth.

Excitement quivered low in her belly, like a shimmering, eager flame. She tensed, afraid of the sensation, and he lifted his head.

Embarrassed now, she sniffed. "I have to get a tissue."

"Here, blow your nose on this."

He tugged the hem of his shirt free from his jeans and offered it to her.

She grinned, and hiccuped. "I've got one in my purse. It's over there, behind you."

He reached back for the purse and handed it to her, watching her solemnly while she rummaged inside until she found a tissue and blew her nose.

"Feeling better?" he asked softly when she looked up at him.

She nodded. "Thanks." Feeling suddenly self-conscious, she added, "I'm sorry, I don't usually make a fool of myself that way."

Her heart missed a beat when he leaned forward and gently wiped a tear from her cheek with his thumb. His fingers grasped her chin.

"I told you," he said, his voice dropping to a husky whisper, "it's okay to cry."

Her breath seemed to freeze, making her lungs ache. His gaze held hers, and in his eyes she saw a question as old as time.

All her instincts told her to move, to speak, to leave while she still had the strength to resist the purpose clearly forming on his face.

His fingers tightened on her chin, slowly drawing her forward, banishing every single thought from her mind except for the fire leaping in his eyes, the touch of his hand on her skin, and the soul-destroying scent of masculine heat.

Inch by inch, he drew closer, until his mouth settled on hers, warm, insistent and incredibly exciting. This was a very different kiss than the last one he'd given her. This was erotic, sensuous, with the hot promise of fulfillment.

She moaned, softly, a quiet sound in her throat.

He lifted his head and looked deep into her eyes, as if trying to see into her soul. "I want you," he whispered.

Her breath caught, and her heart slammed into her ribs. Common sense hammered at her, trying to get through the pounding excitement that shook her body.

"I want you, too," she whispered back.

For a moment longer he stared at her.

She felt as if she were staring into the heart of a volcano, watching its fiery lava swirl faster and faster as it prepared to erupt. She saw the sudden blaze of heat in his eyes and it stopped her breath.

Then he uttered her name, his voice thick in his throat. His hands clamped on her arms, dragging her hard against his chest.

She went willingly, eagerly, desperate for the touch of his mouth on hers again.

Impatiently now, his hands roamed her body and she tugged at his shirt, pulling the rest of it free from his jeans.

The warm, smooth flesh of his stomach excited her. She ran exploring fingers over the soft fuzz on his chest, delighting in the sensuous touch. He allowed her only a moment before he pulled at the buttons of her shirt, almost tearing them off in his frantic rush.

A tiny sound penetrated the hot assault on her senses. Dragging her mouth from his, she whispered, "Wait."

"I don't think I can," he said, his voice low and ragged.

The thrill of knowing how badly he wanted her filled her with a heady sense of power. She pointed at her cubicle door.

Understanding flashed in his eyes, followed by a decisive nod that started another chain reaction in her belly. He reached for the handle to open the door and the two of them squeezed inside.

She leaned across the narrow bed and switched on the lamp in the headboard. "Not much room," she whispered.

"I don't need much room." He pushed her down and straddled her on his knees while he pulled off his shirt. His gaze held hers as his hands moved to his belt buckle.

She kept her gaze on his face while she wriggled out of her shirt. Her heart began hammering again as she reached behind her back for the snaps of her bra.

With a quick movement of his hand, he stopped her. "No," he whispered. "I want to."

She smiled, and reached instead for the waistband of his jeans. Very carefully, she slid them down over his thighs.

All at once, his patience snapped again. In a frenzy of movement he undressed her, and struggled frantically out of his briefs.

The touch of his naked body lowering onto hers brought a whimper of sound to her throat. She cut it off before it could escape.

There was so much she wanted to know about his body. So much she wanted to explore, so much she wanted to give to him.

With hands and tongue, he roamed her flesh in a fever of craving, giving and taking in never-ending waves of pleasure.

He commanded her body now. She was his, to do with as he wanted, as long as he satisfied the pressures his caresses ignited. He was in control, and although her searching hands caused an occasional swiftly drawn breath, she knew she was at the mercy of his knowing touch.

Finally she reached the limits of her endurance. With impatient hands, she gripped his firm buttocks and spread her legs. "Now," she urged in a fierce whisper. "Please, Hank, now."

He hesitated only a moment, poised above her, his chest gleaming with perspiration. He looked down at her, as if wanting to commit the moment to memory, then with a swift, smooth, firm movement, he slid into her.

Never, she thought wildly, never in a lifetime would she experience again the torment of sensations that plundered her body. Wave after wave of hot, raging passion blotted everything else from her mind. She rose swiftly to a climax, and had barely recovered before she was riding the wave again.

Finally, with a convulsive shudder of his body that echoed in the deepest recesses of her mind, his muscles strained for the final thrust. They seemed to be poised together for a moment, on the brink of something ethereal, then in a rushing torrent of release it was over, and he lay spent and panting on top of her.

She closed her arms around him, floating in the pleasant haze of a longing well satisfied.

"Am I too heavy?" he whispered, after his breathing had steadied.

"No, you feel wonderful."

He reached up an arm and switched off the light. "So do you."

She smiled in the dark. "I feel pretty wonderful."

His lips brushed hers, unseen but painfully pleasurable. "The feeling's mutual, hot stuff."

Her smile widened into a grin. "You'd better not call me that in public."

"I'll keep that in mind." He shifted his weight off her, and turned her in his arms to lie with his knees tucked behind hers.

Wondering if she would ever feel the same again, she closed her eyes and gave herself up to the exhaustion creeping over her.

Hank lay for a long time, staring into the blackness. And as the torrid thoughts faded, the cold shock of reason took their place. He felt Jill's body slacken, and heard her breathing gradually slow to the deep, even rhythm of sleep.

Even then he waited, until he was sure she had reached the deepest stage of sleep before he eased out of the bed. He found his jeans in the dark, and decided to leave the rest until the next day. Right now he wanted to get out of that tiny enclosure, before Jill woke up, wanting to know why he was leaving.

He didn't know what he could say to her. He needed the cool, fresh breezes of the night to calm his mind and banish the chaotic thoughts that would not be still.

He let himself out of the camper, under a dark sky strewn with a million stars. Nothing stirred in the parking lot, even the breeze had deserted the quiet night.

He paced the few steps to the edge of the lot, where a grass verge led to a stand of cottonwoods. For the first time in years, he wished he still smoked. For some reason, the thought amused him—the ultimate cliché of a good lay.

His faint smile vanished on the heels of the thought. It hadn't been like that at all with Jill. If it had, it would be easier to forget. But something told him he would never be able to erase the memory of her vital, eager body, every bit as demanding and insistent as his own.

He had never been with a woman who gave so much of herself. He had never known that kind of aggressive give-and-take that had made the experience so incredible.

He had never thought about it much before, but he knew now what it could be like with someone so well matched, so attuned, that each of them knew instinctively how to please the other, while receiving so much pleasure in return.

And the knowing made it all the more bittersweet. He had never known a woman such as Jill. But his brother had known her first. And there were too many bad memories to put Perry's ghost to rest. He would always be there between them.

His curse echoed across the parking lot, dying in the shadows of that warm, summer night. He was beginning to face a truth he hadn't wanted to acknowledge.

He'd blamed Jill all those years for his fight with Perry, because it had been easier than blaming himself. Jill was right. If he hadn't interfered, things might have been different for all of them.

But it was too late to put things right now. He had to put it all out of his mind. It couldn't happen again. He wouldn't let it happen again.

He'd given in to the heat of the moment. They both had. They were both passionate people, caught up in an impossible situation, thrown together in a confined space fraught with tension. It was no wonder their emotions exploded into something he couldn't stop.

He started off at a brisk pace, intent on walking the perimeter of the parking lot before going back to the camper. He hoped that Jill wouldn't demand an explanation for his about-turn. Because no matter how hard he racked his brains, he still couldn't think what to tell her.

Jill formed her own conclusions very quickly the next morning. The fact that Hank had left the bed in the night without waking her, the fact that he barely glanced at her when she went out to make coffee, the fact that he apparently had no intention of discussing what had happened between them, all added up to one thing in her mind.

He'd satisfied his lustful curiosity and was no longer interested in the prey. Hurt and angry with herself for giving in to her emotions, she did her best to ignore him for the rest of the day.

It was easier than it might have been, since she had her hands full with Danny that morning. She had planned on going to the grocery store that afternoon, but Danny's ill-concealed temper worried her.

Nothing she said or did seemed to pacify him. Once more she found herself with a temperamental man-child, whose unpredictable mood ranged from explosive swearing to sulky silence.

Things came to a head when Jill suggested they go with the Wildwoods to a well-known seafood restaurant in the town. Danny adamantly refused to go, saying he couldn't stand being around the group any more than he had to.

"Then leave him here," Hank said shortly as Jill tried pleading with Danny. "Maybe he'll be in a more adult frame of mind if he's left on his own. I'm getting a little tired of these childish outbursts every time he can't get his own way about something."

Any other time, Jill might have agreed. But she was still hurting from his abrupt dismissal of what had happened between them. And her heart still ached for the terrible tragedy Danny had experienced so early in his life.

She leapt to his defense immediately. "Why don't you just go on without us and leave us alone. Danny has enough problems, without listening to you jumping all over him at every opportunity."

She was being unfair, she knew. But she was too angry to care. Right then all she wanted was to be alone herself, where she wouldn't feel the blade of a knife in her heart every time she looked at Hank Tyler.

Hank stared down at her for a moment, his face uncompromising. "Do you want me to bring you something back?" he asked stiffly.

"No, thank you. I'll find something here to tide us over until I can get to the store to shop."

He nodded, and left the camper, banging the door behind him.

Jill allowed the ache to ease up before trying to approach Danny. She needed all her concentration if she was going to bring Danny out of this foul mood. She wondered briefly, if he'd overheard her and Hank discussing the story of what had happened to his parents.

She didn't think he could have. The door of his cubicle had been firmly shut, and both she and Hank had been careful to speak quietly. Still, something had happened to trigger this latest tantrum, and if she was going to get through to him, she needed to know what it was.

She fixed a peanut butter and jelly sandwich, the only thing she could find in the cupboard for lunch, and used up the last of the milk. Danny ate without speaking, staring moodily out the window.

After churning a few things over in her mind, Jill decided to take the bull by the horns. She watched him sit back, wiping his mouth with the back of his hand. "I'm going shopping this afternoon," she said. "Is there anything special you'd like me to pick up for you?"

Avoiding her gaze, Danny gave a decisive shake of his head.

"Look at me, Danny," Jill said, trying to coax him with her voice. "Has somebody done something to upset you?"

His pale blue gaze skimmed across her face. Without answering, he looked back out the window.

"I can't help if I don't know what it is." She waited a moment and, getting no response, added quietly, "Is it something I've done?"

His narrow shoulders lifted in a shrug.

She felt a twist of discomfort in her stomach. Maybe he had overheard them last night, after all. "Do you want to talk about it? Perhaps I can explain if I know what I've done."

Dismay chilled her as he shoved himself to his feet. "I'm tired," he said, pushing his hands into the pockets of his jeans. "I'm going to lie down."

She peered closer at him. "Don't you feel well?"

"I feel fine. Just leave me alone, okay?" He stomped down the camper to his room and went inside, slamming the door shut behind him.

Really worried now, Jill stared at the closed door. It wasn't like him to turn on her that way. She could always coax him out of his bad mood, or at least get him to talk about it. Not since she'd met him had he shut her out the way he was doing on this trip.

She cleared up the dishes and rinsed them off. Maybe she was expecting too much from him, she told herself as she dried the plates and put them away. After all, he was under a great deal of stress.

If it wasn't enough that his entire career could be riding on this tour, there was also the threats to contend with. Even if she had managed to persuade him it was nothing to worry about, she knew it had to be playing on his mind.

And of course there was the trauma of revisiting his hometown. It had to have brought back some terrible memories. All things considered, he'd handled himself far better than she could have hoped.

Still, she couldn't help wishing that he'd been willing to talk about it. Maybe a long nap this afternoon would help to relieve some of his anxieties, heaven knew she had enough of them herself.

She finished putting away the dishes, still fighting a gnawing uneasiness. If he had overheard her discussion with Hank, she would have to insist Danny talk about it, and get it out in the open.

She could understand him not wanting to talk about it to anyone, but he needed to know that people were not going to think any less of him for what had happened. In fact, people would most likely be far more sympathetic and tolerant toward him if they knew how he had suffered.

Everyone but Hank that was, she thought, her brows meeting when she remembered Hank's muttered retort before he left. How she'd misjudged that man.

Now that she thought about it, he should have been back by now. She glanced at her watch. Almost three. He'd left before noon. She needed him to be here before she could go to the store. They'd planned on leaving early in the morning to head home, and she was out of just about everything.

Anxiously she stepped outside the camper, hoping to catch sight of him. The thought occurred to her that he could be in the trailer with Tiffany, but she dismissed that almost immediately.

She was prepared to give him the benefit of the doubt as far as Tiffany was concerned. Even as the thought formed, she saw him striding across the parking lot toward her. She couldn't deny the lift of her spirits when she saw he was alone.

He had also been drinking, she noticed at once. She tried not to sound disapproving when she said, "I'm glad you're back. I have to leave to do some grocery shopping and I didn't want to leave Danny alone."

Hank nodded, and tipped his hat back on his head. "Good old Danny. How is the maestro? In a more amiable frame of mind, I hope?"

"He's lying down. So you won't have to be bothered with him."

"Glad to hear it." He took a step toward her and she backed into the camper, unsure of his intention.

A quick frown passed across his face as he stepped inside. "Did you eat lunch?"

"Yes. Did you?"

"Hamburger. It was lousy."

"Is that why you washed it down with beer?"

She saw his expression change and knew she'd made a mistake. Silently cursing herself for her quick tongue, she moved down the camper to look for her purse.

"You suggesting I drink too much?"

"I'm not suggesting anything."

"Good. I don't like being told what to do."

"Yes, I've noticed." She found her purse and picked it up. "To be perfectly honest, Hank, I couldn't care less what you do with your time. Just as long as you do what I hired you to do, and that's to guard Danny."

"Well, I don't think you have much to worry about there. No one's taken a stab at him yet, and the newspaper story turned up nothing significant."

His voice slurred slightly over the last word and her mouth tightened. "I want to go over it again later. Maybe there's something I missed. In the meantime, I'm going to the store. So if there's anything you want . . ."

"Nothing. Can't think of a damn thing."

"We're out of beer."

Why was she doing this? she wondered. She was deliberately needling him. And judging by the glint in his eyes she'd succeeded.

"I can have all the beer I want once this job is over. I reckon I can hold out until then."

"I'm glad to hear it." She had to push by him, and he made it difficult for her by not moving an inch. Aware of him looking down at her, she felt her face burn by the time she reached the door.

Looking back at him, she said coolly, "Try not to disturb Danny while I'm gone."

He grinned at her, a lazy widening of his mouth that mocked her. "Don't you worry about that, ma'am. I'll take mighty good care not to bother him."

She left without answering, though several possible retorts came to mind.

The store was just a short walk from the parking lot. Mindful of having to carry everything back with her, Jill was careful about what she bought. By the following night they would be home, and she wouldn't have to worry about it anymore. If the letters kept coming after that she'd insist the police look into it as a harassment charge.

She had to admit, as she wandered up and down the aisles, it would be a relief to have this all behind her. She wondered if the talent scout had already seen the show. It was highly likely by now. How long would it take them to make up their minds? Not long, she hoped. The suspense would kill both her and Danny. She'd call the studios if she hadn't heard any news by the end of the week.

Jill looked over the apples piled high in the produce case. She chose four of them and dropped them into the cart. That would have to do it. Any more and she'd break both arms before she got back to the camper.

Maybe she should have asked Hank to come with her. She dismissed the thought the minute it was formed. Apart from having to leave Danny alone, shopping with Hank, and all it represented, was too painful to contemplate. Somehow, shopping for food with a man seemed such an intimate undertaking.

She paid for the groceries and picked up one sack in each arm. Telling herself it would be good exercise for her, she set off back to the camper, where, she promised herself, she would enjoy one of the crisp apples that had looked so good in the store.

She'd almost reached the parking lot when she heard a faint thumping sound, accompanied by raised voices. For some reason her pulse jumped, and she quickened her step. The high wall blocked her view, but the sound had come from the other side, where the camper was parked.

Shifting the weight of the sacks in her arms, she hurried across the street, her heart thumping heavily against her ribs. She could hear the shouts now. It sounded disturbingly like Hank's voice.

She rounded the corner and rushed into the parking lot. Across the tops of several cars she could see the camper now. She could also see Hank, surrounded by all three members of the Wildwoods. They watched him as he pounded on the door with his fist, over and over again.

Jill hurried toward them, her heart in her throat. She could hear what he said now, his voice harsh with rage.

"Open this door right now, you little punk, or I'll damn well break it down. And when I do, your neck is next."

"What happened?" Jill demanded breathlessly as she reached the small group of people.

From inside the camper she could hear Danny yelling, but his words sounded garbled and unintelligible.

Hank stopped pounding and swung around to face her. His eyes looked like silver slits in his angry face. "Your precious, fragile, misunderstood delinquent just detonated, that's what happened. He's locked himself in there and won't open the door.''

"He threw a pot at the window," Tiffany said, her face vibrant with excitement.

"Come on, woman," Gary muttered, tugging on his wife's arm. "Let's leave Jill alone to handle this. No need for us to get in the way."

Jill barely noticed the three members of the group leaving. Her attention was on Hank, and the moaning sounds now coming from inside the camper. "I want to know what happened," she repeated. "Is Danny hurt?"

"No, but he's damn lucky I didn't take a shot at him. He just about broke my shin with his boot."

Jill glanced anxiously at the camper door. "Something must have set him off," she insisted. "I need to know what it is before I can calm him down."

"The problem with that kid is that he's sick," Hank roared. "And you're too damn wrapped up in his career to see it. He's got problems, Jill. Real bad problems, and he needs more help than you can ever give him."

Once more, her frayed temper snapped. "His biggest problem is you, Hank Tyler. You are continually upsetting him. Danny resents you, and I don't know why. It's probably your condescending, egotistic attitude. Which is laughable, when you consider your lousy reputation."

"Fine. If you don't like my attitude, then you take care of this all by yourself. And I wish you the best of luck. You'll need it this time."

She watched him march off, too shaken and anxious about Danny to care much where he was going. Right then she had more pressing problems.

Stepping up to the door, Jill listened for Danny's voice. The silence worried her more than the moaning. She rapped loudly with her knuckles. "Danny? It's me. Open this door please, honey. I want to talk to you."

The silence continued, frightening her.

She pounded louder. "Danny, I'm all alone out here. Everyone's gone. I just want to talk to you, honey. Let me in, please? We can sort this out, whatever it is. You trust me, don't you?"

She waited for several more long seconds, her heart pumping crazily. She'd have to get someone to break down the door if he didn't open it. That would bring all kinds of bad publicity if word got out, but it couldn't be helped. Danny's well-being was the most important thing right now.

She lifted her hand for one more try at persuading him. As she did so, she heard the key turn in the lock. Weak with relief, she waited while the door slowly opened.

Danny's face appeared in the opening. His eyes looked puffy, as if he'd been crying, and his hair hung in a tangled mess to his shoulders.

Tenderness welled up in a rush of sympathy as she pushed the door open wider and stepped through it. "Oh, honey," she said softly, and held out her arms. To her intense surprise, Danny walked into them.

She held him for a minute or two, concerned by the trembling of his frail body, then he straightened and, with a sigh moved away from her.

She watched him sit down, his legs spread out in front of him, his chin lowered to his chest.

"Tell me what happened," she said quietly.

She sat down opposite him, careful not to touch him now. She waited for some time before Danny lifted his chin and looked at her. The grief in his eyes shocked her.

"I woke up," he said, barely moving his lips, "and came out here. I couldn't see anybody. You were gone and I didn't know where Hank was. I got the jitters and I wanted a drink. I went to get the bottle and that's when I saw the papers."

His lip trembled, and Jill leaned forward anxiously.

"Saw what papers, honey?"

"The newspaper copies. They were spread all over the table. I saw my picture when I was a kid, and..." He gulped, and waved his hands as if unable to go on.

"Oh, God." Jill looked over at the table, where several balls of crumpled paper lay scattered across it.

"I was upset, I didn't know anyone knew about... about..."

"It's okay, Danny. Take your time." Hank must have decided to go through the news accounts again, perhaps hoping to find something that would tie in the letters. So why had he left them lying there for Danny to see? Surely he must have known what a shock it would be for him. She felt sick. Poor Danny. It must have been a dreadful shock.

"It hurt to see it all again. Then Hank came back. I started yelling, asking him where he got the newspapers... I didn't want anyone to know..." He paused, struggling to control his voice.

"Oh, honey, I'm sorry. I told Hank to get the copies of the story from the library. Someone told me about it in Goldwater and I wondered if it had anything to do with the letters. I was just trying to help, that's all. I never meant to hurt you, you know that."

"He said terrible things. He said I was sick in the mind and I needed help."

She hadn't known Hank could be so cruel. Inflexible at times, and a little arrogant perhaps, but somehow she thought he had more compassion and understanding than that. It just proved how little she really knew him. Apparently he had more in common with his brother than she'd imagined.

But now that she did know, she decided, it was time to put an end to this impossible situation. There was no point in having him around, if he was upsetting Danny more than the letters were. Besides, the tension between her and Hank had to be affecting Danny, too.

The best thing she could do for both of them, Jill thought with a sharp pang of regret, was to fire Hank. That very night. She'd tell him after the performance. He could find somewhere else to sleep that night and make his own way home. She'd had it. And she no longer wanted to deal with him. It was over.

Chapter 10

"I'm not sick, am I?" Danny asked, his pleading eyes reaching Jill's heart.

She put her own troubles behind her and concentrated on comforting him. "Of course not. Under the circumstances, anyone would have been upset." She looked around, wincing at the damage. "How did all this happen?"

Danny shrugged, looking defiant. "I told him to get out, and it took a little while to persuade him. I guess I got a little mad."

"So I see." Jill looked at the cracked window. "Well, we'll have to pay damages to the rental company when we get back. It will have to come out of your salary."

He scowled, but didn't answer.

Relieved that he seemed much calmer now, Jill asked tentatively, "I hope you still feel up to the performance tonight."

He was silent for so long, she started to worry again. Then he lifted his chin. The look he gave her seemed odd, almost as if he wasn't quite focusing, as though he were looking right through her.

"Oh, yes," he said, his voice strangely flat. "I'm going to be up there tonight. I'm going to be better than you've ever seen me. That's a promise."

She looked at him, uneasy about the subtle change in him. "Good. It's your final performance. Then we can go home."

"Home. Ah, yes." He got to his feet and did a funny little dance. "I can't wait to go home. We're going home." He wandered down to his room, chanting over and over, "We're going home. We're going home."

Frowning, Jill watched him open the door of his room and vanish inside. This was quite unlike any mood she'd seen him in before. She hoped he'd feel better after he'd had a rest.

To her surprise, he reappeared a few minutes later, twitching and dancing toward her with a grin on his face. "It's been a great tour, hasn't it?" he said, flicking his fingers to a silent beat. "A fantastic tour. Danny Webster is going to the top."

"I think it went very well," Jill said carefully.

"Very well?" Danny paused in front of her, then startled her by bringing his face down close to hers. She could see an almost feverish excitement in his eyes. "Is that all you call it? Very well?"

He'd mimicked her voice and, a little sharply, she said, "Let's not get too carried away. The scout has to take his report back to the studios. He might not have seen the show yet. He might even be waiting until tonight, the last show, to see how well you do on the road."

"Well I hope he is."

To her dismay, his excitement died, like a light being turned off. The odd look was back, a kind of deadly stillness in his gaze that chilled her. Still with his face close to hers, he whispered, "Just you wait, Jill. You're going to see Ricky Mason at his most awesome."

Shock rippled through her at the use of his real name, but he seemed not to notice his slip. It must have been the shock of seeing the news story confusing his mind.

He straightened and, turning his back on her, shuffled in a kind of slow dance back to his room, and went inside, closing the door quietly behind him.

Try as she might, Jill could not silence Hank's comments in her mind. *He has...bad problems...he needs more help than you can ever give him.*

She shook her head in an effort to calm her fears. It was true he acted a little odd at times, but he'd been through a terrible shock. He needed a rest, and he'd have one just as soon as they got the matter of the recording contract settled. She'd take him to Hawaii, some warm sun and clean ocean breezes would do wonders for him.

It might even give him a chance to meet someone special. That's what Danny needed, she thought as she busied herself making coffee. Someone to care for, someone with whom to share his triumphs and his disappointments. Someone willing to share his life. Someone to love.

Her mind winged straight to Hank. Stunned, she froze to the spot, the coffeepot held motionless in her hand. She couldn't be in love with him.

If she was, she was in love with a mirage. The man she thought she knew all these years didn't exist. She refused to consider herself in love with a man who didn't have an ounce of sensitivity in his body.

In spite of her denials, her entire body seemed to tingle when Hank returned to the camper later. She had to remind herself of how angry she was with him.

She tackled the problem as soon as he had closed the door. "Danny told me what happened," she said, her voice low and accusing.

Hank moved toward her, one eyebrow tilted at an angle. "What did Danny tell you?"

She tried hard not to let her anger get out of hand. "That you left the camper with all the news reports lying all over the table for Danny to see. That was incredibly insensitive. How could you do that?"

His mouth tightened visibly and she saw the storm signals gathering again in his eyes. "I went to the bathroom," he said, slowly and distinctly. "Like most people, I can't control the moment when nature calls. I didn't know that Danny would choose that moment to come out of his room. I was trying to find something that might help us find the letter writer."

"Oh." With some of the momentum taken from her attack, she had to regroup her thoughts. "He also told me what you said to him."

Hank's expression had turned dangerous. "And what was that?"

Nervously she held her ground. "According to Danny, you told him pretty much what you'd said to me. That he was sick and needed help."

"That *is* what I said to you." Hank stepped closer, until his toes almost touched hers. He seemed very big, and very tough at that moment.

"I did not say one word of that to Danny. He must have heard me yelling at you outside the camper. When I came out of the bathroom Danny was throwing one of his major tantrums. I tried to reason with him, he wouldn't listen. I was afraid he'd hurt himself. I went to get Gary and Slim for help. I thought he might listen to reason from them. I came back and found the door locked. Then you came charging up spitting fire and brimstone."

She stared up at him, at a loss as to what to say next. Even as she wondered how to apologize, she saw his expression soften.

"Dammit, Jill, make up your mind. Who are you going to believe? Me, or a kid who is so screwed up in his mind he can't think straight?"

She backed away from him, half of her mad at this latest affront to Danny, the other half desperately wishing he'd take her in his arms and kiss her problems away.

"I'm sorry," she said stiffly. "I guess Danny got a little mixed up."

"Yeah," Hank said, rubbing his forehead. "He's good at that."

Although the conversation seemed somewhat stilted after that, at least they were communicating by the time Danny reappeared in time for the sound check.

The rehearsal went well, all things considered. Danny sounded in good voice, and appeared fully recovered from the upheaval earlier.

Although he refused to even look at Hank, much less speak to him, he chatted quite agreeably with Slim, and appeared calm and confident.

Jill began to relax. One more show. If she could only get him through this night, she promised herself, they'd be home free. Pain engulfed her when she thought about firing Hank, but she'd made up her mind. For everyone's sake, it was the right decision.

Dinner that night was almost festive, for the Wildwoods at least. They all sat in a corner booth at the Chinese restaurant next door to the theater.

Danny still ignored Hank for the most part, and seemed to have trouble meeting Jill's eyes. He sat quietly, saying nothing, while the Wildwoods joked among themselves. For once the meal was uneventful.

Only one incident unnerved Jill. It came as they were leaving the restaurant. Tiffany leaned on Danny's arm and stood on tiptoe to whisper in his ear.

Gary scowled, but it was Danny's reaction that bothered Jill. He shoved Tiffany away from him far more violently than was necessary and, for a moment, she saw an expression of pure hatred cross his face.

It disappeared so quickly Jill wondered if she'd imagined it, but then she caught sight of Hank's shrewd look in her direction, and knew he'd seen it, too.

She had a few short moments alone with Hank while Danny was getting dressed for the performance. She stood outside the dressing room, trying not to be unsettled by his uncompromising expression.

"Is he going to be all right?" Hank asked, jerking his head at the dressing room door.

"Yes, I think so," Jill said quietly. "He will be if Tiffany stays away from him. I can't believe she still persists in hanging over him, after the way he's treated her."

"Tiffany is one of those people who gets her kicks from tormenting people." Hank shoved his hands into his jeans' pockets. "She probably tortured spiders and flies when she was a kid."

If Jill hadn't been so uneasy she would have smiled at that.

"Danny seems in an odd mood, tonight." Hank frowned down at her. "Maybe I should check in on you later, just to make sure everything's okay."

"No, don't do that." She saw the frustration in his expression, but couldn't see any reason for it. "You know how upset he gets when you're around, I don't need that right before he goes on."

Hank shrugged. "Okay, if you say so. You're the boss."

Feeling uncomfortable, Jill hunted for something else to say. "I have to admit, I'm glad this is the last show. We could all use the rest."

"You got that right."

Tightening her mouth, she decided she might as well get it over with. "I think it would be a good idea, Hank, if you packed your things after the show and found somewhere else to sleep tonight. There's a motel just down the street with vacancies. The Moonlighter. I happened to see it when I came back from the store today."

She could see by his face that she'd shocked him.

"You're not worried about Danny's safety any more, is that it?"

"That's right. After the performance tonight I think we can all relax on that score, don't you?"

He shrugged. "Okay, if that's how you feel. I'm the last person to hang around where I'm not wanted. I'll move out tonight."

He started to turn away and she said awkwardly, "It might be better if you could take the bus back to Cedarvale, or wherever you're going to next. Leave an address with me before you go so that I can mail you a check."

This time she could see the hurt look in his eyes. "I thought I'd signed on for the entire ride."

How she hated this. Why couldn't he just accept her decision and be done with it? "I just think, under the circumstances, it would be better if we part company here, tonight. I think Danny has just about had all the tension he can handle."

"You talking about Danny or yourself?"

She met his gaze steadily, wondering what he was really thinking behind that cool, controlled expression. "Maybe I'm talking about both."

His mouth pulled into a rueful smile. "Lady, when you do something, you really believe in doing it all the way." He walked off, his back stiff, and she stared miserably after him, her heart breaking to see him go.

It was better this way, she told herself as she knocked on the door of the dressing room. Better for Hank, better for Danny and better for her. Now all she had to do was convince herself of that.

Danny opened the door to her knock, and she was surprised to see yet another mood change in him. He seemed highly nervous, pacing around the room humming disjointed phrases from his opening number.

In an effort to calm him, Jill suggested he sit down, intending to talk to him.

"I don't want to sit down. I'm too strung out to sit down." He stood in front of her, an odd, gleaming elation sparkling in his eyes.

She smiled up at him, pleased that he had banished his blues. "You seem very happy that it's the last show. Won't you miss all this excitement after tonight?"

"Excitement? Yeah, I guess I will."

She looked at him more closely. He seemed to be brimming over with some kind of suppressed impatience, as if he were dying to tell her something.

For a crazy moment she thought he might have had word from the talent scout. "Danny, has something happened I don't know about?"

He laughed, a high-pitched, reckless sound that worried her. "Yeah, you could say that."

He stopped his jiggling and leaned over her. "I've got a secret," he whispered.

Frowning, she humored him. "You have? Can you tell me?"

"Yeah." He looked over at the door, and then back at her. With a childish gesture, he put his finger to his lips. "Don't tell anyone, but I know who wrote the letters."

Shock destroyed her breath for several seconds. Incredulous, she stared at him, wondering if she'd heard right. "You what?" she said at last.

He giggled. "I said, I know who wrote the letters."

"Who?"

He shook his head. "I'm not going to tell you."

Angry with him for being so ridiculous, she said sharply, "This isn't funny, Danny. This is much too serious a matter to be joking about it."

His smile vanished immediately, to be replaced by a cold, aloof expression. "I'm not joking." He straightened and moved a few paces away from her.

Folding his arms across his chest, he said quietly, "I can prove it."

"Then who is it?" Jill jumped to her feet, still uncertain whether or not to believe him. It seemed incredible that he could know and not have said anything about it. But if this was just a prank, he was certainly carrying it way too far.

"You wouldn't believe me if I told you. I can show you, then you'll believe me."

"Show me what?"

"The proof. But you'll have to come with me."

She shook her head at him, impatient to put an end to this silly game. "You know we can't go anywhere. You're due onstage in less than twenty minutes."

"That gives us plenty of time. It's right there in the trailer."

Her heart seemed to stop beating. "What trailer?"

He gave her a satisfied smile. Leaning forward, he whispered loudly, "The Wildwoods's trailer, of course. Where else would it be?"

She swallowed several times before she could speak. "You think it's one of the Wildwoods?"

Danny straightened again, giving his head a decisive shake. "I'm not saying any more. You have to come with me to see it."

She thought quickly. If they left now, they could be there and back in ten minutes. "All right, I'll get Hank."

She made a move toward the door but he stopped her with a sharp command.

"No!"

"But, Danny—"

"No Hank. No anyone. Just you and me. We do this on our own."

"Danny, it isn't safe. What if one of them should find us—"

"How can they?" Danny waved an arm at the wall, through which could be heard the faint sound of the group in full swing. "They're onstage for the warm-up, they won't come off until just before my intro."

"How can we get into the trailer? It's locked."

Danny stuck two fingers into the narrow pocket of his shirt and pulled out a key. "We get in with this. Tiffany gave it to me before we left Cedarvale."

She would, Jill thought grimly. "Wait, Danny," she said, feeling more and more uncomfortable about the whole thing. "Let's wait until after the show. We can ask Hank to—"

"How can we do that? They'll be right there after the show. They'll see us go in there."

"No they won't. They'll be packing up the equipment. It will take them at least an hour."

"Yeah? And how can you be sure Tiffany will stay with them? You know she's always wandering off. No, I won't wait until after the show. I want to show you now."

"Danny—"

Her heart sunk when she saw the defiance on his face.

"I'm not going onstage unless you come with me to see the proof."

"All right. But I must insist we take Hank with us. If there's any trouble—"

"Don't you trust me? Are you saying I can't take care of you if someone shows up?"

That's exactly what she was thinking, but she knew better than to admit that. "Of course not. All right. But we'll have to be quick. You have only fifteen minutes before your introduction."

"Don't worry," Danny assured her with a triumphant grin. "We'll have plenty of time."

She followed him out to the parking lot, wishing she could have thought of something to say to discourage the crazy idea. She didn't believe for one minute that Danny had proof of anything, it was probably something quite insignificant that he'd seen and built up in his vivid imagination.

Still, if she wanted a good performance out of him tonight, she thought it wiser to humor him. She didn't need him throwing yet another tantrum just before he was due onstage.

The wind stirred the dust across the parking lot as she walked with Danny to the trailer. Neither of them spoke, and their footsteps seemed to echo behind them, making Jill look nervously over her shoulder.

No one followed them. They were alone in the dark shadows of the parking lot, with only the buzz of traffic on the other side of the wall.

Danny paused at the door of the trailer and looked back at her. "It won't take a minute," he said quietly. "I know right where it is."

They shouldn't be doing this, she thought, trying to dispel the cold shivers of apprehension coursing down her back. It wasn't right. Yet she had to know who had been writing those threats to Danny, and if there was a chance of finding out, no matter how small, she had to take it.

Danny opened the door and motioned for her to go in first.

Reluctantly she stepped up into the trailer, holding on to the door frame for support. Sliding her fingers down the wall she found the light switch and turned on the lights.

"Where is it?" she whispered, although there was no one to hear her.

"Up there." His hand came over her shoulder, pointing ahead of her. "Just keep moving, I'll show you."

She began stepping forward, directing her gaze over every possible surface that could contain the evidence that Danny had insisted was there.

She passed through the kitchen and reached the dining area. "Danny, tell me what I'm looking for. We don't have much time."

She heard the soft click of the door being closed and began to turn. But in the next second the entire trailer plunged into darkness.

For several electrifying seconds she froze, afraid to breath. Then she found her voice. It sounded so weak and quavering in the darkness. "Danny? Are you there, Danny?"

"Yes." He sounded every bit as scared as she felt.

"Did you turn off the light?" You know this person, she told herself firmly. He wouldn't hurt a fly.

"No, I didn't. Someone else did."

Oh, dear God, someone else was in there with them. Someone must have followed them without being seen as they'd crossed the parking lot. Who was it? Gary? Tiffany? Slim? Who?

"Is someone else there?" Jill demanded, forcing an assertive note in her voice.

Silence. Then a soft swish of fabric, as if someone brushed against the long couch.

"Who's there?" Jill demanded. She wiped her damp palms down the sides of her jeans. Her heart thudded so hard she could feel the vibration of it shaking her body.

She jumped violently when a strange, grating voice she'd never heard before came out of the darkness.

"Me."

"Who...who are you?"

"No one you know."

She stared into the pitch-black gulf between her and the voice. It came from the direction of the door. "Danny," she said sharply. "Don't move. Stand perfectly still and don't move."

"O-okay."

She closed her eyes, praying that the intruder wouldn't be able to pinpoint Danny's position from his voice. She had to keep talking, keep his attention off Danny.

"So tell me your name. I assume you have a name?"

"You don't need to know."

Her heart jumped at the menace in the deep voice. It didn't sound like either Gary or Slim. She began to edge forward, silently, one hand outstretched, feeling for the breakfast bar. Beyond it was a set of drawers. There had to be a knife somewhere in there. If she could just find it, maybe she'd at least give Danny a chance to get out of the trailer and go for help.

Feeling a cold stab of fear, she wondered if the intruder had a gun. Forget it, she told herself. Don't even think about it. Just concentrate on talking and go for the knife.

"What do you want?" she asked, and inched forward another step.

"You."

Shock stopped her. "Me? What for?"

"You betrayed me. You shouldn't have done that."

She stood poised, unable to move. The voice had softened, risen. It sounded familiar.

"I don't know what you mean. What did I do? Tell me what I did."

"I trusted you, and you betrayed me. Now I hate you. I have to kill you."

Jill clutched the edge of the bar. She felt sick. Her heart thundered in her ears as she stared blindly in the direction of the voice. She knew who it belonged to now. And the horror of it threatened to destroy her.

Hank stood leaning against the wall, his gaze on the Wildwoods, his mind backstage in Danny's dressing room. Something didn't feel right. He wasn't sure what it was, more of a gut feeling than anything, but he'd had those kinds of pre-warnings before. A kind of tingly feeling in the back of his neck.

Over the years he'd developed a keen sense for anticipating trouble. He knew, seconds before it happened, the moment when a drunk prepared to throw the first punch, when a colt got ready to buck, or when a woman aimed to slap his face—usually undeserved.

He had that same, itchy feeling right now. And he knew why. In the weeks he'd traveled with the group, he'd come to recognize Danny's mood swings pretty well. It had enabled him to sidestep most of the trouble, except for earlier that afternoon when a case of bad timing had led to disaster.

But this odd mood, up one minute, down the next like a bungee jumper, made him real uneasy. It went beyond the usual temperamental insecurity he'd witnessed so far. There was something almost frightening about the feverish glint in Danny's eyes, and Hank didn't like it.

He glanced down at his watch. Ten minutes left before Danny's introduction. He had time to get back there and check on Jill, just to make sure she was okay.

He pushed himself away from the wall, then relaxed again. No. She'd been very clear about how she felt. She didn't want him near Danny, and in a way he couldn't blame her. She'd be all right. She knew how to handle him.

Depression settled over him when he remembered their last conversation. She wanted him out of the way altogether. Fired him. Well, he'd been fired before, he'd get over it.

He dug his hands into the pockets of his jeans. Something told him it wasn't going to be that easy this time. It wouldn't be easy to forget the way her hair curled around her face, or how her mouth tilted up on one side when she smiled.

It wouldn't be easy to forget her soft voice, or the warmth in her eyes when she'd looked at him while he made love to her. And it sure as hell wouldn't be easy to forget the feel of her warm, naked body under him, or the touch of her hands on his bare flesh.

He couldn't seem to get rid of the memories that kept tormenting him. He remembered vividly the feel of her smooth skin beneath his searching hands, the way she moved under him as he explored her body with his mouth, the bite of her fingers on his arms and his back when he entered her.

He closed his eyes, reliving the moment he'd sunk into her warm, waiting flesh, the incredible sensation of being clasped by a warm, wet sheath of sheer pleasure. So much emotion had gone into the moment, emotion that he hadn't even known he was capable of feeling.

How ironic that he should finally discover what making love was really all about, with the one woman who was so wrong for him in every other way. The story of his life.

Damn. He shifted his position and looked at his watch again. Eight minutes. Now he wasn't sure if the nagging twitching in his belly was the thought of never seeing her again, or the persistent feeling that something was wrong.

He couldn't stand around for another eight minutes wondering what the hell was the matter with his instincts. At the risk of getting Jill mad at him again, he had to satisfy that niggling itch.

He had nothing to lose, he told himself as he strode purposefully through the maze of partitions. She was already mad at him, so what did one more reason matter? At least he'd have taken care of that damn twitching in his stomach.

He reached the dressing room and tapped on the door. He waited several seconds, then tapped again. When he got no response the second time, he carefully opened the door and stuck his head around it. The room was empty.

Cool it, he told himself. They've probably gone into the wings already. Danny did that sometimes. Quickening his pace, he hurried out to the stage. A stagehand stood by the curtains, tapping his foot as he listened to the group.

"Did you happen to see Danny Webster out here?" Hank asked, without expecting too much from the guy's response.

"Yeah, I did." The stagehand looked down at his watch. "Must have forgot something. I saw him head across the parking lot with his cute little manager. He'll have to make it quick..."

The rest of his sentence was lost as Hank turned and marched swiftly to the stage door. The sensation in his stomach was no longer a twitch. It was a full-blown feeling crawling with disaster.

He burst through the door and hit the parking lot at a run. He could see no one out there, and the lights were out in the camper. If they were inside, they were in the dark.

He sprinted up to it and pounded on the door. Cursing, he hunted for his key, then twisted it in the lock, muttering furiously at himself when it took two tries. At last he dragged the door open and sprang up the step, flicking on the light as he did so.

His gaze swept the empty space, and at first he felt relief, though he wasn't sure what he expected to find. Then fear hit him again. Where the hell were they?

Had the bastard who'd written the letters caught up with them? Abducted them? His stomach heaved when he thought about the gun. He should have warned Jill. It was too late now.

He pounded his fist against the wall in furious frustration. Dammit, if anything happened to her—

He leaned over to the window, dragging the net curtain aside. He could see the Wildwoods's trailer from here. It was in darkness. No one was in there, all three members were on stage.

Turning, he grabbed the door handle of Jill's room. Without bothering to knock, he yanked it open. Empty. He moved on to Danny's room, and hauled that open. That, too, was empty.

He was about to close the door again when something caught his eye. He moved into the room, staring down at the notebook sticking out from under Danny's bed. It looked familiar.

He pulled it out and flicked through it. Some pages had been torn from the book.

Very slowly, Hank felt in his jeans' pocket for the folded note he'd carried with him ever since Jill had given it to him. Carefully he unfolded it, then fitted it into one of the torn spaces.

Although he knew what to expect, the shock of it still cut through him like a sheet of ice. The page matched perfectly. It could mean only one thing. Danny Webster had been writing the threatening notes to himself.

Chapter 11

"Danny," Jill said, making a desperate effort to keep her voice calm. "This is me, Jill. Your friend. The person who gave you your career. The person who loves you."

"You don't love me. Poor, weak little Danny. He would never have made it, you know. He doesn't have what it takes to be a big star."

Jill's nerves tingled with fear. The voice kept sliding up and down, one minute sounding like Danny, the next, a complete stranger. Yet unbelievably, it was the same person speaking. There was no one else in that trailer with her but Danny.

"He has to die, you know," the voice went on. "I have to kill him. And I have to kill you, too. That's sad, because you're a beautiful lady. I won't like seeing you die."

"Why, Danny?" Jill whispered. "Why do you want to hurt me? I'm your friend."

"You're *not* my friend!"

The voice had risen sharply, sounding more ragged, more agitated, and Jill cringed.

"Please, Danny—"

"Don't call me that. My name is Ricky Mason. I don't like Danny. He kept getting in the way, pretending to be me. He can never be me. He's too weak, too stupid to see people the way they really are. He couldn't see that you were betraying him. But I could. I could see."

With mounting horror, Jill realized the voice was closer. Her fingers found the drawer and silently drew it open. "I don't understand, Da...Ricky. Why do you think I betrayed you? I love you."

"No, you don't love me. You love Hank Tyler. That's who you love. I know you were together. All night. In the same bed. I know you were, so don't lie to me. I hate people who lie to me."

Jill closed her fingers around the handle of a knife. Even as she did so, she knew she could never use it against Danny. She couldn't hurt him. And she just couldn't believe that he would hurt her.

Almost as if he'd read her mind, his voice came out of the darkness again. "I've got a gun. It will be very quick, Jill. I promise you."

No, she wouldn't believe it. He was bluffing. She pulled her hand away from the drawer and slid forward another step. "You don't have a gun, Danny. I won't have one in the camper, you know that."

"I found it. That's something he didn't tell you, did he? I found it in his bag, underneath all the stuff he'd crammed in there."

Bewildered, Jill blinked. "Hank? He had a gun?"

The laughter rippled softly in the darkness, sending more chills down her back. "Didn't know your lover was armed, did you, Jill? You were very stupid to trust him. Just like I was stupid to trust you."

She'd pinned down his voice now. He was closer, between her and the door. And in front of the light switch. She would have to get very close to him to turn it on.

Her mouth felt dry, and she ran her tongue over her lips to moisten them. Whatever she did, she couldn't let him know how terrified she was. He was sick. Hank was right. Deep down she'd known it, too, and hadn't wanted to face it. Not Danny. Not her baby.

She had to get help for him. It was the one last thing she must do for him. But unless she could get through to him, she was in terrible danger.

She moved again, sliding silently closer to where Danny stood. He knew about her and Hank. He was jealous of him. He thought that because she loved Hank, she couldn't love Danny, too.

It was true, she thought, through the haze of fear. She did love Hank. How would he feel, if Danny managed to kill her with the gun Hank had brought along against her express wishes? It was too bad she'd never know the answer to that.

Her heart seemed to have slowed down, it wasn't banging in her ears anymore. She felt frozen inside, as if everything had turned to ice. She had to get through to Danny. If she wanted to live, she had no other choice. She couldn't hurt him.

Again she slid her foot forward, then put her weight on it.

"Where are you?" Danny demanded. "Speak to me."

Her muscles jerked. She hadn't realized she was that close. She tried to remember where the light switch was located.

"Speak to me, dammit, or I'll shoot."

Her blood froze when she heard the click of the safety. "I'm right here, Danny. Listen to me. I know I did something wrong with Hank, but I thought I loved him. I was wrong. I don't. He's going away, Danny. I sent him away. I knew he was upsetting you and that's why I sent him away. And that is the truth, I swear it."

He didn't answer, but she could hear him breathing. Long, shaky breaths, as if he had trouble drawing air into his lungs.

She went on talking, trying frantically to reach the young man she had known and cared for. "Danny, I know how badly you feel. I understand how you feel. But you must believe me. I want to help you feel better. I love you, Danny. I love you as if you were my own son."

Another step. She was close enough to smell the cologne he always wore. One more step and she could reach out and touch him. Please, she prayed silently, let her get to the gun before he could pull the trigger.

She braced herself to take the step when Danny's voice came out of the darkness again. This time there was no mistaking the voice she knew so well.

"I'm sorry, Jill, I really am. But I have to kill you. You did something bad. My mother did something bad, too. I had to kill her, Jill. I had to shoot her and that man she was with. I had to do it, she was bad. She betrayed me. She didn't love me or Daddy anymore."

She thought she was beyond any more surprises. But the shock that hit her at Danny's words almost blacked out her senses. Corey Mason hadn't killed his wife and her lover after all. His eight-year-old son had shot them, and he'd taken the blame.

"That's why I have to kill you, too, Jill. You're bad, like she was."

Jill stood deathly still, afraid to breathe. She had perhaps a few seconds left to say the right words. And they had better be the right ones, because if he fired now, he couldn't possibly miss her.

The precious moments ticked by, while her mind remained a stubborn blank. Then it came to her. "Your mother forgives you, Ricky," she said softly. "Your mother understands why you did it, and she forgives you. But she could never forgive you for killing again. She is asking you to put down the gun, Ricky. She loves you, and she wants to forgive you."

Jill closed her eyes. She hoped it wouldn't be Hank who found her. Even if he couldn't love her, he would never forgive himself for allowing this to happen. Her lips moved silently. *I'm sorry, Hank. I love you.*

The sob that came out of the darkness startled her. Her eyes flew open and she held her breath. A second, agonizing sound of grief melted the ice gripping her body in a rushing torrent of hurt and anguish. Danny was crying.

She moved swiftly, one hand feeling for the light switch. She found it and pressed it down, then turned to take the gun from the weeping young man.

Slipping the safety catch on again, she dropped it onto the couch, then wound her arms around Danny's heaving shoulders. His sobs were awful, and her own cheeks were wet with the tears.

Seconds later the door exploded inward and Hank hurtled through it, clutching his shoulder. He pulled up short when he saw her, and the relief on his face made her smile.

Danny seemed not to notice he was there, his body still racked by the deep, hopeless sobs that tore through her heart. "Call the hospital," she said quietly. "You were right. He needs more help than I can give him."

Hank nodded, his eyes sending her a message of hope. "Are you okay?"

"I'm fine." She jerked her head backward. "You'd better take your gun with you."

Hank swore, and squeezed past her to get it. "If he'd—"

"He didn't," she interrupted quickly. "Someone will have to make an announcement. I'm afraid the letters were right about one thing. Danny Webster has made his last appearance."

For a long moment Hank looked at her, his expression grave. Then he slid by her, giving her shoulders a squeeze with both hands before disappearing out the door.

Gently, Jill nudged Danny down onto the couch, and sat next to him to wait for the ambulance.

The wait at the hospital seemed like hours. People came and went, anxious-looking doctors hurried down the corridors and nurses bustled about with skirts flying, and still no word came on Danny's condition.

Jill sat on a leather couch in the waiting room, trying to read a magazine, while Hank occasionally took a short rest before jumping up to resume his restless pacing.

"You really don't have to wait up with me," Jill told him, after a glance at her watch had told her it was almost midnight. "I can get a cab back to the camper."

His expression, when he looked down at her, was hard to read. "I don't want to leave you here alone."

"I won't be alone. The group should have everything wrapped up by now, I'm sure they'll be here soon."

"Then I'll at least wait until they get here."

She wished she knew what he was thinking. What thoughts were churning in his mind?

Once Danny had been taken away by a sympathetic nurse, she'd had plenty of time to relive the events of that evening. She couldn't forget the look on Hank's face when he'd burst through the door and had seen her standing there.

She'd hoped the blazing relief in his eyes meant that he at least had some feelings for her. Looking at him now, at the withdrawn expression blanketing his rugged features, they might as well be strangers, caught up in a situation that neither of them knew how to deal with.

She looked down at her hands, at the fingers hugging each other. She had felt alone before, but never like this. She had failed somewhere. Danny was beyond her help, and in losing him, she'd lost far more than a client.

She didn't hear the doctor come in, and jumped when a quiet voice spoke her name. "Ms. Preston?"

"Yes, that's me." She stood, anxiety making her words tumble over each other. "How's Danny? Will he...? Is he...?"

"I'm afraid the young man is seriously disturbed. I'd like to speak to someone in his immediate family. Can you tell me how I can get in touch with them?"

"His parents are dead. I'm the closest family he has."

The doctor looked at her solemnly. "I see. Well, Ricky has agreed to seek psychiatric help. I can either put him into the hands of staff here, or have him transferred back to his hometown. He didn't seem to have any preference when I asked him."

"I'd like him to go back to Cedarvale," Jill said without hesitation. "I want to be close by in case he needs me."

"It will be some time before he's allowed visitors. He doesn't want to see or speak to anyone he knows. I'm sorry."

She had to blink hard to prevent the tears from forming. "I still want him nearby."

The doctor nodded. "Very well. I'll have to ask you to fill out some forms, if you want to accept financial responsibility for him."

"Of course." She glanced across at Hank, who stood watching her. "I won't be long."

He gave her a brief nod, and she turned away to follow the doctor down to the reception desk. When she returned, she found Hank talking to Gary, while Tiffany gazed up at him in rapt attention. Slim stood a few feet away, looking uncomfortable.

"I guess this is the end of the road for us," Gary said, holding out his hand to Jill. "Sorry it had to end this way."

Jill shook the proffered hand with a tiny smile. "Thanks. So am I."

"I always did think there was something very strange about that weirdo—" Tiffany began, then broke off when Gary clamped a hand down hard on her shoulder.

"Shut up, woman," he said, scowling a warning at her. "You always did run off at the mouth."

She looked at him in astonishment, her mouth opening and shutting as if she couldn't believe what she'd heard.

Jill looked around nervously, expecting a fight.

"From now on you're gonna start behaving like a wife, or you can find some other sucker to put up with you," Gary said with conviction.

Tiffany shut her mouth.

"Hank filled us in on what happened," Gary went on, ignoring his wife's dumbfounded expression. "I guess there's not much we can do now, so we'll be taking off. I want to get a head start on the road while the traffic's quiet."

Jill nodded, uncomfortably aware that Gary didn't know she wouldn't be traveling back with Hank. "I'll settle up with you once I get all the accounts in order."

"Sure." Gary turned to Hank and held out his hand. "Nice meeting you, guy. For a rodeo rider you make a damn good manager."

Hank looked surprised as he shook hands. "Thanks. I'll keep that in mind."

Gary touched the brim of his hat in farewell, grabbed Tiffany by the arm and marched her, unprotesting, to the door. Pushing himself away from the wall, Slim winked at Jill, nodded at Hank, then followed the two of them out.

"Something tells me," Hank murmured, "that Tiffany will have to toe the line in the future."

Jill smiled wearily. "You know something? She'll love it. That's all she needed, someone to take charge of her. As long as Gary keeps the upper hand, they'll make it."

He nodded, his gaze intent on her face. "Want some coffee?"

Her treacherous pulse leapt with hope. "That sounds good."

She followed him down to the cafeteria, trying hard to hold down the crazy expectations that refused to be ignored. She waited at the table in the half-empty room, while Hank bought the coffee and carried it back to her on a small round tray.

He'd bought donuts, too, but she was too drained and exhausted to eat. She wondered if she looked as haggard as she felt, and when she spied his gaze on her, hoped she looked better than she feared.

"Are you okay?"

The sympathy in his voice threatened her composure. She waited a moment before nodding. "I'm okay."

"It's been a rough night."

"Yes." She ran a finger up and down the handle of the mug, afraid to look at him.

"Will you be okay to drive back to Cedarvale? It's a full day's ride from here."

Her spirits sank. She wondered what he'd say if she told him she didn't feel up to driving all that way by herself. He'd most likely offer to drive back with her.

She was tempted. Oh, so tempted. Time together without Danny's ever-present resentment and suspicion. Time to talk about the past and maybe come to terms with it. Time to find out if what she felt really was the lifetime kind of love she thought it was, or just an attraction for a man who was everything his brother hadn't been. The kind of man she wished she'd married.

But she couldn't put him on the spot that way. It had to come from him, because he wanted it, not because she'd forced him in to it. She had been the one to bring them together again. Now it was up to him whether or not they did something about it. And she would have to accept whatever he decided.

"Oh, sure," she said, with a casual shrug. "I'm used to driving and I enjoy it. I'll get some sleep tonight and leave in the morning. I'll be fine."

His pause went on a little too long, but still she couldn't look up.

"Okay. I'll call a cab, then go back with you to pick up my things. I'll call the motel at the same time and book a room."

She nodded. After another long pause, he got up from the table. She watched his lean figure walk away from her, and the ache began.

He barely spoke as the cab drove them back to the theater parking lot. They were almost there when he said abruptly, "So what will you do now?"

She kept her eyes on the street lamps flashing by as she answered. "I'm going to find another singer. That's what I do, remember?"

"Yeah. I remember. It's who you are."

So he did understand. She had only recently realized it herself. That her need to find young talent and develop it to its full potential was a replacement for the tiny life she had lost. She was trying to fill the need she had been denied, the chance to see her child mature into a responsible adult.

She had failed with Danny. One day she would convince herself that it wasn't her fault, that Danny's life had been destroyed the moment he took his father's gun from the wall. But right now, the failure hurt.

She had only a few moments alone with Hank in the camper as he gathered up his belongings.

"If I forget anything," he said, "just ship it to the rodeo association. It'll find me."

Her throat felt tight, and something cold and heavy had settled in her stomach. "I'll do that." She forced a smile. "You want me to send your check there, too?"

"Yeah, that'll be fine." He lifted his bag and looked down at her. "I guess I'll be off, then."

She nodded, and moved to the door to open it.

He reached her side and paused.

When she made herself look up at him, she saw, for the first time, a deep regret in his silver gaze.

"I know what you must think of me," he said quietly, "and it's probably well deserved. But I can't leave without telling you that I never meant to hurt you. What we shared that night meant a great deal to me. I hope you know that."

A great deal. But not enough. Perry was a formidable wall between them, and his brother's resentment was too deeply imbedded to break it down.

She felt the weariness seeping into her bones. All she wanted to do now was lie down and try to escape from her misery into sleep. "It's all right, Hank. We're both consenting adults."

He looked down at her for another long moment. "Goodbye, Jill. Take care of yourself."

"You, too." She watched him walk out of her life, and a large chunk of her heart went with him.

He cursed himself a thousand times that night for being such a coward. He knew now that he loved her. Maybe he always had. But he was his father's son, and the apple never fell far from the tree.

His father had left his wife and sons because the call of wide-open spaces and free living had been too strong to ignore. He hadn't been able to commit his life to the ties and bonds of married life. He had been a drifter when he'd met Hank's mother, and not even the love of a woman could hold him down for long.

He'd broken his wife's heart when he'd left, and she'd never recovered. She'd never looked at another man and she'd died alone. Deep inside Hank was the terrible fear that he would make the same mistakes.

Perry had walked out on Jill, unable to settle down, and Hank wasn't sure that he could, either. Jill wanted kids, she needed kids to give her the happiness she deserved. And he loved her too much to take the chance of hurting her the way his father had hurt his family. She was better off without him.

And only he would know how very much it hurt him to let her go.

A month later Jill asked to see Danny's doctor. She wanted to know how Danny was progressing, and she wanted more than the brief bulletins they gave her over the phone.

Dr. Paul Stellman was a man about her own age, serious, dedicated, and with kind blue eyes that smiled at her from behind his glasses. She found him perfectly willing to answer all her questions.

"You were a big influence in Ricky's life," he said, glancing down at the open file in front of him. "He talks about you sometimes."

She looked at the psychiatrist in surprise. "He's talking about me? Then he must be getting better."

"I didn't say that." Dr. Stellman folded his hands and propped up his chin with his thumbs. "He is still unable to face reality."

"Oh." She still couldn't get used to hearing him referred to as Ricky. To her, he would always be Danny. Ricky Mason seemed like another person, far removed from the vulnerable, scared, talented man-child she'd loved.

"In a way," Dr. Stellman said, "Ricky had escaped from reality many years ago. He created Danny Webster, a totally new personality, to escape what he had become...a murderer."

Her shocked cry escaped into the quiet room. "I'm sorry. I just can't associate the person I knew with that word."

"I don't blame you. We all have trouble accepting a child being capable of murder. Yet, in every sense of the word, that's exactly what it was. And Ricky had a double-edged guilt. His father had gone to prison for the crime that Ricky committed and then committed suicide. It was just too much for a small boy to accept."

She was dreadfully afraid she was going to cry again. She seemed to do that far too much lately.

"A part of Ricky wanted to blame his mother for what happened," the doctor continued. "Because of that, he was unable to respond to women. It's remarkable that he responded to you. You must have reached a chord that was inaccessible to anyone else."

"His music," Jill said softly. "He lived for his music, as I did once."

The doctor nodded. "Yes, that was probably it. Anyway, at first, the substitution of the alter ego worked. Ricky became Danny Webster, and started to reestablish a life for himself. He even began to achieve some success, thanks to you.

"But Ricky was strong. He didn't want to lose his identity. He had to destroy Danny Webster in order to get it back. At the same time, Danny fought for the one thing that had given him a measure of security. He wanted that fame and fortune very badly.''

"Poor Danny," Jill murmured. "No wonder he was so temperamental. His mind must have been in so much confusion."

"Yes, it was. Especially when the guilt started to take over, and Ricky became a real threat. He wrote the letters to draw attention to the battle going on inside him. It was a cry for help, directed at the one person he figured could help him. His protector. You."

"Oh, God. And I failed him."

"You couldn't be expected to know what was going on in his mind. When you became involved with Hank Tyler, Ricky saw that as a betrayal, the way his mother had betrayed him. When he saw Hank reading the newspaper stories of what he'd done, it was the final straw. It sent him over the edge. You had committed the ultimate betrayal. You had revealed his worst nightmare to the enemy."

Tears spilled down her cheeks, and she groped in her purse for a tissue.

"I don't want you to take that as an accusation," Dr. Stellman said in his kind voice. "I'm just trying to explain what was going on in Ricky's mind. You have nothing to reproach yourself for. No one could have possibly understood the kind of battle he was fighting."

"I can't help feeling responsible...."

"Don't. Believe me, it won't help Ricky or you to blame yourself for what happened. Once Danny Webster realized what was happening, it came down to a final struggle between the two personalities. Fortunately, for both of you, you said exactly the right thing to reach him."

Dr. Stellman smiled. "He must have loved you very much," he said softly.

"I loved him, too." She blew her nose loudly. "Can I see him?"

The psychiatrist looked at her for a long moment. "Yes, I think that would be all right. Just for a minute, that's all. His withdrawal is a necessary transition before he can begin his journey back to full health. And I should warn you, he might not acknowledge you. If that happens, please don't let him see you're upset. He can't handle any more guilt."

Neither could she, Jill thought, tucking the tissue in her pocket. That thought alone would keep her strong.

She followed Dr. Stellman down the silent, white corridors, her footsteps echoing eerily behind his measured stride.

He paused in front of a pair of swing doors. The windows had wire-reinforced, frosted glass.

Jill felt a shiver of apprehension. "It won't upset him, will it? Him seeing me, I mean?"

The doctor shook his head. "I doubt he'll even know you're there. But just in case, don't call him Danny. We are trying to erase all traces of Danny Webster from his mind."

"But won't I remind him?"

"I don't think so. If he recognizes you at all, he'll remember you as a friend. That's the way he talks about you. As his friend. If I wasn't sure of that, I wouldn't be letting you in to see him."

Feeling a little more reassured, Jill braced herself.

Dr. Stellman pushed open the door. "He's over by the window, in the corner."

"You'll come with me?" Jill asked in alarm.

"No. I think it's better if you do this by yourself. But I'll be in the room, just in case. Don't worry, Ricky is very docile."

Jill smiled. "I wasn't worried about that. I just don't want to say the wrong thing."

"Just say whatever's in your heart. But don't expect too much."

She nodded and walked into the room. It was spacious, with dove-gray walls and bright blue drapes at the barred windows. Patients sat at several tables, some together, some alone. All were quietly absorbed in some kind of activity.

Jill looked over to the corner, where a lone figure sat at an easel. His blond hair had been cut, and was neatly combed back from his face. It gave him a more mature look, and his features looked stronger, somehow.

Pulling in a deep breath, Jill walked slowly across the room. She paused by his shoulder, and watched him daub a streak of red paint across the maze of colors on the white paper.

At first it looked like a typical effort from a kindergartner, but as she looked more closely she could see the shape of guitars, musical symbols and notes, and in the very center, a group of clamoring hands raised in the air.

Tears pricked her eyes and she blinked them back. For his sake, she had to be strong. "Hello, Ricky," she said quietly. "It's nice to see you."

The paintbrush paused in midair, then continued to stroke the paper.

"I like your painting," Jill said, leaning forward for a better look. "It's about music, isn't it?"

Ricky's head nodded up and down, and his beautiful smile spread over his face. "I like music."

"So do I." It was painful to see him this way. It was painful to know he didn't recognize her. She struggled to sound cheerful. "You paint very well. You must do a lot of it."

He didn't answer, seemingly absorbed in his work.

"Are you happy here, Ricky?"

Again his head nodded enthusiastically.

"I'm very glad. Can I come and see you again?"

She thought he wasn't going to answer that, but then a quiet "Yes" escaped.

"Good. I'd like that. Maybe next week. Perhaps you could paint another picture for me?"

"Okay."

He'd sounded matter-of-fact about it, and she decided it was time to leave. Her heart ached for him, and she longed to touch him, but she knew it would be a mistake. He never had liked people to touch him. She could understand why now.

"I have to go now. Thank you for showing me your painting. I'll look forward to seeing you again soon."

She turned away, then froze as he said quietly, "Have you seen Hank?"

She spun around to face him, half-afraid of what she might see. Danny's face looked back at her, older with the new haircut, but with the same vulnerable look in his pale blue eyes.

"No," she said carefully, aware of her voice trembling. "I haven't seen Hank since I got back from the tour. I don't expect to see him again."

"He loves you, you know. He's just afraid to admit it."

She stared at him, and as she did so, she saw the intent expression in his eyes fade to a blank, vacant stare, and she knew that he'd drawn the curtain across his mind once more.

He turned back to his painting, and swished the brush around in a jar of blue water, turning it purple. He loaded the brush with paint and, very slowly, drew a thin white line around the raised hands.

"Goodbye, Ricky," Jill said unsteadily, and escaped from the room.

She thanked the doctor, promising to come back again the following week. And then she went out to her car, and sat there until the storm of weeping had passed.

Hunting for tissues in her purse, she reflected ruefully that for someone who never cried, she'd spent the past four weeks making up for that in a big way.

Blowing her nose, she wondered why people said they felt better after they'd cried. She always ended up with sore eyes, blotchy skin and a headache.

She drove home slowly, reluctant to be alone in her apartment. It was too easy to dwell on her misery, and too hard to keep her mind on her job.

The nights were the worst, long hours when her mind wouldn't let her rest. So many times she relived the past, wondering if she could have done things differently.

The days slipped by, but the memory of Danny's words kept coming back to haunt her. They had been important enough for him to break through the mental fog that imprisoned his mind. Yet she couldn't help wishing he'd never spoken them.

In an effort to forget, she toured the bars, looking for another singer among the hopefuls that climbed up in front of a mike determined to realize their dreams.

Each time she walked through a tavern door, she half expected to see Hank sprawled at the bar. Or on the floor. Part of her dreaded the thought of seeing him again, reawakening the heartache.

Another, small, persistent part of her longed to see his lean figure propped up at the bar, his hat tilted back on his head, his gray eyes looking at her through the smoky haze.

After a while she stopped scanning the room to see if he was there. Certain that she would have seen him by now, she assumed he had gone back to Wyoming. His suspension was just about up; he'd probably gone back on the rodeo circuit.

The next time she saw Danny, he answered her in mono-
syllables. He gave no sign of recognizing her, and she left,
resigned to the fact that it could be many weeks before he
did so again.

Still his words continued to torment her, until finally she
could stand it no longer. She could do one last thing for
Hank, to make up for all the misery she had caused him
over the years.

Using her contacts, she tracked Perry down in Nash-
ville, where he was appearing regularly at a small theater.
And on one warm September morning, she flew out from
Colorado on her way to Tennessee to see her ex-husband.

Chapter 12

Jill sat in the darkened theater, listening to the solid beat of the excellent group backing Perry. She could see why they were so popular. They created an infectious excitement in their sound that had the audience tapping their feet and clapping, though with more enthusiasm than timing.

Jill waited until the theater had cleared before making her way backstage. She had to push through a small knot of people standing outside the dressing rooms, but when she gave the security guard her name and explained who she was, he let her through.

One of the band members opened the door to her knock. He was tall and dark, with a lean, hungry look that reminded her of the man she was trying so hard to forget.

"I'd like to speak to Perry," she said, smiling up at him.

"Uh, he's busy right now. Who shall I say was asking?"

"Just tell him it's his ex-wife."

She almost laughed at the look of astonishment on his

face. He looked over his shoulder. "Hey, Perry, there's a gal here who says she used to be your wife."

The chattering inside the room halted. Jill waited, wishing she were anywhere but there. She was beginning to have second thoughts about the whole idea.

Then a voice she remembered well said slowly, "Jill?"

He appeared in the doorway, looking older and heavier than she remembered now that she was up close to him. On stage he'd looked no different than the day he'd walked out.

"Hello, Perry," she said, doing her best to smile. "I'd like to talk to you. It's important."

"It must be, I reckon, for you to drag yourself all this way to see me. Wait here, I'll get my jacket."

He looked nothing like Hank, a fact for which she was deeply grateful as she faced him across a table in the fast-food restaurant. His features were softer; he had his mother's light blue eyes. He sat munching on a hamburger, and offered her a fry.

She shook her head, waiting impatiently for him to finish eating before she said what she'd come to tell him.

"You shoulda had one," Perry said, after swallowing the last bite. "They're good." He wiped at his mouth with his napkin and crumpled it into a ball. Dropping it onto his plate, he leaned back and looked at her.

"Well, you got my curiosity jumping like a frog on a hot skillet. What's so all-fired important you come hundreds of miles to tell me?"

Now that the moment was at hand, she couldn't think where to start. After selecting and rejecting half a dozen sentences, she blurted out, "It's about Hank."

Perry stared at her for a long moment. "What about Hank?"

"I've…seen him, lately. About a month ago. In fact, he came on a road tour with me."

Expressions crossed Perry's face in quick succession.

When she saw relief, Jill realized he thought she'd come to tell him Hank was hurt. Or worse. It also told her what she wanted to know. Perry still cared about his brother.

The astonishment that had ended up on his face still hovered there. "A road tour? What happened to the rodeo? Are you still singing? I thought you gave that up."

Slowly, halting every now and then to find the right words, Jill told him a version of the truth. She left out Danny's story.

She told him how she'd found Hank in the tavern and hired him as road manager for Danny Webster and the Wildwoods. How they'd shared a camper and ended up in bed with each other. How she'd fallen desperately in love during those weeks, and had hoped that Hank could love her back.

"I think he might have loved me," she said as Perry listened silently to her quiet voice. "But something was in the way. He has never been able to forgive me for causing trouble between you two. His resentment just went too deep to wipe out the memories. I haven't seen him since the tour, and I'll probably never see him again."

"So what do you want me to do?" Perry said in a cold, hard voice that sank her hopes. "Go beg him to forgive and forget and take up with you again?"

She felt warmth creep across her cheeks. "Of course not. I don't expect you to mention me at all. I told you all this for one reason only. Hank must love you very much to carry this much resentment against me all these years. I wanted you to know. I hoped it might make you realize that it's time you two forgot your grievances and got back to being brothers."

Perry sat drumming his fingers on the table, his face closed to her behind his brooding expression. She thought of Danny, and pain knifed through her. She had failed Danny. She would not fail again.

"He needs you," she said, mentally crossing her fingers. "He is a very unhappy man."

"He always was." Perry looked up and gave her a rueful smile. "I admit, I gave him cause enough times."

"It hurt him dreadfully when you wouldn't talk to him at the funeral."

Perry shrugged. "There wasn't a lot I could say."

"Yes, there was. You could have told him you were sorry for all those wasted years and that you wanted to make up for them. You could have told him you've missed him and want him back in your life."

"And what if he doesn't want that?"

She smiled. "Oh, he'll want that. He's changed, Perry. He still likes to have his say, but he's not nearly as belligerent as he used to be. The years have mellowed him."

Perry picked up the saltshaker, and started twisting it around in his hands. Hands that trembled just a little bit. "Yeah, well, to be honest, I ain't been too happy since the funeral. I mean, we're still family and now that Mom is gone, there's just the two of us left. I guess it's time we mended our fences."

"Then you'll go and see him?"

"Yeah, I reckon. I'm working weekends but I can get someone to pinch-hit for me, give me a week or two to track him down."

"He might be back on the rodeo circuit. I don't think he's in town."

"Don't worry, I'll find him. Anyone as ornery as my brother can't hide their tail for long."

He seemed excited now at the prospect of seeing Hank. She felt good. At peace. Whatever came of the meeting between the brothers, she'd given them the chance to work things out. She'd done her best to make up for the trouble she'd caused. Now it was up to them.

"So when's your flight back?" Perry asked as he drove her back to her hotel.

"In the morning. I have my eye on a new singer, and I want to be there to catch her act on Saturday night."

"What happened to Danny Webster, then?"

She closed her eyes briefly. "Danny got out of the business. He just decided it wasn't for him."

Perry nodded. "Too bad, after all the work you must've put in. But it happens sometimes. Can't take the heat, some of 'em."

"Yes," Jill said quietly. "I guess the pressure was too much for him. He had the talent but not the stamina."

"Tough break."

"A very tough break."

She hoped that Hank wouldn't tell him about Danny. Though the story was bound to break sooner or later. Tiffany wouldn't be able to keep juicy gossip like that to herself for long.

Perhaps by the time Danny was well enough to leave the hospital, it would be old news, and someone else would be on the chopping block.

She went to see Danny soon after she got back from Tennessee. He seemed pleased to see her, but remained behind his self-imposed barricade. There were no glimpses of the up-and-coming country singer who had shown such promise, and in a way, she felt relieved. Danny Webster had died that night in the Wildwoods's trailer, and she hoped that someday, Ricky Mason would find his way back to peace and fulfillment.

She met Dr. Stellman on the way out. "I wanted to thank you," she said when the doctor greeted her with a smile. "Ricky looks so much better and seems very happy."

"Yes, he does. He still has a long way to go, but there are definite signs of improvement."

It hurt to say the words, but she'd made up her mind and there was no going back. "I think it would be better if I don't see him again. I'm afraid I'll remind him of the past."

Dr. Stellman nodded gravely. "I think that would be best. As a matter of fact, I'd planned on discussing it with you soon. I'm glad you brought it up."

"So am I." She smiled to cover the grief. "I'll miss him, but I want what's best for him. I know he's in good hands."

"We'll take care of him. He's a very strong young man. He'll do just fine."

"Yes," she said quietly. "I really think he will."

She walked out into the cool October sunshine, hoping that the ache in her heart would soon heal. She had lost so much that summer. It was time to start again.

Two days later she signed a contract with a new singer. A young girl with a voice that vibrated with such intense emotion when she sang it almost brought tears to Jill's eyes.

Deciding to celebrate that night, she bought a bottle of champagne and her favorite pâté. She had a steak in the freezer and salad in the fridge. Tonight she was going to dine in style, even if she would be alone. For once she would forget the neighbors, turn up the CD player and listen to her favorite country singers.

Getting into the right mood was difficult, but the new blue silk negligee she'd bought to cheer herself up helped, and she sprayed perfume down her cleavage for good measure.

The steak went into the microwave oven to defrost, and she chose the CD she wanted, turning up the volume as she pressed the play button. The slow, sultry beat of country blues filled the room, and she glided across the floor in time to the music.

For one brief moment her body ached for the feel of Hank's arms around her, then she shut off the thought. That was a sure path to depression and she'd been down that one far too often lately.

She turned up the volume another notch and swayed sensuously into the kitchen. Humming along with the music, she took the champagne out of the fridge, hoping she wouldn't have trouble popping the cork. Champagne wasn't something she'd had a whole lot of practice opening.

She stood the bottle on the counter and looked at it thoughtfully. As long as she didn't point the thing at her face, it should be okay to give it a shot in the kitchen.

Trying to remember how the waiters did it, she braced the bottle on her thighs and pushed at the wire with her thumbs. It refused to budge. No matter how hard she pushed, how loud she cursed, the cork refused to budge.

Shaking the bottle in her frustration, Jill glared at it. "I'm not going to give up," she told it out loud, "so you might as well surrender." Dumping it on her thighs again, she jabbed at the wire.

The cork flew out with a loud pop, and champagne poured in a frothy stream down the bottle and over her knees. Cursing, Jill placed the bottle on the counter and reached for a towel. As she did so, she heard the faint chime of her doorbell.

Probably a neighbor, come to complain about the noise, she thought guiltily. Mopping at the front of her negligee with a towel, she crossed the room to the door and flung it open.

He stood in the doorway, looking down at her, his gaze slowly traveling down to the dark, damp patch below her knees. She didn't know what to do with her hands. The reminder that she wore nothing under a very slinky, silk negligee brought hot color to her cheeks.

She stood as still as her unstable legs would let her and twisted the towel into a tight knot. "Hank," she murmured breathlessly. "What a nice surprise."

And what an understatement. She felt devastated by the shock of seeing him again. He wore jeans and a brown suede jacket over a cream shirt. He was bareheaded, his dark hair neatly combed and longer than she remembered. He looked gorgeous, and unbelievably nervous.

"I'm sorry, I seem to have caught you at a bad moment." Again his gaze traveled over her, setting off all kinds of warning signals.

She backed away, gesturing with an unsteady hand. "No, please, come in. I was opening a bottle of champagne. I'm afraid I made a mess of it. Half of it's on the floor."

He paused just inside the room. "Then I am interrupting something. Maybe this had better wait—"

She looked up at him, wrinkling her brow. What on earth was the matter with him? She'd never seen him this way. He stood there, looking around her small but cozy living room as if he'd never seen it before.

"The only thing you're interrupting is a celebration for one. And I've always said, it's more fun to celebrate with company. Besides, I can't drink all that champagne by myself and I hate to pour good stuff down the drain."

He gave her a slow grin that threatened to put her on the floor. "Always was partial to champagne."

"Good, then you can pour. How do you feel about pâté?"

"I haven't had more than a nodding acquaintance with the stuff, but I'm willing to give it a shot in the interests of celebrating."

"Good. Sit down there while I change into something a little less comfortable." She felt his warm gaze on her all the way across the room as she crossed to the door.

Inside the security of her bedroom she stared at her flushed face in the mirror. *Don't do this,* she silently warned her image. *Don't leave yourself open to that kind of pain again.*

Yet how could she ignore the wild thumping of her heart, and the hot blood racing through her veins when he looked at her with that warm interest in his incredible gray eyes?

Don't be a fool, she warned herself again. But her hands trembled as she pulled on a pair of black slacks and buttoned the gold buttons of a yellow silk blouse.

She whisked a comb through her dark curls and dabbed a light coating of lipstick on her mouth. She wished now she hadn't gone so heavy with the perfume. She wished she'd had the strength to tell him she was busy and didn't have time to talk to him.

She wished he'd given her some warning, so she could have spent more time getting ready. She wished she wasn't getting a schoolgirl fluttering in her stomach that threatened to tie her tongue in knots.

She wished to hell he hadn't come at all, starting up a whole new bombardment of emotions, just when she was beginning to forget the old ones.

And she wished, with all her heart, that she wasn't so crazy about him she couldn't see straight.

Squaring her shoulders, she summoned all her courage and prepared to go back into the living room.

She found him sitting on the couch, staring at her landscape of the painted desert. "I like that," he said as she walked into the room. "It's restful."

He'd taken off his jacket and laid it across the arm of the couch. He looked disturbingly at home.

"Yes, it is. I love the colors in it."

He nodded. "Nice."

She stood awkwardly in the middle of the room, wondering exactly why he'd come.

He turned his head and caught her staring at him with a moonstruck look on her face. "I'll get the champagne," she said quickly.

"What are we celebrating?"

She was halfway across the room and she paused to look back at him. "Oh, I found a new singer. Her name is Cathy Summers and I think she's going to be very successful."

She thought she saw a glimpse of disappointment in his eyes. Then he said quietly, "That's great, Jill. I know that it must have been hard for you."

"It was." She sent him a smile. "I'll be back in a minute."

After mopping up the floor, she set out two of her best glasses next to the champagne bottle. She found a box of crackers in the cupboard that she hoped hadn't been there too long, and quickly spread pâté thickly on several of them.

Her mind worked busily on all the possible reasons for Hank's visit. Had Perry found him? Had they made up? Was that why he was there?

Maybe he hadn't received the check she sent to the association, and didn't know how to go about asking her. That would explain why his gaze kept sliding around the room in an effort to avoid looking at her.

She would not allow herself to think of the one reason that would change her entire world into a magic place. She would not allow the hope to soar, only to have it extinguished again. She could not go through that kind of pain again.

Absorbed in her thoughts, she jumped nearly out of her skin when his deep voice said behind her, "Have you heard how Danny is doing?"

The kitchen was way too small for the two of them, she thought, picking up the plate of crackers. "Yes, I have. Pour the champagne for me, please, and I'll tell you all about it."

He picked up the bottle and examined it. "Reckon you didn't lose too much of it. Good stuff, too."

"You know me, only the best." Her laugh sounded forced, and she hurried into the living room, doing her best to steady the rapid beat of her heart.

He followed her, carrying the champagne. His hands were perfectly steady, she noticed, as he set the glasses down on the coffee table. But when she looked at his face she could see a muscle twitching in his cheek.

He sat opposite her on the edge of a chair, his knees bent as if he was ready to spring up at any second.

She offered him the plate of crackers and he took one, experimenting with a small bite before popping the rest of it into his mouth.

She waited from him to swallow it.

"Good," he said, brushing her face with his gaze.

"I like it." She leaned forward and lifted her glass. "To Cathy Summers."

"And to Jill Preston."

She smiled at that, and sipped the bubbling liquid, her eyes on his face. His gaze met hers, and lingered for a heart-stopping moment before sliding away again.

Putting down his glass, he said casually, "So tell me about Danny."

She told him, leaving out the words that Danny had spoken to her. Danny had been wrong about Hank. He wasn't afraid to admit how he felt. He just couldn't bring himself to love her. She knew that now.

"So Danny Webster is dead," she said, finishing her story. "And one day, Ricky Mason will be well enough to start a new life."

"I'm glad to hear it. That kid has a lot of talent."

"I don't know if he'll ever be strong enough to use it," Jill said sadly. "He has a long road to travel."

"So did Perry, but he made it on his own. Ricky will make it."

Now that he'd brought up the subject, she couldn't hold back the question any longer. "Did Perry contact you?" she asked, half-afraid of the answer.

"Yeah." Hank drained his glass and set it down on the table. "Thanks to you. That's why I'm here. I wanted to thank you for what you did. Perry said you went to see him, and talked some sense into him. I appreciate it."

She smiled. "It wasn't difficult. I think Perry was more than ready to make up. He just needed a little nudge in the right direction."

"Well, that couldn't have been easy for you. I just want you to know that we are both very grateful."

Now she was the one who found it hard to meet his gaze. She played with the stem of her glass as she asked the question. "So, I take it you are real brothers again?"

"Yeah. As a matter of fact, Perry is thinking of forming a new band. He wants a different sound, more of a modern country rock, and he's asked me to manage it for him."

"In Tennessee?"

"Yeah. That's the place to be if you're starting fresh."

She tried not to let him see how his words disappointed her. She hadn't realized how strong the hope had been. "But what about the rodeo? How will you fit that in?"

"I'm giving up the rodeo." His mouth tilted in a rueful smile. "It's like you said that day in the elevator. I got to thinking about all that pounding and grinding when I hit the dirt, and all those strong, young guys coming up behind me."

"I didn't mean—"

"I know what you meant, and you were right. But it isn't just that. It's the other thing. The reputation that they hung on me for being a fighter. I'm getting tired of having to defend it all the time. I'm just getting too old in the teeth to risk losing them anymore."

She wanted to laugh in spite of her misery. "Too old? I never thought I'd hear you admit that."

"Well, it's like the gunslingers of the Old West. All the young sharpshooters are real anxious to prove their mettle against the fastest gun. They figure on claiming the title for themselves. So they challenge the guy with the toughest reputation to a shoot-out. The old gunslinger doesn't want to fight, but what can he do? He's facing a man with a gun and he either shoots first or he dies."

"And you are like the gunslinger."

"Right. The hell of it is, the older he gets the more unsteady his hand becomes, the more fuzzy his eye. He knows that one day he's going to lose. And one day he does. I figure on quitting while I'm ahead. Before someone does some serious damage."

"So you're going to Tennessee with Perry." Her fingers grasped the stem of her glass so tightly, she was afraid it would break.

"I didn't say that."

She looked up quickly, and once more saw his gaze sliding away from her. "You're *not* going with Perry?"

He pushed a foot out in front of him, nudging the soft, tufted rug in front of the fireplace. She saw his fingers tapping a light tattoo on his knee, and the hope began to build again. Very slowly and carefully, but it was there.

"See, it's like this," Hank said, staring at the landscape on the wall behind her. "I have the darnedest trouble dealing with people. I'm not too careful when it comes to treading on people's toes. I tend to say what I think, and the words come out before I've given much thought about how it sounds."

She started to smile. "Really? I hadn't noticed."

He ignored her gentle sarcasm, and watched the toe of his boot as he slowly drew it back from the rug. "Yeah, well, that doesn't work too well with most people. And it's just plain suicide with show people. They have mighty thin skins."

"They do, indeed. But you'll learn. It just takes practice, that's all."

He shook his head, still not looking at her. "No, it takes a special kind of person. Like you. That's why I'm here."

She suddenly felt afraid to breathe. Afraid that if she did, she'd break the fragile bubble of excitement that had begun forming around her.

"Just what are you trying to tell me, Hank?"

He looked up, then, and she thought she would drown in the wonderful, warm, beseeching look in his eyes. "I want to start my own management company, Jill. And I want to do it right here in Cedarvale. These past weeks without you have been lonely as hell. I missed you. I reckon what I'm trying to tell you is that I love you."

He sat back and passed a hand across his forehead. "There, dammit, I said it."

She got to her feet, masking her joy with a purposeful look. "Say it again."

He looked at her warily, uncertainty written all over his face. "What?"

"Say it again." She stood looking down at him, not quite close enough to touch him.

"I said, I love you, Jill."

"That's what I thought. Now tell me, Hank, why it took you so damn long to say it."

His slow grin spread all over his face as he got to his feet. Putting his arms around her, he said softly, "Because I'm a lot better at showing than I am at telling."

She wound her arms around his neck and went up on her toes. With her mouth just inches from his, she whispered, "So show me."

His mouth felt so good on hers. So warm, so familiar, so demanding. She felt his hands moving over her body, creating spasms of pleasure that manifested in sensual murmurs of satisfaction deep in her throat.

She drew her hands to the front of his shirt and began to unbutton it. He had her blouse open before she'd reached the third button.

It amazed her how fast he could arouse the hot need in her. And how impatient he was with the necessary details, like getting her clothes off her. She stopped him before he unsnapped her bra.

"I do have a bedroom," she said breathlessly.

"I know. I want you now. Right here." His hands worked at his belt while he captured her mouth again, nipping her lower lip before sliding his tongue inside.

His kiss lasted long enough for him to get out of the rest of his clothes.

She came up for air, gasping. "There's plenty of room in my bed."

"I told you, I don't need room." He dragged her against his chest and unsnapped her bra.

"It's more comfortable—"

He smothered the rest of the sentence with his mouth, and drew her panties down over her hips.

She steadied herself with her hands on his shoulders as she stepped out of them, then gave herself up to the sheer, mind-searing touch of his hands, his mouth and his body.

When at last they lay spent and breathless on the rug together, she said dreamily, "You're full of surprises, Hank

Tyler. That was the last thing I expected when I saw you in the doorway."

"Yeah?" He turned his head and looked at her, his grin transforming his face. "Well, I gotta tell you, lady, when I saw you standing there in that filmy thing with nothing on underneath, I almost took you right there and then."

She grinned back. "Yeah, I was afraid you'd noticed."

"I noticed."

"Good."

"Then when you said about the champagne, I thought you were expecting someone else. The thought of you getting dressed like that for another man just about blew my fuses."

She rolled onto her side and propped her face on her hand. "Would you have fought for me?"

He pretended to think about it. "I reckon it depends on how much younger and stronger he was than me."

"I'm not worth risking your teeth, is that what you're saying?"

"Lady, you're worth risking my entire body. But it wouldn't be much good to you without some life in it." He drew a finger down her breast, sending a shaft of pleasure winging down her body.

She responded by tracing a sensuous path down his chest to his belly. "Well, my love, you don't have to worry. There isn't a man alive who could come close to matching you in my eyes."

He captured her fingers and brought them to his mouth. "I'm sure happy to hear it. Right now I don't have the strength to fight a flea."

Laughing, she reached for her clothes. "In that case, I'd better feed you. How does stir fry sound?" It was the only way she could think of to stretch the steak.

"It sounds real good." He sat up, and ran his hands through his thick hair. "Need some help?"

She let him scrub carrots and wash celery. It felt so good, the two of them together in the kitchen, talking and laughing while they prepared a meal together.

She tried not to think beyond that night. He had said nothing more than that he loved her, and for now that was enough. She would take what he had to offer and enjoy it while she could.

They talked about the music business while they ate dinner, discussing the latest trends and future stars appearing on the record labels. It was an animated discussion, and one Jill enjoyed immensely.

Afterward they sat side by side on the couch with a cup of coffee, and the television tuned in to the country music channel.

"You surprise me," Hank said, setting his coffee cup down on the table. "I would never have figured you as being so domesticated."

She wrinkled her nose at him. "It was a matter of necessity. A half-dozen road tours in a camper and you learn to take care of yourself pretty well."

"Yeah. I guess you do."

His face grew serious as he looked at her, and her heart skipped a beat. "Is something wrong?"

"I was just thinking about how close I came to losing you. I was a damn fool."

She shrugged. "I guess we both had some growing to do."

Leaning back, he folded his arms behind his head. "I never figured on settling down in one place. I was too much like my Dad, always looking for new roads to travel and new faces to spit into. I didn't think I'd ever change."

"I guess we have to want to change. It's like giving up smoking. You can't do it until you want to badly enough."

"Yeah." He turned his head and smiled at her. "I guess I never figured on meeting you again. I never did quite get you off my mind. Every now and then something would trigger a memory and I'd see your face as plain as if you stood right there in front of me."

"I thought about you a lot, too. I followed your career on the rodeo circuit, and every now and then I'd see a picture of you, and I'd wonder if you were happy."

"Never was, I guess. I reckon that no matter where I went or what I did now, you'd always be on my mind." He lowered his arms and sat up. "Jill, how would you feel about coming into the business with me? If you're gonna be a permanent fixture on my mind, you might as well be there in my life, as well."

She stared at him, wondering exactly what he meant by that. He had to be the most enigmatic man she'd ever met. He drove her crazy wondering what he was really saying.

"I mean," he went on, "if I'm managing a band, I'm gonna need singers. And if they're female I'm gonna need a woman along if we go on the road, and—"

"You just want Cathy Summers," Jill said with a grin. "That's a sneaky way to land a good singer."

"I want someone who's gonna keep the musicians in line. You'd be perfect for the job."

She laughed. "I'd love the job. But you're the one who needs keeping in line. I'm not sure how good I'd be at that."

"Well, there's one way to make sure."

Once more, his gaze kept sliding away from hers. Her heart started the familiar pounding as she waited.

He laced his fingers together and stuck them between his knees. "You could marry me. I reckon that would keep me in line better than anything."

This was a ridiculous time to cry. Especially for someone who hated to cry. "Mister," she said softly, "that's an offer I can't refuse."

He looked up, and his heart was in his eyes. "I'm sure glad to hear it," he said, his grin spreading across his face. "I'd have hated like hell to hire Tiffany."

She reached for him, winding her arms around his neck. "Come here," she whispered. "I'm going to make you forget all about Tiffany."

And she did.

*   *   *   *   *

HE'S AN

AMERICAN HERO

A cop, a fire fighter or even just a fearless drifter who gets the job done when ordinary men have given up. And you'll find one American Hero every month only in Intimate Moments—created by some of your favorite authors. This summer, Silhouette has lined up some of the hottest American heroes you'll ever find:

July: HELL ON WHEELS by Naomi Horton—Truck driver Shay McKittrick heads down a long, bumpy road when he discovers a scared stowaway in his rig....

August: DRAGONSLAYER by Emilie Richards—In a dangerous part of town, a man finds himself fighting a street gang—and his feelings for a beautiful woman....

September: ONE LAST CHANCE by Justine Davis—A tough-as-nails cop walks a fine line between devotion to duty and devotion to the only woman who could heal his broken heart....

AMERICAN HEROES: Men who give all they've got for their country, their work—the women they love.

IMHER05

INTIMATE MOMENTS®

Silhouette®

What a year for romance!

Silhouette has five fabulous romance collections coming your way in 1993. Written by popular Silhouette authors, each story is a sensuous tale of love and life—as only Silhouette can give you!

Three bachelors are footloose and fancy-free...until now.
(March)

Heartwarming stories that celebrate the joy of motherhood.
(May)

Put some sizzle into your summer reading with three of Silhouette's hottest authors.
(June)

Take a walk on the dark side of love—with tales just perfect for those misty autumn nights.
(October)

Share in the joy of yuletide romance with four award-winning Silhouette authors.
(November)

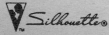

A romance for all seasons—it's always time for romance with Silhouette!

PROM93

Silhouette Books has done it again!

Opening night in October has never been as exciting! Come watch as the curtain rises and romance flourishes when the stars of tomorrow make their debuts today!

Revel in Jodi O'Donnell's STILL SWEET ON HIM—
Silhouette Romance #969
...as Callie Farrell's renovation of the family homestead leads her straight into the arms of teenage crush Drew Barnett!

Tingle with Carol Devine's BEAUTY AND THE BEASTMASTER—
Silhouette Desire #816
...as legal eagle Amanda Tarkington is carried off by wrestler Bram Masterson!

Thrill to Elyn Day's A BED OF ROSES—
Silhouette Special Edition #846
...as Dana Whitaker's body and soul are healed by sexy physical therapist Michael Gordon!

Believe when Kylie Brant's McLAIN'S LAW —
Silhouette Intimate Moments #528
...takes you into detective Connor McLain's life as he falls for psychic—and suspect—Michele Easton!

Catch the classics of tomorrow—*premiering* today—
only from Silhouette

**Silhouette Books
is proud to present
our best authors,
their best books...
and the best in
your reading pleasure!**

Throughout 1993, look for exciting
books by these top names in
contemporary romance:

DIANA PALMER—
Fire and Ice in June

ELIZABETH LOWELL—
Fever in July

CATHERINE COULTER—
Afterglow in August

LINDA HOWARD—
Come Lie With Me in September

When it comes to passion,
we wrote the book.

BOBT2

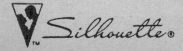

**Relive the romance...
Harlequin and Silhouette
are proud to present**

by Request

A program of collections of three complete novels by the most requested authors with the most requested themes. Be sure to look for one volume each month with three complete novels by top name authors.

In June: **NINE MONTHS** Penny Jordan
Stella Cameron
Janice Kaiser

Three women pregnant and alone. But a lot can happen in nine months!

In July: **DADDY'S HOME** Kristin James
Naomi Horton
Mary Lynn Baxter

Daddy's Home... and his presence is long overdue!

In August: **FORGOTTEN PAST** Barbara Kaye
Pamela Browning
Nancy Martin

Do you dare to create a future if you've forgotten the past?

Available at your favorite retail outlet.

REQ-G

Fifty red-blooded, white-hot, true-blue hunks from every
State in the Union!

Beginning in May, look for MEN MADE IN AMERICA!
Written by some of our most popular authors, these
stories feature fifty of the strongest, sexiest men, each
from a different state in the union!

Two titles available every other month at your favorite
retail outlet.

In September, look for:

DECEPTIONS by Annette Broadrick (California)
STORMWALKER by Dallas Schulze (Colorado)

In November, look for:

STRAIGHT FROM THE HEART by Barbara Delinsky
(Connecticut)
AUTHOR'S CHOICE by Elizabeth August (Delaware)

You won't be able to resist MEN MADE IN AMERICA!

If you've been looking for something a little bit different and a little bit spooky, let Silhouette Books take you on a journey to the dark side of love with

▼ SILHOUETTE® *Shadows*™

Every month, Silhouette will bring you two romantic, spine-tingling Shadows novels, written by some of your favorite authors, such as *New York Times* bestselling author Heather Graham Pozzessere, Anne Stuart, Helen R. Myers and Rachel Lee—to name just a few.

In July, look for:
HEART OF THE BEAST by Carla Cassidy
DARK ENCHANTMENT by Jane Toombs

In August, look for:
A SILENCE OF DREAMS by Barbara Faith
THE SEVENTH NIGHT by Amanda Stevens

In September, look for:
FOOTSTEPS IN THE NIGHT by Lee Karr
WHAT WAITS BELOW by Jane Toombs

*Come into the world of Shadows and prepare
to tremble with fear—and passion....*

SHAD3